The

BOY
IN THE
ATTIC

BOOKS BY IMOGEN MATTHEWS

The Girl Across the Wire Fence

WARTIME HOLLAND SERIES
The Hidden Village
Hidden in the Shadows

IMOGEN MATTHEWS

The

BOY
IN THE
ATTIC

bookouture

Published by Bookouture in 2022

An imprint of Storyfire Ltd.
Carmelite House
50 Victoria Embankment
London EC4Y 0DZ

www.bookouture.com

ISBN: 978-1-80314-635-5
eBook ISBN: 978-1-80314-634-8

This book is dedicated to Alba and Ludo.

ONE

ILSE

January 1945

Snow had fallen thickly overnight, the third time in as many days. The iron-hard ground lay frozen under a pillowy white blanket, disturbed only by the occasional sudden gust of wind that sent sparkling snowflakes swirling up into the frigid morning air.

Ilse watched from the kitchen window, momentarily entranced by the fairy-tale scene. But as pretty as it looked, it was a nuisance for anyone who needed to be out and about, even those who still had the stamina to walk more than a few paces along the unswept streets. After yesterday's snowfall, she had put off venturing outside, but after today's she couldn't delay any longer. If she didn't get out soon on her trusty battered bike with her old childhood wooden sledge strapped to the back, she and her parents would starve. It was as simple as that.

Ilse shivered and hurried over to the rack by the door and lifted her woollen navy coat from its peg. It was the last purchase she and her mother had made at the Bijenkorf depart-

ment store just months before the war started. She remembered
that crisp autumn day so clearly and with such fondness. She
and her mother had taken the train to the Rotterdam Centraal
station and walked arm in arm along tree-lined Coolsingel
Street towards the imposing emporium, excitedly discussing
which departments they would visit first and what they
intended to buy. They'd treated themselves to rich fragrant
coffee and apple cake topped with whipped cream at the smart
restaurant on the second floor, before travelling up in the lift to
the coat department on the third floor. Ilse had tried on coat
after coat that the attentive shop assistant had picked out from
the immaculate displays, until she settled on one in navy-blue
wool that flicked out at the knee and was tied at the waist with a
matching belt. It was perfect. But Ilse had been worried it was
too expensive, until her mother, delighted at her choice, had
told her it would be a good investment. Little did they know
how essential this coat would become, serving Ilse well during
the long cold winters. Now after five years, it was showing its
age, despite Ilse's efforts to patch up the elbows and disguise the
frayed collar and cuffs. She shrugged it on over the fitted dress
she'd made from a pair of dull pink curtains she'd found in the
attic and which she'd dyed to a soft dove grey. She had also put
on extra layers against the cold, a woollen vest and one of her
mother's old cardigans. And from the pockets of her coat, she
pulled out her dark-brown suede gloves, which her mother no
longer had a use for, and the fur hat that had once belonged to
her grandmother.

At the sound of shuffling footsteps approaching from the
corridor, Ilse pinned a smile to her face and turned to greet her
mother. She wasn't going to let her see how worried she was
feeling. Every time she caught sight of her mother it pained her
to see her so small and thin, and she couldn't help but think how
old she now looked. Her dignified mother, who used to take
such care over her appearance, going to the hair salon once a

week to have her beautiful chestnut hair washed and styled just so, stood before her daughter, her hair now hanging grey and limp around her drawn face. Recently, Ilse had been shocked to see how her mother's skin had taken on a worrying yellow tinge and her eyes, once a sparkling blue, had lost their lustre. Ilse pursed her lips in determination. She couldn't bear to see her mother succumbing to the effects of so little food and vowed she must do better.

Ilse crossed the kitchen and kissed her mother on both cheeks. For a brief moment, the older woman's face brightened and her chapped lips spread into a smile.

'I was thinking how well navy suits you. It was a good choice, wasn't it?' She gazed fondly at her daughter.

Ilse laughed. 'An excellent one, especially given the weather. Now, I must be off, as I've found a place not many people know where I can get hold of firewood. I've also heard that there are carrots and sugar beets at a farm on the road to Leiden. I'd better set off before anyone hears about it.'

'Leiden? That'll take you all day, won't it? And in this weather.' Her mother's voice drifted off as she gazed out of the window with a frown. It had begun to snow again.

'I'll warm up once I get going, so you don't need to worry. Just think, we'll have wood for the stove and can bring Pa downstairs.' Ilse looked anxiously at her mother, desperate for a reason to cheer her up. But if she didn't go out right now, all there was left to eat was less than half a loaf of stale bread made from dried peas and a handful of potatoes left over from Ilse's last trip out.

Her mother sighed as she crossed the cold tiled floor in her tattered slippers and reached up to one of the pegs for a dark-red damask stole that hung there. 'Ilse, take this, will you?' She held out the heavy garment in both hands.

Ilse remembered the look of delight on her mother's face when Pa had presented her with the stole one Christmas Eve.

Ilse had been just twelve and enchanted by the gift, which her father had found in a souk in Algiers when he and his wife had both performed at the opera house during their last season on tour. From that moment on, her mother had always worn it over her evening dresses whenever the two of them had gone out to soirées and dinner parties. How could Ilse take something that had been so precious to her as if it were some discarded old thing?

'I can't, Mama. It's yours,' she began, her voice faltering. She could feel tears pricking at the back of her eyes.

'Take it, please. I have no use for it now.' Her mother folded it over twice and wrapped it gently round her daughter's neck, tying it securely. 'Now, please... be careful.'

TWO

'Hello, Ilse. You're not going out in this, are you?' said a man's voice behind her. It was Mr Bakker, her next-door neighbour.

'Try and stop me,' said Ilse, irritated at the interruption, as she was having trouble fastening the sledge to the back of her bike. In the short time she'd been outside, her fingers had become so cold and stiff that she was now unable to secure the rope.

'Here, let me help.' Mr Bakker came over for a closer look.

Ilse stood up from crouching, feeling a little embarrassed at her brusqueness toward her kindly neighbour. Her family had always relied on Mr Bakker, who often helped out with various jobs around the house. His skills as a carpenter had been particularly useful in constructing a large space beneath the floorboards of the sitting room for the valuable jewellery and silverware a young Jewish couple had left in their safekeeping hours before their arrest and deportation to Auschwitz. Those last words spoken by Rachel Cohen to her mother still played on Ilse's mind: *It's just a precaution and we'll be back for our belongings in a few days*. But more than a year had passed and still there was no word. Every time Ilse thought of this kind gentle couple and their certain belief that they would return, she was gripped by the most terrible sense of foreboding.

The hiding place under the floorboards was also where Pa had insisted on keeping their wireless set in defiance of a Nazi directive to hand them in, when he had realised how determined the Germans were to remove every last vestige of freedom from the Dutch. He was well aware that anyone found hiding a wireless faced a large fine, or even death, but told his family it was a risk worth taking: the wireless set was their only connection with the outside world. And as the weather worsened, each evening just before nine Mr Bakker and his wife crept through the concealed door he'd constructed in their adjoining fence and in through the back door, where they joined Ilse and her parents to listen to the crackly voice broadcasting from London on the BBC for any news of the Allied advance into occupied Holland. This tiny glimmer of hope was virtually all that sustained them through those dark cold winter months.

'That would be very kind,' Ilse said, grateful for Mr Bakker's offer of assistance. She brushed snowflakes from the shoulders of her coat and briskly rubbed her hands together to get some feeling back into them.

He chatted while he worked, asking after Willem from across the road, who was now working for the Germans and hadn't been home in over eighteen months. 'It's a terrible thing to see so many promising young men like Willem forced to do the jobs the *moffen* won't do because their own men are over here fighting us. How is Willem coping?'

Ilse hesitated, for she didn't much like talking about Willem's circumstances with anyone, but made an exception for Mr Bakker, whom she knew she could trust. 'I think he's treated reasonably well, though the conditions sound gruelling, especially now it's so cold. At least he's no longer clearing rubble after bombings. In the autumn, he was moved to a factory operating machinery making parts for rifles.' She thought of Willem toiling from early morning till late afternoon, returning exhausted to camp only to have to carry out more chores. He wrote her of his relentless days, but he never complained and always signed off cheerfully with words of hope that it would soon all be over and he could return home. He'd often alluded to the two of them being together, but Ilse tried not to think about that. As much as she liked him as a friend, her feelings for him stopped short of considering herself to be his girlfriend. But she knew that to say as much would be a crushing blow to him, especially on top of all he was going through.

'That should do it,' Mr Bakker said, satisfied with his handiwork, and stood up. 'And how are your parents?' He turned his kind eyes towards Ilse. 'I suppose it's too cold for them to get out.' He glanced up at the leaden grey sky. The snow was falling less thickly now.

Ilse followed his gaze. 'They haven't been out in weeks and it's not just the cold. There's so little to eat and the only food I can get hold of has little nutritional value. How are you and Mrs Bakker keeping?' she said quickly, realising that they must be suffering too.

He gave a small shrug. 'There's only the two of us. We do what we can to conserve our energy. The cellar's almost bare, but we still have a little rice and some dried beans.'

'I hope the weather will put people off going out into the fields. I'll see if I can bring back some root vegetables for you and Mrs Bakker.' She spoke brightly as she searched for some small way in which to repay his kindness. This was all she could think of.

'You mustn't bother about us. We can manage. Now, please don't waste your time standing around chatting to me.' He gestured for her to leave. 'Look after yourself.'

Ilse mounted her bike and turned to smile at him, before pedalling the bike and sledge onto the snow-covered street. She proceeded slowly and concentrated hard on avoiding the icy patches where the snow had been flattened by people's footsteps. Once she reached the main road leading toward the lowlying land reclaimed from the sea, it was easier going and she was able to relax. It had left off snowing, the clouds had parted and the sun shone down on the vast glistening snowscape that vanished into the distance on either side of the road. She passed a handful of people, wrapped up from head to foot against the cold, pushing empty carts and prams and all heading in the same direction in their relentless search for anything that could pass for food or fuel.

'*Goedemorgen*,' Ilse called out cheerfully each time she passed someone.

'*Goedemorgen*,' each person replied, as if it were completely normal to be out so early on such a bitterly cold winter's morning.

Ilse knew exactly where she was going and it wasn't along the road these people were walking. She used to cycle this same route to Leiden, full of optimism for the course in medicine she had started and looking forward to spending time with Connie and her other university friends. It had all been so promising, till one day she turned up to find the place in uproar. A leading professor had just delivered an inflammatory lecture against the dismissal of Jewish colleagues, and the professor of medicine, whose lecture she had come to attend, instead held forth on the unsustainability of the theory of racial doctrine. These two men's courageous actions enraged the Nazis, who promptly closed the university, leading to thousands of students joining the resistance. Although Ilse deplored the actions of the Nazis, she chose not to become embroiled in the activities of her fellow students – as an only child, her parents depended on her and she simply couldn't take the risk.

When she reached the place she was aiming for, she dismounted and pushed her bike and sledge over the snowy ground to a clump of willow stumps lining a narrow water channel, now completely frozen over. Her hands had warmed up and she was able to unfasten the sledge. Parking her bike in a dip, where it couldn't be seen from the track, she swapped her shoes for skates from her saddlebag and gingerly clambered down the side of the ditch, dragging the sledge onto the ice. She stopped a moment to tie the rope onto her belt, giving little thought as to how she would manage once the sledge was weighed down with firewood. Then with a tentative prod of the ice with the tip of her skate, Ilse decided it was safe to set off. She glanced along the length of the frozen water channel that disappeared in front of her in a long straight line and began slowly, getting used to the weight of the sledge at her back. She took long swishing strides – left, right, left, right – as the sledge whirred softly behind her. All around her it was perfectly white and perfectly still. She had never encountered such deep, magical silence.

After a while, she picked up speed and leant forward with her hands behind her back, just like the long-distance skaters who took part in the famous Elfstedentocht race that took place only when the canals and waterways linking eleven rural towns and villages froze over. She'd been lucky enough to see the race once, when her father had taken her to watch the event in Sneek in Friesland in sub-zero temperatures. She remembered the roar of the crowd as groups of skaters came soaring past at a terrific speed, and jumping up and down in her father's arms when their favourite competitor, the son of a friend of her father's, had appeared on the horizon leading the pack. Now as she sped over the ice, she imagined taking part in the race, being part of a team, travelling at speed and revelling in the thrilling, magical atmosphere.

After skating for more than an hour, she reached a bend in the channel. She was glad to stop as she felt stiff, but it was only after gliding to a halt that she noticed that the copse of trees, where she'd previously stopped, was no longer there. *Someone must have beaten me to it*, she thought with a grimace. She untied the rope from her belt and slung it round a freshly sawn tree stump. Shielding her eyes, she looked about her for any signs of life, but she was completely alone. There were a few small sticks littering the ground, which she gathered up and tied to the wooden slats of her sledge with a length of string from her pocket. It was so little fuel; it would barely bring any warmth into the kitchen. An image of Pa came to her, huddled beneath three blankets, too cold and weak to venture downstairs, and it almost made her cry.

'Right. Keep going,' she told herself firmly with a big sniff. It was still early and if she concentrated, instead of enjoying herself on the ice, she would find enough wood to fill the stove. With a renewed determination, she set off more slowly, keeping an eye out for anything suitable for burning, but it was as if something or someone had made a complete sweep of the area and removed every last tree or bush. Every now and then she stopped to collect up twigs, but she knew that the pitiful bundle of dry wood in her hands would flare and burn in an instant.

Disheartened, she decided she must waste no more time but go looking for food. The way back, into the bitterly cold wind, was much harder going and her earlier exhilaration soon evaporated. The sun disappeared behind a bank of clouds and the frozen landscape had turned featureless and forbidding. Tired and hungry, she arrived back where she had started, wishing that Mr Bakker were here to help her with the sledge, before she remembered her promise to bring him back a few root vegetables. But the thought of searching longer and harder made her even more exhausted; she needed a rest, however brief. She sat down on a willow stump and fumbled in her pocket for the small package she'd brought containing a crust of stale bread smeared with a tiny amount of margarine. Her stomach still rumbled after she'd swallowed it down, but that was too bad.

She tried to picture the carrots, onions and maybe even the potatoes she would find, and how her mother would make her favourite dish, *hutspot*, for dinner, just like old times.

It was getting dark by the time she arrived home, wheeling her bike along the street, which had turned treacherously icy. The sledge bounced and scraped along behind her, a constant reminder of how little she'd managed to forage during the long hours away from home.

She glanced up to see her mother's worried face peering through the curtains and then, when she caught sight of her daughter, gave a cheery wave. Her expression broke into a relieved smile before she disappeared from view.

Ilse knew she'd be full of anticipation for stoking a fire and cooking a decent hot meal for the first time in weeks, and hated that she'd have to disappoint her. She steadied herself with a long breath as she prepared to tell her mother only part of what had happened out on the polders. If her mother were to know the danger Ilse had put herself through to hunt for a few misshapen turnips, she was certain she wouldn't be allowed out again. The saving grace was the two decent-sized logs strapped onto the sledge; she consoled herself with the knowledge that they would heat the kitchen for several days and provide the means for cooking a warming soup, however few ingredients they had to bulk it out.

Her mother, waiting inside the kitchen, held out a steaming cup of weak tea. 'Well, what did you manage to get?' she asked, hope brightening her eyes.

Ilse could hear the excitement in her voice as she took the cup, wrapped her numb fingers around it and took a long sip. The warm sweet liquid seemed to permeate her whole body. Her mother must have added a drop of the precious sugar syrup from the half-used bottle she kept at the back of the kitchen cupboard, and she was grateful for it. After a moment, Ilse felt revived enough to be able to speak about her trip, but she didn't want to disappoint her mother by telling her how little food she'd managed to scavenge.

'It took a while to find any wood, but I've got two logs I can saw into smaller chunks. And there's some kindling.' She blew on her tea and took another sip, not wanting to meet her mother's eye. She hoped she wasn't about to question her about where the wood had come from.

* * *

Ilse had given up the idea of finding more firewood when she'd arrived at the field where dozens of people were already hard at work pilfering turnips. They appeared to have done a good job of stripping the top half of the field, so she walked her bike and sledge to a less populated spot, where a middle-aged woman in a threadbare coat and headscarf was on her hands and knees, scrabbling at the frozen soil. She looked up and through pursed pale lips warned Ilse that there had been sightings of German soldiers in the vicinity. Ilse thanked her and immediately set to work clearing snow with her hands and using her small trowel to search. But her delight at unearthing what she thought were turnips soon turned to disappointment when she realised that what she held in her hands were stones.

When the Germans came roaring into sight on their motorbikes, she'd only managed to dig up half a dozen of the knobbly vegetables, some not much larger than a plum. Hastily, she tumbled them into her pannier, and fled towards a tumbledown barn, where she was able to hide her bike and sledge around the back. She peered out at the scene unfolding: men and women were screaming and running in all directions as the group of German soldiers, maybe half a dozen or more, shouted and fired warning shots into the air. As she cowered out of sight, waiting for the danger to pass, she spied a stack of logs piled against the wall. Wasting no time, she secured a couple to her sledge, not daring to stay and take more. There was a rough track running away from the barn, so she took her chance, mounting her bike and pedalling away as fast as she could. She'd had a narrow escape from being noticed by the Germans and was forced to take a detour in case she ran into any more danger. But all the way home, she berated herself that she hadn't got there sooner and had so little to show for her efforts.

She drained her cup. She couldn't put off telling her mother any longer. 'Ma, I'm afraid there wasn't much left by the time I got to the fields. There were so many people there – I can only think someone must have tipped them off. I did find a few turnips though, but that's all.'

Her mother put her palm to the side of her face as she processed this information. She looked crestfallen. 'Well, never mind. You were unlucky. And the wood will go a long way to make up for the lack of food. I'll make a soup and thicken it with a little flour and we'll have a fire tonight. I'm sure Pa will come down and join us.'

Ilse nodded, but inside she felt as if her heart was breaking.

THREE

ANNA

March 2001

It had gone six by the time Anna arrived at the stylish Soho bar. She cursed herself for cutting it so fine, knowing as she did that it always took twice as long to get into central London for early evening; and it hadn't helped that the bus had broken down halfway along Oxford Street. She'd run from John Lewis, across the red lights at Oxford Circus and all the way to Dean Street, arriving hot, sticky and flustered.

The door of the bar flew open and four young women came tottering out in vertiginously high heels, clearly drunk, and cackling at the tops of their voices. Anna stood aside in dismay as a cacophony of deafening music and loud voices hit her from inside. She almost didn't go in, but she wasn't going to let Caro down – it had been her idea to meet close to her office and she would already be waiting inside for her. Pushing her wavy auburn hair away from her face and trying not to think what a mess she must look, Anna strode inside with determination. The bar was packed with office workers, judging from their attire, and she had to squeeze past several groups to get to the seating area beyond. Pure relief washed over her when she spied Caro at the back, sitting at a small brass-topped table with a bottle of wine in an ice bucket. She couldn't help notice Caro's glass was almost empty.

'I'm so sorry I'm late,' Anna shouted, trying to make herself heard above the din, as she sank onto a plush red velvet chair.

'Not a problem. Good thing I was early. I got the last table,' shouted Caro back. She sloshed wine into both glasses. 'Pinot Grigio.' She held a glass out to Anna. 'So, what kept you?'

Anna didn't answer immediately as she took a long sip, letting it slip down, followed by another. It had been a long day and finally she could relax. 'Bus broke down on Oxford Street,' she said, screwing up her face.

Caro frowned in sympathy, and they chinked glasses.

'And I left home late,' Anna confessed. 'I've been chasing this interview with Pierre Blanchet all week and his PR kept fobbing me off. Then, guess what? At a quarter to five, the master perfumer finally came on the line and well... I couldn't refuse to speak to him, could I?' She smiled and finished her glass. Caro held the bottle up for a refill.

A strand of glossy chestnut hair fell across Caro's cheek and she brushed it back behind one ear. If it had been anyone else, Anna would have been jealous of those good looks, but she knew that behind her best friend's glamorous exterior lay a kind, generous woman who was fiercely loyal. They'd known each other since sixth form, long before Caro had embarked on her career in advertising, where she'd risen through the ranks to become an account director for a successful global conglomerate. She said she loved her job, the shoots in exotic locations, the conferences, and even the long hours, but she was in her late twenties. Anna sometimes wondered if it bothered her that her relationships never lasted longer than a few weeks. Whenever they discussed their futures, Caro only ever talked about her ambition to become a senior partner in an advertising firm, never about finding someone to settle down with.

Anna couldn't have been more different – she'd been made redundant at twenty-four from a dull market research job she didn't care about. She'd worked as a freelancer ever since, writing reports on beauty and well-being and picking up commissions for magazine features. Work could be erratic and there were weeks when she hadn't much on followed by others when she'd be inundated by a pile of deadlines, but she liked it that way – all that mattered was that she was her own boss. And having Hugo around, of course, even though he seemed to be away in Boston more than he was at home. 'It's just temporary. It won't be for more than six months,' he had said to Anna before his first trip to help establish the US office of his law firm. But a year had passed and Hugo still left her every Sunday night, returning on the red-eye flight into Heathrow on a Friday morning, so exhausted that the weekend passed by in a blur until it was time for him to leave again. Anna was left wondering if she was destined for the kind of long-distance relationship she'd read about and abhorred.

'Was the interview worth it?' Caro tilted her head and gave Anna a searching look.

'Are you kidding? Who wouldn't want the opportunity to speak with the maestro who has no fewer than three of his creations in the top best-selling perfumes list this year?' The wine was going to Anna's head and she was unable to keep a note of sarcasm from her voice. She'd asked herself that very same question – was it worth it? – as she'd run in a fluster out of the door at five fifteen.

'So how's your week been?' Anna went on absently, making a mental note to call Hugo when she got home, if she hadn't heard from him by then.

'We won the pitch,' said Caro, as an enormous cheer went up from the crowd at the bar.

'What?' said Anna.

Caro leant forward. 'We won the pitch,' she said more slowly, emphasising each word.

'Wow, that's fantastic news,' said Anna, with genuine pleasure. Caro had been working on the three-way pitch for a French high-end jewellery brand for weeks and Anna knew winning meant so much to her.

'I've never been so scared in all my life, standing in front of the whole marketing department in their Paris office and presenting my ideas for the campaign. Even the managing director popped in towards the end – she's English, but incredibly chic, and it was slightly unnerving her being there. It felt like being interviewed, but far worse, as I was the one doing all the talking, and it wasn't till I'd finished that anybody spoke. But they loved my presentation and even clapped at the end. Then there was the agonising wait. They took their time coming back to me, but it was so worth it when they called to say we'd won the pitch.' Caro drew in a breath. Her cheeks had grown quite pink. 'And my boss wants me to work out of our Paris office. Isn't it amazing?'

Anna kept on smiling. Of course it was amazing, but she was unable to ignore a worm of anxiety starting up in her stomach. First Hugo as good as moving to Boston and now Caro moving to Paris. Her two best, her two only, friends. But she wasn't going to show it.

'This calls for a toast,' Anna said decisively, and grabbed the bottle. It was empty. Laughing, she insisted she buy another, but it meant queueing at the bar, where she had to wait ages to be served, while the office party continued in full swing around her. She tried to pass the time by checking her phone, but there were no messages from Hugo or anyone else. Why would there be, she thought bitterly, when Hugo was working in his Boston office thousands of miles away and her only other friend was sitting across the room. But her mood lightened after she'd finally got hold of the bottle of bubbly and two glasses and made it back to their table.

'To my amazing talented friend,' said Anna, toasting Caro with her glass. She took a sip and enjoyed the sensation of bubbles bursting against her tongue.

'Did you know that Paris is only three hours from London?' said Caro happily. 'Say you'll come and stay once I'm set up in an apartment. It'll be so much fun and we can do all the touristy stuff together.'

Anna drained her glass and felt a rush of fuzzy warmth towards Caro for including her in her plans and for being such a kind and generous friend. 'Definitely,' she said. 'I'd love to.'

An hour later and with the second bottle finished, Anna stood up to go and had to steady herself on the edge of the table. 'I'm not sure I should go back on the bus,' she said.

'Then we'll share a cab,' said Caro, who thought nothing of jumping in a cab whenever it suited her. 'I'll get it to drop you off first.'

'Are you sure? You don't have to,' said Anna.

'Of course I do. Come on, you.' Caro took Anna's arm. The two women left the bar a little unsteadily and walked towards the bright lights of Shaftesbury Avenue and Theatreland, where Caro hailed a black cab, and they headed through the traffic for home.

Anna climbed out of the cab and turned to wave Caro goodbye. She swayed a little as she climbed up the steps of the block of flats where she and Hugo lived. She wished they hadn't shared that second bottle, and also regretted not eating anything before setting out. She aimed her key at the lock but missed, and kept jabbing until it finally made contact. As she stepped into the dark hallway, the automatic ceiling light clicked on, casting a ghostly glow onto the letters and flyers strewn over the grubby mat. Not bothering to stoop down to see if any were for her, she started up the two flights of stairs, her only thoughts to get inside her flat and flake out on the sofa.

After wrestling again with the key, she managed to push open her own front door, with a long sigh of relief at being back home. The answering machine on the telephone table blinked at her. She hadn't been expecting anyone to call, so she ignored it and walked into the kitchen, where she poured herself a large glass of cold water from the tap. She drank it down, took two slices of bread from a packet on the counter and dropped them into the toaster. While she was waiting for the toast to pop up, she went back to the answering machine and pressed the message button. For a few seconds all she could hear was a hissing sound, and she was about to delete the message when her mother's panicky voice filled the hallway.

'Anna? Anna? Are you there? Pick up, will you?'

There was a pause and Anna thought she had hung up. It wouldn't be the first time. Her mother hated leaving messages, so something must be badly wrong for her to do so. Anna held her breath till her mother started speaking again.

'Anna. It's your father. Call me, will you, as soon as you get this.' And the voice faded out.

Anna's breath came fast as she punched the button to listen again in case she'd missed something, but there was nothing more. Her hand shook as she jabbed out her mother's number and waited impatiently for her to pick up, as various dread-filled scenarios raced through her mind. Had her father had an accident, a heart attack, a stroke even? Or had he left Mum for another woman? No, that last thought was unthinkable.

There was a click and there was her mother's voice again. 'Hello? Anna, is it you?' She sounded tearful. Anna's chest tightened.

'Mum! What's happened?' she shouted, her head now

completely clear, as if her evening downing wine with Caro had never taken place.

'Dad is dangerously ill. He's been taken to hospital... in Kuala Lumpur. He's been there all week at a conference.' Anna could hear her mother's shuddery breath, before she carried on, 'Phil, his work colleague, he's been so kind. He's been with Dad at the hospital and says he's being looked after. But I'm so scared. I don't know what to do.'

'Mum, it's OK. But tell me, what's wrong with Dad?' Anna's heart pounded in anticipation of the worst possible news.

'They're doing tests and think it's pneumonia. I don't know any more than that.'

Anna let go of her breath. Pneumonia can't be as bad as a heart attack, can it? She knew little about the illness, other than it was something old people got, but her father wasn't old. She remembered that her great-aunt Lucy had passed away a few days after contracting pneumonia – but she'd been in her nineties.

'Let me come over, Mum. I can get the Oxford Tube. It runs all night.' Anna didn't fancy making her way over to Shepherd's Bush and waiting for a night bus along with drunken rowdy students on their way home after a night out in the capital, but she couldn't very well not offer.

'No, darling, it's far too late. I feel better now I've spoken to you. Come tomorrow, will you?'

Anna heard her mother blow her nose and felt a twang of guilt as she agreed, but insisted her mother should call her back if she heard anything more from Phil.

Hanging up, Anna decided she needed a cup of tea. She was still shaking at the news. It was inconceivable that her father could suddenly have fallen ill. He was never ill; he always looked after himself, hardly drank and was paranoid about his fitness, going out running at least three times a week.

She went back into the kitchen and caught sight of the toast, which she'd forgotten about. It looked cold and unappetising. She threw it away and was filling the kettle when her mobile rang.

'Hugo! Thank God it's you!' Anna cried out in relief at the sound of his voice.

'What is it, hon? You sound upset.' Hugo's voice was faint and she could hear people chatting in the background. She glanced at the clock over the cooker. It glowed 22.45. He'd still be in the office, she guessed, calculating five hours back for Boston time.

'It's Dad. He's been taken ill in Kuala Lumpur and had to go to hospital. Mum's in pieces, so I'm going over tomorrow to be with her. I don't know for how long, so I'll miss you on Friday. I'm so sorry.'

There was a silence from Hugo. All she could hear was muffled background chatter and laughter.

'Hugo? Are you still there?'

'Yeah, sorry. Someone just asked me something. Listen, I'm really sorry to hear about your dad, but don't worry about Friday. That's why I was calling. My boss has arranged a client dinner tomorrow night, so I won't be back till Saturday morning anyway. I'll come over to Oxford, if you want.'

It was Anna's turn to go silent. How could Hugo be so offhand when it was obvious she was in the middle of a crisis? She began to shiver and drew the sides of her blouse tighter together. 'No, you don't have to. I can manage with Mum. Why don't you call me when you land?'

'Yeah, I'll do that. And Anna, try not to worry too much. I'm sure your dad'll be fine.'

FOUR

Anna stood in front of the locked door of her father's study, the key clenched in her hand. Fortunately, her mother had found it hanging on the key rack in the kitchen where her father had put it, the day he'd left for his fateful business trip. So much had happened since then, she reflected, that it seemed much longer, almost a lifetime ago. 'Come on, Dad. We can do this,' Anna muttered under her breath as she slid the key into the lock.

Everything had been left untouched since he'd left: his black swivel chair was pushed underneath the pine work surface that occupied an entire wall. A sleek silver iMac computer was positioned in the centre. Above the desk was aluminium shelving that stretched to the ceiling, clearly where her father kept everything of importance. The top shelf was crammed with rows of books and below it was a shelf full of labelled box files; on the bottom shelf was family-related stuff, like the wonky blue dish she'd once made in pottery, now containing golf tees, receipts and a National Trust membership card. There was a silver-framed photo of herself aged about fifteen, standing between her father, who was making a silly face at the camera, and her grandmother. Mum had taken the photo. She remembered that trip well – it was one of the times Dad had taken them to see her grandmother, who lived in a tiny village in Friesland in the north of the Netherlands. The photo was taken not long after her grandfather had died and she remembered how sad she'd felt that she'd never see him again. Her grandmother was kind and fussed over them with delicacies she'd been especially proud of, some based around raw fish, which Anna had been too polite to refuse. Conversation had been limited, as her grandmother had no English to speak of and spoke in an unfamiliar dialect, but Anna found she could get the gist of what she said to her father as some words were similar to English.

Anna picked up another faded colour photo and examined it. It had been taken at the back of her grandmother's house on the edge of the water, with the small white skiff that had once belonged to her grandfather moored there. Anna was sitting on the bank next to the Dutch boy who often used to visit with his parents. Luuk, his name was; Anna smiled, remembering how she used to look forward to their visits. She'd enjoyed having someone her own age to hang around with; he'd taught her how to fish and steer her grandfather's skiff. *How long ago can that have been*, Anna thought, with nostalgia and sadness.

The chair glided smoothly over the wooden floor as Anna pulled it from under the desk. A smile lifted the corners of her lips as she sat down on the chair, set up for her father's tall frame. She pumped the lever at the side till she was in the proper position to sit with her hands resting comfortably on the desk. She sat there for several long minutes, gazing around and trying to imagine her father, his brow furrowing as he tapped away at his computer. But she found she couldn't, for his study was his private space; she had always respected that and never came in here.

Glancing at her watch, Anna sighed. She knew she had to get on with her own work; she had several pressing deadlines. It

had been her mother's idea for her to take over the study,
despite Anna's protests. Barely a week had passed since the
funeral and everything was still so raw for them both. By staying
at the house Anna could spend more time helping her mother
through this awful time, so she was willing to do it. She
unzipped her laptop bag, opened the lid of her computer,
logged on, and was soon lost in writing the article she needed to
hand in by the end of the day.

* * *

It was three weeks earlier. Anna stood in her mother's large
basement kitchen drinking the mug of strong tea her aunty Jane
had just handed her. She'd sugared it and Anna winced slightly,
but after she'd taken a few sips the sweetness soothed her. She
was exhausted, but she knew her mother was too after long days
and nights of caring for her husband, now an invalid in a bed
made up in the living room. Aunty Jane had insisted her mother
take a break and was plying her with sweet tea and buttered
toast at the scrubbed pine kitchen table. But once again, there
was his voice, and she caught her sister's eye.

'Shall I go?' said Jane, putting down her own cup of tea.

'No, I'll do it. He only wants me,' Anna's mother said with a
heavy sigh, as she got wearily to her feet and headed off to
attend to him again.

Anna exchanged a look with her aunt, a look that spoke of
intense anxiety. They both knew her father was not doing so
well.

The hospital in Kuala Lumpur had allowed Anna's father to
travel home after ten days. The tests they'd run had proved
inconclusive. His dangerously high temperature had come
down and a chest X-ray confirmed the signs of inflammation on
his lungs. It may get worse, he'd been told, but they were happy
to discharge him so he could fly home. Phil had stayed on after

the conference to accompany his colleague to the airport and onto the thirteen-hour flight back to London. He'd even insisted on driving him back home to Oxford, so he could give Anna's mother the details of the sudden illness that had led to his hospitalisation.

The night before he was due home, Anna had arrived with a small suitcase, expecting to spend a few days until her father had settled in. But when he'd shuffled through the door, supported by Phil, and looked up at her through hooded eyes with only the whisper of a smile, Anna had known instantly that he was a lot sicker than anyone had been prepared to admit. She watched as he winced in concentration, putting one foot in front of the other, stopping to catch his breath only for it to develop into a deep hacking cough. Phil shot her a sympathetic look, but she was so overcome with shock she didn't know what to do. Her mother took over and helped her husband over to the sofa. She'd made it up with extra cushions and a blanket, which he'd clutched to his chest as he sank down. Almost immediately he'd fallen asleep.

'I'd get a doctor to look him over,' Phil had said with a worried frown. 'He wasn't able to settle on the flight, despite the medication to relieve his cough and help him sleep.'

Anna's mother had tried her best to get Phil to stay for a meal as a thank you, but he declined, saying he needed to return home to his own family in Bristol. The past couple of weeks had clearly taken it out of him too.

Two days later, Anna's father was back in hospital, where he went downhill rapidly after coughing up blood and being put on oxygen to help him breathe. The call came at midnight and they headed straight to his bedside. At 3 a.m., Anna and her mother sitting either side of the hospital bed, each holding one of his clammy hands, he drew in his last breath.

* * *

Anna corrected a few typos in her article and printed it off, before giving it a final read through. She hunted around on the shelves for a stapler but couldn't find one. She kept looking, pulling open drawers and rummaging through an assortment of pens, pencils, packets of envelopes in various sizes and several unused lined notebooks, but no stapler.

What does it matter, she thought, as she tapped the sheets of paper on the desk so they were aligned, and folded the left-hand corner over to secure them.

She sat back and swivelled the chair round to face the window overlooking the garden, which was waking up after winter. Daffodils swayed gently in the spring breeze and a profusion of yellow and purple crocuses nestled below her childhood apple tree, which was on the verge of bursting into delicate pink and white blossom. *How Dad loved his garden, and he won't ever see it again,* thought Anna sadly, and quickly twisted away from the view. Not wanting to linger any longer among the things that brought back such bittersweet memories, she stood up abruptly... and something caught her attention that she hadn't noticed before.

The cylindrical tin stood at the back of the middle shelf, just visible behind several box files. Pulling it out, she smiled at the old-fashioned blue-and-cream picture of a man holding a tray of what looked like buns, which he was placing into the mouth of a wide baker's oven. Above the picture were the words *Twentsche Beschuit,* and underneath, *Bolletje.* Anna knew it was Dutch. She vaguely recalled seeing a similar-looking tin, containing circular rusks, that her grandmother always put out on the breakfast table.

Intrigued, but feeling slightly guilty to be going through his private things, Anna tried to prise open a corner of the lid with her fingernail, but the metal stuck fast. Her nail broke, but she didn't let that deter her; she was more curious than ever to find a way to open the tin. She'd noticed a silver letter opener in one of the drawers and was sure it would do the job. She carefully applied the tip of the blade to the bottom of the lid and it began to ease open. A musty smell hit her nostrils, suggesting it had been left languishing on the shelf for a long time. She peered inside, but there didn't appear to be much, apart from what looked like a blue silk scarf, folded over and over into a small square parcel. Anna lifted it out and placed it on the desk, noticing something solid in its centre. Gently unfolding it, she found a tiny coin medallion threaded onto a silver chain. She held it up for closer inspection and saw *Sixpence* inscribed across the bottom below the date: *1942*. It was slightly bent and looked as if someone had tried to beat it back into shape and had punched a small hole for the chain.

Anna cupped the necklace in her hand and let the metal warm against her palm. Was this an old heirloom that her father had forgotten about after shoving it to the back of the shelf? Or was it there because he didn't want anyone to know about it, and this was why he never wanted anyone to come into his study? But why? Anna turned the tin upside down, hoping to find some clue, but it was empty. She wasn't sure what to do. Telling her mother might upset her even more so soon after Dad had passed away; but Anna knew she couldn't just forget about what she'd found. She glanced around at the bookshelves and the large number of box files and wondered if one of them might provide the answer. Then just as she reached up to bring down the first file, she heard her mother's voice calling her to lunch. She hesitated, then decided to leave it where it was for now. Turning her attention to the medallion still lying on the desk, she grasped it in her fist, before wrapping it back in the scarf and returning it to the tin. The box files would have to wait.

FIVE

ILSE

Ilse had a plan, but if she told her mother about it, she would only worry unnecessarily. Her mother worried a lot more since the Bakkers at number ten were raided, starting at the slightest noise in the street, convinced it would be their turn next. Everyone was nervous they would be next. But Ilse couldn't let the thought of *moffen* forcing their way into their home to intimidate her. If she and her parents were to survive, she had to get out each day and make sure she returned with enough food for the three of them to have an evening meal of sorts – that was all that mattered.

'I do believe it's not so cold today.' Ilse stood staring out of the kitchen window at the drips of water forming at the ends of icicles. She knew it was wishful thinking, as the kitchen was still icy cold, like the rest of the house. Since before Christmas, they'd closed off most of the rooms, using just two bedrooms, the bathroom and kitchen, in an attempt to save heat. *What a joke*, thought Ilse, trying to make light of the fact that they had no means of heating their house now the Germans had cut off supplies of oil, gas and electricity. The one saving grace was the small contraption Mr Bakker had rigged up for them, consisting of a foot-high tin cylinder with an inner compartment into which slivers of woodchips were fed. By balancing a cooking pot on top, they could at least boil water and heat soups.

Ilse rubbed her hands together and turned to her mother. 'I need to get going. I've heard that the butcher in town is opening for an hour this morning. I've no idea what meat he has or if I'll even get any, but it's worth a try. Wish me luck.'

As she leant in for a kiss, her mother grabbed hold of her daughter's cold hands in her own and stared into her eyes. 'You shouldn't have to do this. At your age, you should be out living your life, not foraging for food to keep us alive. We're too old...'

Ilse cut her off. It was unbearable to hear her mother speak like that, even though she knew it was true. She often thought of her lost student years and that she would have been nearly four years through her degree on her way to being qualified to be a doctor. 'No, Mother. This is what I need to do for the three of us and I wouldn't have it any other way.' She kissed her cheek. 'Make sure Pa eats some of the leftover soup, won't you?'

Her mother nodded. 'You're so good to us,' she said, her eyes welling up.

Ilse hurried along the almost deserted streets, clutching the tips of her coat collar together against the cold wind. In her other hand, she grasped tight her woven shopping bag containing the fine woollen scarf Willem had given her for her twentieth birthday. They'd been walking back from celebration drinks at the Bruin Café with all her student friends when he'd surprised her, stopping at the bridge over the canal and pulling the beautiful cherry-red scarf from his pocket. At that moment, a breeze had whipped up, lifting it between his fingers into a gorgeous crimson swirl, before he was able to tame it by draping it across her shoulders. She remembered how he'd reined her in with the scarf so their noses touched. 'Happy birthday,' he'd whispered, before kissing her chastely on the lips. He'd told her he hadn't wanted to give her his present in front of everyone in case they jumped to conclusions. It was so like Willem, so sensitive and self-effacing, and so unwavering in his love for her.

Less than six weeks later, along with thousands of other young Dutch men, he received his summons by the German authorities to go and work in Germany. Willem spent the next few agonising days discussing his options with her, but none of them made any sense. If he refused to go, he ran the risk of being arrested and shot, but if he went into hiding he feared his family would suffer reprisals. And hiding had its own dangers: he had no connections or ration coupons; who would take him in? It was a frightening time for them both and Ilse was scared for him. Eventually, Willem decided his only option was to go. In his first letter home he told her that when he'd arrived at the station the place was swarming with armed guards, making him and all the hundreds of men gathered there feel like criminals. They'd set off, not knowing their destination till they arrived in Lübeck, where they were taken to a labour camp and the hard labour began.

The wind stung her face, making her eyes water, but the tears she blinked back were for those sweet innocent times together, when a world of possibilities lay before them. Or so they had imagined before the war had so cruelly intervened. That late winter's morning, she'd thought briefly about wearing the scarf one last time, but had decided against it. She didn't want her mother asking any questions.

Ilse put the scarf from her mind and concentrated on putting one foot in front of the other till she arrived at the house of Mr Vos, her father's friend who used to come to the house to play clarinet while her father played the piano. How she loved to hear the strains of Mozart's 'Aria Grazioso' from *Don Giovanni* drift up to her room at the top of the house where she sat poring over her medical books. Ilse couldn't remember when he'd stopped coming, but nowadays the absence of music in the cold house haunted her.

She knocked quietly, not wanting to shock Mr Vos into thinking he was receiving an unwelcome visitor, but nothing stirred; he couldn't have heard. She knocked a little louder. A concerned face appeared at the window to her left, recognised her and broke into a smile. Moments later, he appeared at the door.

'Ilse, how good to see you. How are you, and your mother and your father?' Mr Vos was a tall man of about fifty with thick, unkempt grey hair. Ilse smiled, warmed by the familiarity of him, thinking how he still looked the same as he always had, though it was obvious the weight had dropped off him.

'As good as can be expected, Mr Vos. Perhaps it's best if I come in a moment?'

'Of course, how rude of me not to offer. Can I make you a coffee? I'm sorry, but I only have the acorn kind.'

Ilse shook her head to decline as she followed him into the long dark hallway hung with landscape paintings and an ornate antique Frisian *schippertje* clock ticking softly at the far end. She didn't want to put him to any trouble, and besides she really couldn't stay long if she was to get to the butcher's on time.

She reached into her bag and brought out the scarf, which she'd wrapped in brown paper and tied with twine. 'You can look at it if you like,' she said, holding out the package.

'My wife will be back any minute, so I'll take your word for it. Wool, is it?'

'A fine weave. And it's hardly been worn.' She lifted one corner so he could take a peek.

He smiled approvingly. 'She won't have been expecting such a birthday gift as this. I'm sure she'll be delighted with it. And thank you.' He turned and walked off into the kitchen, returning with a brown stone bottle of jenever.

'Here you are. It's a good one, so mind you get something decent with it.'

Ilse hesitated, knowing that by taking the bottle he would be denying himself the opportunity to get hold of food for himself and his wife.

He seemed to sense her reluctance in accepting the bottle, and placed it firmly in her bag. 'There are more where this came from, but please don't go shouting about it,' he said quietly. 'And if you and your parents ever find yourselves in need, don't hesitate to ask.'

The queue snaked down the street. Ilse's heart sank. She knew she'd missed her chance of getting anything, but she couldn't give up now. She took her place behind a woman wrapped in a shawl who was holding hands with a tiny blue-lipped boy wearing a man-sized cap. He didn't complain, merely looked from his mother to Ilse with solemn grey eyes as they slowly edged forward towards the open door. No one spoke. What was there to say, thought Ilse, not allowing herself to dwell on the very real possibility that she would walk away empty-handed.

When the woman and the boy came out of the shop, she shook her head sadly at Ilse. Ilse felt her insides clench. That poor little boy... what would they do now for food? If it hadn't been for her own starving parents, she would have thrust the bottle at her and run back home. But instead, she gave the woman a sympathetic smile and walked through the door.

The butcher had served Ilse's family all his life and his tired face lifted into a weak smile when he recognised her. He showed her his palms and said he was sorry, he had not a scrap of meat left.

'Do you really have nothing?' Ilse said boldly, as she lifted her bag onto the counter with a clunk. 'I do have this.' She kept her eyes on his as she showed him the top of the bottle.

The butcher let out an exasperated sigh. 'If I could count the number of bottles of jenever I've been offered today, I'd be a rich man... or very drunk.' He gave an embarrassed laugh, but Ilse stood her ground, stony-faced.

'So you have absolutely nothing? My father...' Her breath caught in her throat. '... I don't know how much longer he has, but I want him to taste real food one last time.' She hated having to voice what she feared, but what else could she do? It wasn't a lie, even though she knew he himself wasn't telling the truth. So she placed the bottle onto the counter – a superior-quality gin, the likes of which no one had seen since before the war – and pushed it towards him.

He sniffed a long breath in, as if imagining the sharp aroma of gin. Ilse waited, hoping he would be tempted. Then, without looking her in the eye, he leant down and pulled out a package from under the counter. 'This is absolutely my last cut. It'll be enough for a couple of meals if you're careful.'

He didn't elaborate and Ilse didn't want to ask what meat it might be. She'd heard about the pet dogs that had gone missing. She pursed her lips into a tight smile and thanked him, then dropped the packet into her bag and walked out of the shop.

The queue outside was as long as when she'd first arrived. She couldn't bear to walk past the line of long-suffering desperate people, so she hurried away in the opposite direction.

SIX

It wasn't until the following morning that Ilse told her mother how she'd come by the meat. She hadn't wanted to confess, but her parents were so buoyed up by the nutritious meal she was able to put on the table that she knew she had to tell her. One good meal was never going to be enough. Once they had tasted the morsels of meat and gravy mashed into a mix of potato and turnip there was no turning back.

'Do you really think I didn't guess?' said her mother, after Ilse had told her about exchanging her precious scarf for the jenever. 'I've been thinking about doing the same myself, but can't quite bring myself to part with our valuables. But soon we'll no longer have any choice – money buys next to nothing these days.'

Ilse nodded, thinking about the small wad of guilder notes her mother had pressed into her hand the previous week. She'd arrived at the baker's to discover that the only bread on sale was a dense dark loaf costing forty guilders. She'd swallowed hard as she'd passed over the money, a small fortune. It wasn't that her parents couldn't afford it – like many Dutch families they were reasonably well off – but there was virtually nothing left in the shops once food supply lines had been cut off due to the German blockade of rail and water routes, leaving millions of people in the grip of famine. What little food was available had become so expensive that money no longer had any currency.

So, piece by piece, Ilse bartered the silverware handed down from her grandmother to her mother and that one day would have passed on to her, and the intense physical pain she'd felt handing over the scarf that first time soon faded. Six silver teaspoons gave them half a dozen eggs and she exchanged the small silver bowl bearing her grandparents' initials for a wedge of hard cheese – these were the hard decisions they were forced to make.

And then, as the shops closed their doors, even that method of obtaining food was no longer an option. There was simply nothing left to buy or exchange as barter.

Once more, Ilse went off on her ancient bike to forage for food wherever she could find any. And she wasn't the only one. The vegetable fields were filled with people, all desperate to dig up anything they might grate, grind up or boil. Often Ilse would return home, her hands red-raw with all the scrabbling through the dirt and only a few knobbly tubers to show for her efforts. But she had her bike, which meant she could go further into the flat polders than those who had travelled on foot from the towns.

One day, after searching for hours and finding nothing, she was about to return home when she came across a group of three women, all stooped over and digging. She wheeled her bike alongside them and glanced at the brown-and-creamy-white bulbous things that lay at their feet. Of course she knew what they were, but she asked all the same.

The oldest-looking of the three women straightened up. She looked so weary. 'Tulip bulbs. We've been told they're nutritious. What else are we to do when there's nothing left to eat?' She sighed heavily and went back to her work, muttering to the other two women, who were filling a small handcart beside them.

Ilse hadn't known that tulip bulbs were edible, but she wasn't going to pass up the opportunity. She moved to another part of the field and set to work digging. The ground was frozen hard, but once she'd penetrated the surface, she unearthed dozens of bulbs, some already sprouting tiny yellowy-green shoots, which had been planted in rows. Working fast, she soon filled her panniers. There would be more than enough for herself and her parents, as well as some for the Bakkers.

More people arrived on foot as she pedalled away with her haul. Her heart was lighter than it had felt in weeks, even though she knew that what she was doing was theft. She couldn't wait to get home and present her mother with her haul.

But the reaction she received wasn't at all what she'd been expecting. Her mother wept when Ilse presented her with the tulip bulbs.

'No, no,' she said, wiping away her tears. 'Is this what we're now reduced to eating?'

Ilse stared at her, feeling deflated. 'I thought you'd be happy. There's more here than I've ever managed to bring back before. What else was I to do?' she said in frustration.

Her mother's tears still came. She wasn't to be placated. 'Ilse, I know you're only doing your best, but can't you see how desperate things are? And when there are no more tulip bulbs, what then? Tulip bulbs, we can't eat tulip bulbs...' She kept shaking her head as if she couldn't countenance the idea.

'Well, that's all there is, so you'll have to put up with it. It's the only food we have.' Ilse grabbed the pannier and shoved it beside the stove, then scooped out several handfuls of bulbs to fill her shopping bag. 'I'm going next door. I'm sure Mr Bakker will be grateful.' She walked out of the kitchen door, slamming it behind her, then immediately felt guilty about leaving her mother in that state. She understood her despair, but in the heat of the moment had felt sorry for herself. She was the one who left the house each freezing cold morning on a bike that was falling apart, not knowing where or if she'd be able to scavenge food, and in the knowledge that one of these days she would return empty-handed. Had her mother any idea how hard it was for her?

Later that evening, with food warming their bellies, Ilse and her mother had both calmed down. Pa, who had come to sit with them for meals since Ilse had brought back the meat, was in good spirits and his cheeks even had a bit of colour in them, though this might have come from the soft light of the flickering candle, their only source of light after dark. The three of them sat round the table, enjoying a surprisingly good soup Ilse's mother had created from a small chopped onion and grated tulip bulbs and flavoured with a pinch of curry powder.

Ilse felt tempted to say, 'See? Tulip bulbs aren't so bad after all,' but she desisted. Instead, she talked about what else they could do with the bulbs, such as roasting them and using the coffee grinder to make bulb flour. 'Imagine, we'll be able to make a cake,' she said, though she knew that was probably going a bit far. As much as she wanted to enthuse about her discovery and what it would do in terms of keeping her parents alive, she knew there was only so much one could do to make these dull bulbs taste better.

Word spread about this unexpected new source of food and soon the roads leading to the bulb fields were packed with people wheeling prams, rusty old pushchairs and wooden carts piled up with bags, tin bowls, even suitcases. In fact, they brought anything they could fill with tulip bulbs.

Ilse made several more trips out to the polders and each time she had to fight for her patch among dozens of men, women and children, all desperate for their share. She no longer returned with her panniers full, but she had gathered enough to last the three of them for several weeks. By then, surely spring would be on its way, the weather less harsh and life a little easier? With that thought in mind, Ilse hummed quietly to herself as she climbed the stairs from the cellar where she'd laid out the bulbs in the dark and dry. Then she heard her mother calling her name. She emerged through the cellar door to where her mother was standing with two letters in her hand.

'A letter for you; Willem, I think, from the handwriting. Here you are.' She handed Ilse the envelope, which looked as if it had been opened and stuck down again. Ilse sighed, knowing that some German official had been reading their private letters and looking for anything that could be found incriminating. She knew Willem couldn't tell her what things were really like for him, so he never said much about himself. He would ask after her and her parents and end by saying how much he missed her. Still, boring as his letters were, Ilse was comforted to hear from him, though she was finding it increasingly hard to imagine a time that they would be together again. Her mother was still looking at her, perhaps hoping Ilse would open the letter and read it aloud. But Ilse refused to be drawn in, and tucked it into her skirt pocket for later. 'Who's the other letter from?' she asked.

'It's from Clara,' her mother said, and from the way she pursed her lips Ilse suspected it was serious. These days, the arrival of a letter could so easily bring devastating news.

'What is it?' said Ilse, fearing the worst. She thought of Clara, her mother's oldest friend, who lived some distance away in Hilversum where she and her husband, Hans, ran a busy doctor's practice from their house. And of Connie, their daughter, the friend she'd been at university with till it was shut down by the Germans. She hadn't heard from Connie in a while, she realised, and dread swept through her that something terrible must have happened.

'It's nothing to worry about,' said her mother, noting her daughter's worried expression. 'Clara's asking if you'd be prepared to go and help as a medical assistant at the sanatorium. There's been an outbreak of TB and the place is severely short-staffed. Clara and Hans are doing all they can to help when they're not seeing to their own patients, but it sounds as if they're having to work all hours. She thinks it'll only be for a few weeks.' She refolded the letter and slid it back into the envelope. 'You'll be good at it, Ilse, and you'll gain valuable experience. It's been so long since you were forced to give up on your studies, it's time you did something for yourself.'

Ilse knew her mother was right, but was torn as she took in the implications of leaving. After all her efforts to keep her parents alive, she simply couldn't abandon them. 'I would go, and it's what I've been studying for, but how will you manage? You can't go hunting for food while the weather's so cold.'

'We'll manage, darling. Don't forget we have a cellar full of tulip bulbs to last us for weeks. I admit you were right about them, even though they'll never be my first choice of food to eat. And there are still a few tins and dried beans in the cellar. Mr Bakker is next door and he'll look out for us. Take Clara up on her offer. It may only be for a few weeks until the weather improves.'

Ilse felt something shift inside her. If she didn't go, she would probably regret it. Although she was the one bringing in the food, she was only too aware hers was an extra mouth to feed. If she wasn't here, then the piles of bulbs lying on racks below their feet would go so much further. She knew her mother would never have put it that way – she was urging her to go because she wanted the best for her daughter. But more than anything, Ilse longed to escape this relentless life of misery, be with her best friend, Connie, and laugh and laugh like they used to when they were free as birds. And her mother knew that.

Ilse suddenly recalled something. 'When I was down in the cellar earlier I came across that tin of De Gruyter chocolate bars Pa laid down at the beginning of the war,' she said. 'Do you remember it? It's never been opened.' They both laughed at the memory of her father always putting off the day when they would share round such treasure.

'I promise we'll keep it till you come home. Don't you worry, we'll manage, my sweet Ilse,' her mother said, and held Ilse to her bony chest.

SEVEN

ANNA

Anna returned to her London flat, promising her mother she'd be back after the weekend.

The past days had been difficult for them both, as they were taken up with ploughing through endless paperwork relating to her father's death. They had found it emotionally draining and agreed they should give it a break for a few days. Anna was also missing being in her own space and looked forward to seeing Hugo after nearly a week apart. Aunty Jane had agreed to come and stay with her grieving sister over the weekend, so Anna was able to put aside any feelings of guilt about leaving her mother. It would be a relief to have time alone to process her thoughts about the meaning of the silver necklace, and to prepare herself for any possible revelations about her father's past.

She arrived back at the flat on Friday morning, glad to have the whole day ahead so she could get things straight before Hugo arrived. She knew he'd be tired after flying into Heathrow on the early-morning flight and going straight to the office to put in a full day's work. If only things didn't have to be like that, she thought wistfully, as she went about putting the dirty dishes left in the sink into the dishwasher. Why couldn't they just be like any other normal working couple and make more time for each other?

On the spur of the moment, she decided to book the new Italian restaurant she'd read about in the local paper; it was on the river at Richmond and had received excellent reviews.

Hugo walked through the door just after five, looking exhausted. He left his small suitcase in the hallway and went straight to the fridge for a cold beer, which he drank down in several long mouthfuls. 'I so needed that,' he said, wiping his mouth on his sleeve. He smiled at Anna, who was waiting for him to say hello. Did he not even think to ask how she was when he knew full well how upset she'd been about her father's death? She pursed her lips, waiting for him to show her some sympathy.

'I've had a pig of a week. Don't let me even think about work this weekend,' he said, seemingly unaware of her mood, as he helped himself to another beer from the fridge. After he'd finished that one, he went over and scooped her into a tight hug.

'Stop it! You're hurting me,' she cried out, still annoyed at him, but unable to stop laughing as he alternately squeezed and tickled her.

'I'm glad to be home,' Hugo breathed in her ear.

Anna felt the tension that had been building all week melt away. Perhaps life had become just a bit too serious recently.

The evening was warm for early May and the towpath was filled with runners, dog walkers, couples pushing toddlers in strollers and people on their way for a drink or supper at one of the many riverside bars and restaurants. Anna and Hugo sauntered along hand in hand, not talking much, but enjoying that delicious end-of-the-week feeling and the promise of two free days to come. They took their time, stopping to watch two scullers swoosh past side by side, their oars slapping the water perfectly in harmony; then again to look at a swan family with five fluffy grey cygnets grazing close to the far bank.

Anna had booked a table on the waterside terrace with views towards Richmond Bridge and downriver to Petersham Meadows. As they were being shown to their table, it occurred to her that they hadn't been out for a meal like this in more than a year.

'I've missed us doing this,' she said, turning to look at Hugo, who was already examining the wine list with great enthusiasm.

He didn't seem to hear her. 'There are some great reds, but you'll want white, right?' He glanced up briefly, before reading out the description of several wines that appealed to him.

'You choose, Hugo. I'm just happy to be here with you right now.' Anna breathed out and sat back in her chair, allowing herself to be calmed by the peaceful view of cows grazing in the meadows.

Hugo knew a lot about wine and always chose well. He selected the Sicilian Chardonnay from Palermo, saying it would make a good aperitif. Anna smiled indulgently and gave his hand a squeeze. 'Isn't this lovely?' she said, sweeping her hand in front of her.

'Couldn't be better,' said Hugo, finally taking in the view and grabbing her hand so he could press it to his lips.

While they waited for their order to arrive, he said, 'There's an antiques fair on in Burford tomorrow. I thought we could drive over and spend the day there. What do you think?'

'Oh, lovely,' said Anna, feigning enthusiasm. She'd been looking forward to having a quiet weekend at home, but it didn't seem to be what Hugo had in mind. He always had to have something on the go; if it wasn't work-related then he'd be pursuing some project or other. This time it was about hunting out nineteenth-century landscape paintings for next to nothing in the hope he'd be able to sell them on eBay for a fortune. To her irritation, he'd only lost money, although not too much.

Frankly, she didn't see the point of it all and was beginning to think they had more differences than interests in common.

The waiter arrived with the wine and an ice bucket. He made a great show of extracting the cork from the bottle and waiting while Hugo fussed over tasting it before declaring that it was acceptable.

Anna waited till this performance was finished before continuing their conversation. 'Burford sounds lovely, but it seems a shame to be inside when the weather's so good,' she said, gazing into her glass and swirling her wine round and round. 'Maybe we can combine going to Burford with a bit of a walk and a pub lunch?'

'OK, if that's what you want. But I don't want to pass up the chance of getting a bargain, so we'll need to leave early. Seven thirty, I'd say.' Hugo took a deep mouthful of wine and looked at her. 'Anna, don't be like that. It'll be fun.'

Anna realised she must have been pursing her lips. His words had made her tense up, but she was in no mood for an argument. She wanted the evening to be perfect, a reminder of the Friday nights they used to spend together when they first got together – the excitement of being just the two of them with the whole weekend stretching out ahead.

EIGHT

Early the next morning, Hugo dropped Anna off in the centre of Burford's pretty town centre, just as it was starting to come to life and the shops were unlocking their doors ready for a busy Saturday's trading. He spotted a small café with tables and chairs in front, and promised to meet her there in a couple of hours.

'That should give me plenty of time to get the pick of the bunch before the hordes turn up. Be good,' he said with a cheery smile, before swinging the car round and heading off to find a place to park.

Left to her own devices, Anna soon forgot about her disappointment at having her weekend hijacked. As much as she would have liked to have spent the morning with Hugo, the idea of wandering around the boutiques and artisan shops was considerably more appealing than pretending to be keen about some second-rate paintings. Feeling a little guilty that she thought that way, she bought Hugo a selection of cheeses from a delicatessen specialising in local produce, before treating herself to a couple of bottles of bath soak and body lotion made from Cotswold lavender. But after an hour or so of sauntering in and out of the shops she became bored and decided to sit at the café they'd agreed to meet, where she ordered a cappuccino and croissant.

She was popping the last of the croissant into her mouth when her mobile phone rang.

'Mum! Is everything all right?'

'Everything's fine, darling.' Anna could hear her mother draw in a breath. 'I've been sorting through your father's things...'

'Mum, we agreed you'd wait till I come back on Monday,' Anna said with an exasperated sigh.

'Something's been nagging me. It's something you should know that Dad mentioned in the weeks before...' Her voice faltered and she corrected herself. 'Some weeks ago.'

The croissant Anna had just eaten suddenly felt heavy on her stomach. 'What is it?' she said quietly, suddenly worried that her mother had stumbled upon something that had upset her.

'It's about his parents. This might come as a shock to you. He was going through some of his mother's old correspondence and was surprised to come across a sealed letter addressed to him, just before she died a couple of years ago. It must have lain hidden all this time, mixed up in a lot of papers. Anyway, he opened the letter and discovered he'd been adopted.'

'What?' said Anna in disbelief. 'You mean Oma wrote that in a letter and never talked to him about it?'

Anna heard her mother let out a sigh. 'Yes, that's right. Perhaps she didn't think it was important, but changed her mind when she became ill, and wrote the letter before she died.'

'That's quite a bombshell. Did she say who his biological parents were? Mum, did you read the letter yourself?'

'No. Your father translated it for me. It was quite short. She regretted not telling him sooner, but hoped he didn't think badly of her for not doing so.'

'It was a bit late for that!' Anna scoffed. 'How did Dad take the news?'

'Shocked and upset, as you can imagine.'

'Poor Dad! I wish he'd spoken to me about it.'

'He meant to, but it was shortly before he went to Kuala Lumpur and he was under a lot of pressure at the time. I came into his study late one evening and found him looking up stuff on the internet about who his biological parents might be. He had all kinds of theories. He assumed his real mother was Dutch, because he'd been brought up in the Netherlands, but he had no idea who his real father was and was beginning to speculate that he might even be German.'

'Really?' Anna exclaimed. 'On what grounds?' She found it hard to imagine having a tall blond-haired German for a grandfather, the polar opposite to the kindly rotund man she knew as Opa. And her father certainly hadn't looked very Germanic with his dark hair and fine features, she thought, letting her mind wander.

'It was just a hunch. He'd been reading about the number of war babies born to Dutch mothers who'd been in a relationship with a German soldier. It seemed to be the only plausible reason to be given up for adoption.'

'Oh, Mum.' Anna sighed, sensing there was more to this than she was letting on. She glanced at her watch. She didn't want Hugo turning up in the middle of this conversation. But there was no sign of him yet.

Her mother went on, 'Well, he found out nothing about his father, but he discovered that his real mother lived in a small town called Rijswijk.'

'Rijswijk,' Anna repeated, but suspected they were both pronouncing it incorrectly. It was another of those tricky Dutch words her father used to tease her about. She regretted never learning the language as a little girl, but she had found it hard when no one apart from her father had spoken it. Perhaps it was time to give it a go. 'So, what was her name?'

'I'm sorry, Anna. He might have said, but I'm afraid I've forgotten. He said he'd go into it more when he returned home from Kuala Lumpur. You see, all this investigation into his family meant he was behind with his presentation, and he was anxious to get back to it. I thought he'd put the matter to one side, so it was a shock when I was sorting through his desk drawer and found an old document case I thought he'd thrown out years ago. Inside were train and boat tickets to Holland made out in his name. He must have booked them just before leaving. They're dated 29 May – that's only a week away. He must have been intending to visit his real mother.'

Anna swallowed hard, wondering if she'd heard her right. 'So, you think he was going to find the mother he'd never met and was going to confront her about who his real father was?'

'He must have been,' her mother said, her voice high, clearly trying to hold back her tears. 'It's so sad he was getting close to the truth. But maybe it's for the best.'

Anna was concentrating so hard on what her mother had told her that she didn't notice that Hugo had arrived, until he came up behind her and planted a kiss on her cheek. Taken by surprise, she started and frowned at him, before cupping her hand over her mobile and mouthing, 'My mother.'

Hugo pulled down the corners of his mouth, which irritated her, so she turned her back on him to carry on her conversation. It bothered her that her mother sounded so resigned. Didn't she realise how important this piece of news was? That it wasn't just about Dad's relatives, but Anna's too?

'Mum, I'm out with Hugo right now, but we must talk more. Can I call you later?'

'Sorry, darling. You go off and have a nice day with Hugo and don't worry about calling me back. I'm seeing you on Monday, aren't I?'

'OK, Mum. But wait until I come before you go through any more of Dad's things. I don't want you being on your own and getting upset.'

'I'm fine, darling. Jane's about to turn up, so there'll be no time for that. Don't worry about me. Love you.'

'Love you.' Anna switched off her mobile and suppressed a sigh as she turned to Hugo.

'What's all that about?' he said, just as the waitress arrived to take his order for coffee. 'Can I get a large latte and blueberry muffin? Anna, what do you want?'

What she really wanted was a stiff drink. Her mind was reeling and she had no idea what to make of her mother's announcement. 'Another cappuccino, please,' she said to the waitress. Anna just wanted her to leave them alone and was relieved when she walked away.

'Look what I've managed to get,' Hugo said. He seemed to have forgotten that Anna had been talking urgently to her mother a moment ago. He laid a bundle of three pictures tied up in brown paper on the table. He fumbled with the string and peeled back the paper to reveal three perfectly pleasant English landscapes of hills and rivers. 'Guess how much I paid for them?' He looked at Anna with all the expectancy of a small boy wanting praise.

Anna forced her attention to the paintings and picked each one up in turn. 'Fifty pounds each?' She had absolutely no idea.

'You're way off! I got all three for eighty! How about that?' he said, looking exceptionally pleased.

'That's... amazing,' she said. 'And how much do you think you'll make?'

'They're signed on the back, so they may have some provenance. Wouldn't it be great if they were worth something?' He began wrapping them up again as if they needed protecting.

Anna looked away and gazed into the middle distance, thinking about what her mother had just told her. Her father had bought a ticket to Holland and was planning on going to meet his mother. Surely that meant he had contacted her already? If that were the case, his mother would still be expecting his visit. But she wouldn't have known that her son had died, and when he didn't show up she'd probably worry, or think he'd lost his nerve about coming. Anna couldn't let that happen. She knew she had to go in his place.

NINE

ILSE

It was a cold early-spring day, but memories of summers past filled Ilse's head as she walked along the long tree-lined private road leading to the Van Dongens' sprawling house. When Ilse had been a young girl, her parents had come here to spend the summer holidays with their friends, whose daughter, Connie, was exactly her age. Growing up, the two only children were so close, they were almost like sisters. Although they went to different schools in different towns, they ended up studying at Leiden University at the same time. They'd been so excited at sharing digs together. But it didn't last, for within a year the Germans had closed the university. Initially, the girls stayed on, studying under the tutelage of older students; it was a bonus that they were allowed to take their first-year exams at the University of Nijmegen. By then, they'd imagined the war would be truly over and they could return to Leiden, but in the meantime life, under the Germans, had deteriorated considerably. With academic institutions, including libraries, no longer open to students, Ilse had no choice but to return home to care for her parents, while Connie took an administrative office job in her home town of Hilversum. In her letters to Ilse she didn't much talk about her job, which she dismissed as boring, but about her circle of friends and the evenings they went dancing together, just like in the old days at Leiden. It was a world away from Ilse's and made her nostalgic for their brief, carefree student days. Back then, their only worries were waking up in time for lectures and making sure they got their essays completed on time.

Ilse admired the houses in this road; they were all imposing, each with a big expanse of manicured lawn and shrubbery out front. She could only guess at how rich the people must be who resided there. She kept on walking till she saw the *paddestoel*, a red-and-white signpost in the shape of a toadstool denoting the start of the cycle path she and Connie often used to take through the woods, ending up for a cold drink at the pretty woodland village called Lage Vuursche, home to the country residence of the Dutch royal family.

She arrived at the end of the road. On her right was a painted sign of yellow sunbeams above the word *Zonnenstraal*, pointing towards the sanatorium where tuberculosis patients were sent to convalesce. Just visible through the tall pine trees was the sun-filled terrace on which patients lay on hospital beds, being attended to by a nurse. Ilse turned to walk up the wide drive and moments later the Van Dongens' large gabled house came into view. Her feet crunched on the gravel path leading to the front door and from somewhere within came the sound of hurrying footsteps. No sooner had she lifted her hand to ring the bell than the door flew open and there stood her dear friend Connie, whom she hadn't seen in more than two years. Tall and slender, just like her mother, she had short wavy fair hair that framed her smiling face. Ilse couldn't help but feel cheerful whenever she was in her friend's presence.

The two girls shrieked in delight and fell into each other's arms, hugging each other tight. Connie felt so solid, so reassuring, just as Ilse remembered. She knew instantly it had been right for her to come. She came out of the hug as Connie's mother, Clara – also tall and fair-haired – appeared in the hallway.

'Dear Ilse, come here,' she said, opening her arms wide. Ilse stepped into her embrace and briefly laid her head against her shoulder. She was determined to keep her emotions in check, but it was hard. Being here reminded her of happier times: the familiar medicinal smell mixed with wood polish, the loud tick of the clock, positioned opposite the front door so patients could check the time when they walked in, and listening to Clara's low calm voice – all this gave her a warm feeling that everything would be fine.

'It's so good of you to come and help. They're rushed off their feet at the sanatorium as they've doubled the number of patients in the past month and they can't get enough staff. I've told them you won't be able to start till after the weekend. That'll give you time to settle in.'

'I'll do everything I can to help. I haven't much practical experience though.'

Clara gave an airy wave of her hand. 'Don't you worry about that. You'll pick it up soon enough.'

'Come on in, Ilse. We've so much to catch up on,' said Connie impatiently. She linked her arm through Ilse's and took her into the spacious living room with its large picture window overlooking the lawn. 'Pa, look who's here,' she said to the figure deep in an armchair, engrossed in a newspaper.

'Why, Ilse!' Hans van Dongen lowered his paper and beamed at Ilse. 'Was the journey awful?' He frowned.

'The journey was fine. Just long. The train kept stopping in-between stations for no good reason and I had to show my ticket at least four times.'

'Well, you're here now,' Hans said, rubbing his hands. 'And just in time for lunch. You'll be hungry, I suppose?'

Ilse pressed her lips together and caught Connie's eye.

Connie raised her eyebrows with an expression that spoke of knowing how tactless her father could be. She herself knew that Ilse was hungry, starving in fact. But surely Connie's father also knew that food shortages where Ilse lived were much worse than in this part of the country? Ilse gave him a smile as Connie took her arm again, and the two girls went through into the dining room.

'Typical Pa. Just ignore him,' Connie said in a whisper, and gave Ilse's arm an encouraging squeeze. Ilse leant towards her friend, not offended in the least, just happy to be back in Connie's company without the responsibility of finding food to put on the table. Her stomach rumbled in anticipation of a proper meal, her first since bartering her precious scarf for the unidentified meat that she and her parents had devoured as if it had been the best meal they'd ever eaten.

The table was set for lunch. Ilse's eyes widened at the spread: a loaf on a cutting board, margarine in a glass dish, a plate of sliced cheese, an open jar of gherkins, a jar of jam and a tumbler of milk beside each place setting. Where had all this food come from? Her insides clenched, knowing her parents would probably be doing without a midday meal in order to make do with the little food they still had.

'You sit next to Connie,' said Clara, gently touching Ilse's arm.

Remembering to smile, Ilse took her seat.

'Apologies for the bread. It's a bit stale but it's edible,' Clara said, sawing a thick slice from the loaf and placing it on Ilse's plate. 'Help yourself to cheese and gherkins.'

'Here, let me,' said Connie, taking over and laying a slice of cheese on top of Ilse's bread. 'Gherkin?' she said, spearing one from the jar.

'No thank you,' Ilse said, looking at her plate. She no longer felt hungry. It just didn't seem right to be eating this much in one sitting. So instead, she sipped her milk; it tasted creamy, almost too rich. Her stomach cramped. Putting down her tumbler, she decided she had to say something. 'I'm not used to eating much at lunchtime. Do you mind if I have half a slice of bread?'

'I'm sorry. I wasn't thinking. I should have asked you first,' said Connie's mother, reddening a little as she took back the bread and replaced it with a smaller piece. 'Will this do?'

Ilse, who hated causing a fuss, became aware of all their eyes on her. She felt ungrateful turning down the offer of food, when her own parents were having to make do with so little. Instead, she accepted the food graciously, and made a point of commenting on how delicious it was.

After lunch, Connie took Ilse upstairs to the room she'd be staying in. It was just as she remembered it from all those summers ago; there was the bed, neatly covered with a pale-yellow candlewick bedspread positioned under the window, the white-painted dressing table with its three-paned mirror and the tall dark wardrobe in one corner beside the pedestal washbasin. Even the comforting smell of the room was familiar, taking her back to happy times.

The girls had much to catch up on and spent the afternoon up in Ilse's room reminiscing about university and bringing each other up to date with all that had happened since they'd last been together. But it wasn't long before Ilse broke down in tears, as she let out everything she'd been bottling up all this time. Handing her a handkerchief, Connie listened quietly as Ilse described how hard life had been in Rijswijk, where all food shops had closed and people were scavenging for scraps they would never have considered giving even to their dog. The worst of it, she continued, was that on more than one occasion she had seen bodies in the street, lying where they had fallen down dead from starvation and the cold. Connie had no words. She allowed Ilse to finish up before holding her for a long time, waiting for her sobs to subside.

'It's being here with you now that makes me think I shouldn't have left my parents to fend for themselves,' said Ilse at last, lost in her misery. 'I feel I've abandoned them – maybe I should just go back.' But she was aware her words didn't carry any conviction. She willed Connie to contradict her, to say she must stay – because this was where Ilse wanted to be, free from the burden of responsibility that had been weighing her down for so long. Reaching for the handkerchief again, she blew her nose. All at once she became aware of a noise above her head. A creaking sound that began in one corner of the ceiling and ended up in the other, as if someone was trying to walk across the floor without being heard.

'What's that noise? Is someone up there?' Ilse said, forgetting her tears. The creaking came again.

'It's probably Ma looking for something in the attic. Nothing to worry about,' said Connie airily. 'Now listen, Ilse. You've only just got here and you'll feel differently in a few days.' And she leant over to give her friend a warm hug.

'Thanks, Connie. I promise I won't talk about it any more. Now, what about you? I want to hear what you've been up to.' Ilse sat back, feeling much calmer.

Connie paused, as she became distracted by a sudden gust of wind, peppering raindrops against the windowpane. 'I never told you that the tutor I worked with after Leiden became a close friend. Well, more than that.' She gave Ilse a meaningful look. 'It didn't last, but during that time he introduced me to a group of students who listened to illegal BBC war news broadcasts in secret and helped to spread the word about what the Germans were getting up to.'

'Were you involved too?' asked Ilse, wondering why Connie had never mentioned any of this before.

Connie shrugged. 'Everybody was, and Bert was very persuasive. It was an exciting time and it felt good to be doing something constructive after the *moffen* had taken away everything that was of value to us. Anyway, it didn't last and after I returned home I lost touch with Bert. So Pa found me the job at the town hall offices, working as an administrative assistant to the mayor. It's mainly typing up letters and memos and filing, but it's a job.' She shrugged again, then leant forward with a conspiratorial smile. 'Now you're here, things are definitely looking up. I know just the thing to cheer you up.'

'What's that?'

'I want you to meet some friends who are really good fun. We go dancing every week and it's just like the old days in Leiden. I know you're going to love them. Tell me you'll come along.' Full of enthusiasm, Connie swung her legs off the bed, pulled Ilse to her feet and began to swing her round.

'OK, I will,' said Ilse, catching her breath. It felt good to laugh again.

TEN

ANNA

'Ilse Meijer.' Anna's hand trembled as she read the name out from the sheet of paper she was holding up. She'd almost given up looking for any evidence when she'd found the note paper-clipped to a sheaf of admin her father must have been intending to deal with on his return. The name was written in her father's distinctive cursive style. Under the name he had written 'Degree awarded Leiden, May 1950.' Below that was an address in Rijswjik, Holland.

Ilse Meijer... surely this had to be her grandmother?

Anna stared at the paper. 'Mum, look here – I've found a name and address.'

Her mother was sorting through one of the many box files filled with photocopies of articles and papers related to her late husband's work. She looked up as a chorus of twittering started up from the apple tree outside the open window and a flock of sparrows ascended into the warm spring air. Anna frowned at her mother, who was distracted by the birds and had a distant look on her face. 'Don't you want to see?' she said, a little too sharply.

'Sorry.' Her mother swung her attention back to the room with a look of confusion.

Anna was frustrated by her vagueness and had to tell herself it was to be expected so soon after losing her husband in such tragic circumstances. They'd been looking through files all morning and nothing of any interest had turned up. All they'd found was work-related stuff that no longer had any value and would need to be chucked out. *It must be hard discarding a life,* Anna told herself, and she resolved to be gentler with her mother.

'The name is written here: Ilse Meijer. Are you sure Dad never mentioned her name?' she said in a softer voice.

Her mother frowned. 'I've already told you. He might have done, but I can't say I remember.'

'But he did tell you she lived in Rijswijk, so maybe that's when he mentioned it?' Anna said patiently.

Her mother paused and stared into the middle distance. 'I really should write and tell her what happened.'

Anna followed her mother's gaze out of the window towards the branches of the apple tree swaying gently in the breeze. 'Mum,' she began with a sigh. She was concerned for her mother's state of mind, but was determined not to be deterred from her mounting desire to do the right thing by her dad. 'I've been thinking. I've decided to take a few days off work and travel to Holland on Dad's ticket. Now I've got an address, I can go and find out if Dad's mother really does still live there. And if she does, I'll be a step closer to finding out about who his father was too. It's important to me, but I want you to be OK with that.'

Her mother turned back with a worried frown. 'But she doesn't even know her son has died. And then you turn up – the granddaughter she never knew she had? Is that such a wise idea?'

Anna stared at her, surprised to hear her speak that way.

'Probably not, but Dad isn't around to go and meet her. All I'm doing is carrying out what he wasn't able to. I imagine he would have wanted me to go through with this.'

It felt good putting her thoughts into words, to have a purpose and go in search of the family she never knew she had. If only she'd had the chance to talk it through with Dad, she thought; but it was too late now. She'd have to do this alone.

Her mother leant forward and placed her hand on Anna's arm. 'I can see this means a lot to you, darling. If this is what you want, do it. It would actually be a weight off my mind on top of everything else.'

Anna was relieved her mother hadn't taken it the wrong way, but didn't like the idea of her staying in the big house on her own with all her memories. 'Thanks, Mum. It is what I want to do. But please go and stay with Aunty Jane while I'm away. I can ask her—'

'Don't be silly. I was going to go anyway,' said her mother, smiling indulgently at her daughter.

Her mother went off to make them both a cup of tea. Anna stayed behind in the study, saying she'd tidy up. She waited till she heard the slap-slap of her mother's sandals on the treads of the wooden stairs before she went to the middle shelf and reached behind the box file for the old Dutch tin. Prising open the lid, she shook out the blue scarf and the silver chain with the dented medallion dropped into her hand. She rubbed the tarnished surface till it began to shine, caught by a sunbeam streaming in through the window. Holding it up to her neck, she decided against putting it on in case the catch wasn't secure. She couldn't bear the idea of losing something so precious, even though she still had no idea why her father had kept it and what significance it had. There was another reason: she didn't want it to be the first thing her grandmother saw when they met. Before showing her the keepsake, she needed to find out her grandmother's reason for abandoning her baby and giving him away.

And then there was the other important question that had been niggling her: Who was her grandfather and had he had any say in the matter? As she rolled the medallion back and forth in the palm of her hand, she wished there was some way it would yield its secrets. Then a doubt crept into her mind. What if she was wrong in thinking there was a connection between this necklace and her grandparents? What if there was another reason her dad had kept it hidden away in secret – had he been given it by someone he loved other than her mother? Pushing the thought aside, she folded the medallion back into the scarf and zipped it into the inner pocket of her handbag.

Taking a last look around the office to make sure that everything was tidy before she went downstairs, Anna went to close the desk drawer, but noticed that something was jamming it. She bent down and felt around. After a couple of tugs, she managed to ease out a scuffed black leather folio case that had seen better days. Instantly, she knew it was the document case in which her mother had discovered the train tickets. Turning it over, she was able to make out her father's initials, now faded with age. Despite its condition, it was a handsome piece and typical of her father's love for things well made. It must have served him well over the years, she thought with sadness. As she opened it up, she found the zip to be in good working order; it slid round three sides of the case with ease. But there was nothing much to see. She could see the outline of where a notepad must have been and the pen holder was empty, suggesting he had stopped using it some time ago. Nor was there anything in the left-hand flap where he must have put the tickets. Anna kept examining each of the pockets to see if there was anything more. And then she saw it: a blue envelope addressed to her father at his London office. Her heart gave a painful jolt as she stared at the unfamiliar handwriting. Her mind still swirling with the possibility that her dad had been cheating on Mum, she immediately assumed it must be from a woman he'd been seeing. On the reverse, she read the return address and surname – it looked familiar, but she couldn't immediately place it. Flipping it back over, she saw the post-mark was dated several weeks before her father had left for Kuala Lumpur.

With her heart in her mouth, she slid out the single sheet of blue paper and her eyes were drawn to the signature. *Of course – I should have guessed*, she thought. Breathing out in relief, she scanned through the letter, but could only make out one or two of the words. Her Dutch had never been strong; she wished she'd bothered to learn more when her father had offered to teach her. Then she noticed the telephone number just before the sign-off. Folding the letter back into its envelope, she slipped it into her bag at her feet, just at the moment that her mother walked in carrying two mugs of tea.

ELEVEN

'Is that Kersten?' Anna said into the phone, her heart in her mouth.

'Ja. That's me. Who is this?' said the voice she hadn't heard in nearly fifteen years. She thought back to when she'd seen Kersten, her husband, Markus, and their teenage son, Luuk – it was the last time they'd all had a summer holiday together at Anna's grandparents' house.

'It's Anna Dekker. You remember me?'

'Anna, of course! What a wonderful surprise to hear from you! Is everything all right?'

Anna heard anxiety creeping into her voice.

'I'm afraid I have some bad news about my father. He caught pneumonia when he was in the Far East and... he didn't survive.' Anna fought to hold back her tears.

There was a sharp intake of breath down the line. 'Paul? I can't believe it. I only saw him a few weeks ago. We were at a conference in Lisbon and were both so pleased to meet again. I even wrote inviting him to visit me. I was so happy to make contact after all this time. But, Anna, you and your mother must be devastated. When did it happen?'

Anna filled her in on the details of the funeral and apologised that she hadn't been in touch, saying she had only just found her number among her father's belongings.

'Kersten, there's something I want to ask you.'

'Please do. What is it?'

'Did you know that Dad was adopted?'

'Adopted? No! Are you sure? He never mentioned it to me.'

'He didn't know himself until recently. It was in a letter from his mother that she'd written and it turned up unexpectedly. The thing is, Dad started looking into who his real mother was, and had booked a ticket to go and meet her. She lives in Rijswijk. That's where you live, isn't it?'

'Wow, this is a lot to take in. But yes, that's where I live.'

Anna went on, 'So I've decided to travel on his ticket and go to see her for myself. Could I drop in and see you?'

'Of course, you must! When are you coming?'

'The day after tomorrow. I'm sorry it's such short notice.'

'I'd be so pleased to see you. And I'll see if Luuk can come and meet you too. I know he'd love to see you again.'

After she hung up, Anna felt a whole lot better for the conversation. Kersten and Luuk had been such firm friends of the family. Despite her sadness, she found herself looking forward to catching up with them again.

The day she was due to leave for the boat train to Harwich and overnight ferry to the Hook of Holland, she called Caro. They'd been in touch regularly since the funeral, which Caro had attended, but hadn't had a chance to get together. Caro was so busy with her new job, staying over in a boutique hotel in Paris during the week, that Anna hadn't yet told her of her plans to go to Holland.

'Caro, it's Anna.'

'Hey, it's so good to hear from you. How've you been?'

Anna let out a sigh. 'I hardly know where to begin. So much has happened, but I haven't got much time to tell you now. To cut a long story short, I found out that Dad was adopted. I'm leaving in half an hour to go to Holland to search for my Dutch grandmother. Dad bought a ticket to go himself just before he died and it's got today's date on it. I've decided to go in his place.'

Before she could say any more, Caro squealed. 'You are? But that's amazing. And she knows you're coming?'

Anna hesitated before speaking. 'No. I only have a name and an address. It's not clear if the name I have for her is even correct or if she's still living there.'

Anna waited for Caro to tell her she was an idiot, but she didn't. Instead, she said, 'You're so brave. I'm not sure I'd have the nerve to turn up at some stranger's house and confront them about my dad. Wow, that takes some guts.'

Anna laughed. She loved it when Caro spoke like this, fast and so full of enthusiasm, and making her feel as if she was doing something remarkable. Maybe it was remarkable, she thought, with a shiver that brought a smile to her lips. Drawing in a breath, she prepared to tell Caro about Kersten and that she was hoping she might provide some useful information about her father. As she spoke to Caro, she glanced at the medallion that lay in front of her on the coffee table, nestling in the blue folds of the scarf. 'There's something else,' she said as she picked it up and clenched it tight. 'I was going through Dad's things and found an old sixpence on a silver chain. I'm sure it's something to do with Dad's past, but I can't work out how it's connected.'

'That's so interesting. Do you think it's anything to do with his mother?'

'I'm hoping it is. And his father too. I know even less about him, and that's not much.' She gave a short laugh. 'But it's all

I've got that might link Dad to his family. Caro, I'm scared. I desperately want it to be relevant, but what if it's not?'

'Course you're scared, but just imagine if it is something. I can't believe your grandma will be anything less than thrilled.'

'Perhaps, but she may not want to relive painful memories. Don't forget she must have had a reason to give Dad away when he was a baby. I'm sure it's something to do with Dad's father, though I've no idea what. What if he'd run off and left her to fend for herself and the baby? That could well have been a reason.'

'Stop creating scenarios in your head. You won't know unless you go and find out. It's exciting and such an adventure for you. For what it's worth, I think you've nothing to lose and everything to gain.'

Of course Caro was right – she'd just needed to hear her say it. 'Thanks, Caro. I must go, else I'll miss the train. And I can't do that.'

'And, Anna?'

'What?'

'Promise me you'll call me as soon as you have any news.'

'I will.'

Anna ended the call, relieved that she could rely on Caro's support at this time. The past weeks had been traumatic and she hadn't felt she could confide in her mother, who also needed time and space to grieve.

But what about Hugo? She realised just how little she'd told him, even when she'd had the chance. She kept telling herself that it was because he was away so much in Boston and she hadn't wanted to bother him, believing he had more important things to think about. There'd been the opportunity to tell him when her mother had called as they'd been having coffee in Burford, but the timing had been off. She assumed Hugo had been so tied up with his own interests that he wouldn't want to know, and then she'd let the moment slip. Since then, there had never an opportunity to talk to him about it, and now he was back in Boston. So she ended up texting him, saying she was going to Holland for a few days and hoping to track down her grandmother, but would be back before he came home. She knew it was a cowardly thing to do, but resolved to have a face-to-face conversation with him when she returned.

TWELVE

Once a year in the summer holidays, Anna and her family had used to visit her dad's parents in Sneek, up in the north of Holland in Friesland. They'd lived in an old farmhouse backing onto the lake and Anna's room was up a steep wooden staircase leading to the attic, with a tiny window overlooking the water. She would always keenly anticipate Kersten and Luuk's arrival, and loved it when all the family, Kersten, Markus, Luuk and her grandparents included, took off on long bike rides along the canals and waterways that linked picture-perfect towns and villages all the way to the provincial capital Leeuwarden.

Now, as Anna boarded the boat train for Harwich at Liverpool Street station, she felt a wave of nostalgia mixed with sadness for those happy times. It made her realise just how close her father had been to his adoptive parents, and she wondered why they'd decided to keep the truth of his background from him all those years. *This should have been Dad's journey*, she mused, as the train pulled slowly out of the station. He'd been so close to discovering the truth about his past, but now he never would know.

Anna turned her attention to the practicalities of her own

journey. She'd booked a room for three nights in a hotel in the old town of Delft, giving her time to acclimatise herself and pluck up courage to seek out Ilse Meijer's house on the Emmastraat in Rijswijk, though every time she thought about turning up there, her heart began to race and her mouth went dry. She had no idea what to expect, and dreaded the possibility that Dad had got it all wrong and she'd receive a cold reception from the woman he'd understood to be his mother.

Anna settled back in her seat to read her book, looking up every time a station was announced and the train stopped. She knew that when they reached Manningtree, the stop before Harwich, she would need to close her book and put it away.

The night boat was much as she remembered it, noisy and packed with families and fractious kids, youngsters with backpacks sitting around on the floor of the lounge and burly lorry drivers sitting at tables in the cafeteria drinking tall glasses of lager with two inches of foam on top as they demolished large plates of fried food. She was relieved to get inside her windowless single cabin and shut the door. She sat on the narrow bed and ate the sandwich she'd brought with her, waiting for the engines to start up, signifying that the ship was backing out of port and turning round to set off across the North Sea.

The overnight crossing took six hours and Anna intended to get a reasonable night's sleep. But as soon as she lay down, she became aware of every small noise – low voices from the cabin next door, a baby crying further down the corridor, and then the steady rumble of engines that used to send her straight to sleep but now had quite the opposite effect. She lay wide awake and tense for what seemed like the whole night until a jingle burst forth from the tannoy in the ceiling above her bed, the announcement to wake up and go to the restaurant, where breakfast would be served. Anna groped for the light switch so she could look at her watch, and groaned. She'd forgotten that Dutch time was an hour ahead. She reluctantly accepted that it was all part of the experience of travelling by boat to Holland and, by the time she had picked up a coffee in the port and found a seat on the blue-and-yellow train bound for Rotterdam, she was feeling in much better spirits.

It was still early, just after eight, and it felt good to have the whole day stretching ahead of her. She gazed out at the familiar Dutch landscape slipping past and sipped her machine coffee, which tasted remarkably good. The endless rows of brightly lit greenhouses full of tomatoes, cucumbers and peppers were soon replaced by endless emerald-green polders dotted with black-and-white cows and the occasional windmill. The scene was so unmistakeably Dutch and always filled her with a sense of long-ing; but today the feeling was so much more intense, knowing she was making this journey on behalf of her father.

When she reached Delft after changing trains in Rotter-dam, there was no time to dwell on the reason she had come. The train station was bustling with commuters and she needed to orientate herself to find her hotel. She took a taxi to the old town centre, and stepped out in front of the hotel just as the church tower chimed nine. The hotel was a narrow building with tall, elegant windows on three floors, tapering to one small window at the top below gables that mirrored other townhouses in the street.

Anna pushed open the glass door and walked into the plush-carpeted vestibule, where a young woman was sitting at a computer behind the reception desk. She looked up and smiled.

'Do you speak English?' Anna asked tentatively, out of cour-tesy, though it was rare for a Dutch person in a city such as Delft to say they didn't.

'Of course. How can I help you?' said the receptionist.

'I have a booking for three nights. I know I'm early but...'

'You came on the night boat from *Engeland*?' The only trace of Dutch in the way she spoke was her pronunciation of 'England'.

Anna nodded.

'It's no problem. If you'd like to check in your details here, you can leave your luggage with us till your room is ready at two p.m.' She was the model of efficiency as she laid a form out on the counter and indicated with her pen the details Anna needed to fill in.

Back out in the square, Anna looked about her, unsure what to do next. She'd forgotten she'd be arriving so early. She had intended to spend her first morning familiarising herself by wandering about Delft, but first she needed breakfast. Her stomach rumbled, reminding her she hadn't eaten anything since the sandwich she'd had in her cabin. There was no shortage of cafés surrounding the square. She chose one with a view towards the imposing town hall, where she ordered a breakfast of bread, Gouda cheese, jam and coffee. When the church clock struck ten, Anna sighed – there were only so many coffees in cafés she was prepared to drink. She walked to tourist information office at the station and enquired about buses to Rijswijk. She was surprised to discover that Rijswijk was just a ten-minute journey away, with buses every few minutes. A bus was about to leave, so there was no reason to delay any longer.

Anna bought a ticket, boarded the bus and sat herself towards the back. She began examining the map she'd been given by the helpful man at tourist information, and noticed a stop for the Rijswijkse Bos. She knew the word meant 'forest', so guessed it would be some kind of urban park. That was where she would get off, take a walk among the trees to gather her thoughts. She was folding the map back up when a middle-aged woman with a pleasant smile took the seat next to her. 'Engels?' she said, with a lift of an eyebrow.

Anna frowned slightly, wondering if it was so obvious she was English, before realising it was the map that gave her away. She nodded.

'Is it your first time going to Rijswijk?'

'Yes. Perhaps you can tell me if the Rijswjikse Bos is a nice place to walk.' She hoped her pronunciation wasn't too bad.

'Oh yes. It's our "green lung", I think that's how you English describe it? We like to walk there to escape from the town. Are you going to Rijswijk only for that reason?'

Anna knew Dutch people could be direct, but wasn't she being just a bit too nosy? She glanced at the woman, but her grey-blue eyes seemed honest enough; Anna was alone and didn't know any Dutch people, so she decided to tell her a little more, but not too much. 'Actually, I'm visiting a relative I've never met before.'

'That's interesting. Where does your relative live?' the woman said with a tilt of the head.

Anna shifted in her seat, wondering if she'd said too much. 'Close to this park – *bos* – I think. I can walk from here.'

'If you have an address, I can show you where to go.'

Anna didn't want to appear rude by refusing the woman's offer. She wished she hadn't embarked on this conversation; but maybe there'd be no harm in telling her where she was going. And it might even be of help. 'It's Emmastraat,' she said.

The woman clapped her hands. 'I live in that street! What is your relative's name?'

'Ilse Meijer. She's elderly and I think she lives on her own.'

'I'm afraid I don't know anyone of that name, but I don't know everyone in the street. But I can show you the way there.'

'No thank you, that won't be necessary. She's not expecting me till this afternoon,' Anna lied quickly. 'I want to spend a bit of time by myself.'

'Oh,' the woman said, and her smile abruptly vanished. Anna wondered if she had offended her, but the woman went on, 'I live at number twenty Emmastraat if you need any help. Look, this is your stop,' she went on, promptly standing up to let Anna off.

'Thank you for your help. You've been most kind,' said Anna, and gave her a brief smile as she squeezed past.

She was glad to end the conversation and get off the bus. The woman waved through the window as the bus moved off and Anna waved back. Maybe she was just being friendly after all, she thought.

The park was delightful, a little oasis of green in the middle of the busy town. Anna felt herself relax as soon as she walked through the gates and followed a tree-lined avenue down to a duckpond, where she sat on a seat. There were few people about, just the occasional jogger and a young woman with a small boy in a pushchair feeding bread to the ducks. The sun broke through the tops of the trees and Anna lifted her face towards it, enjoying the warmth.

Ilse Meijer, who are you? she wondered. *Did you never want to find the little baby boy you gave away?* These questions were too personal to ask, even if Ilse Meijer was prepared to speak to her. But now that Anna was so close to meeting her, more questions flooded her mind that she knew she would never dare voice. *Did she ever think about the son she abandoned? Did she even love him...?*

Anna sprang up from her seat. She had done enough musing and needed to face the truth. Walking briskly back to the entrance, she didn't allow herself to hesitate a moment longer. Within minutes she arrived at number four Emmastraat and stood on the pavement, looking up at the neat terraced house with its big picture windows, a woman's bicycle leaning against the dividing fence and a trimmed hedge at the front.

Heaving in a deep breath, she walked up the brick path, raised her hand and rang the bell.

THIRTEEN

ILSE

From the outside, it looked like an ordinary house with nothing to suggest what went on after hours when the blackout blinds came down on the outside world. Ilse looked questioningly at Connie, thinking she must have been mistaken in coming here, but Connie winked and confidently pressed the doorbell. Moments later it opened a crack to allow the two women to enter. It was pitch-dark inside the hallway, but a faint light at the far end beckoned them into a spacious room with a bar at one end. Ilse could make out in the shadows a dozen or so people sitting at tables, each with a flickering candle that threw dark wavering shapes onto the ceiling. Connie moved through, stopping briefly to greet people she knew with a word here, a laugh there. They drew level with the bar, where a young man with slicked-back hair was pouring out drinks.

'Good evening, Connie,' he said, eyeing her from beneath long black lashes.

'Ah, good evening, Anton,' she said nonchalantly, before swivelling round to survey the room.

'Connie, *wie geht's dir, liebchen? Wie hast du mitgebracht?*'

Ilse hadn't noticed the tall young German approach. She

took an instant dislike to him – the insincere smile that stopped short of his glacial blue eyes, and his penetrating gaze that made her squirm uncomfortably. And she also disliked the way he didn't bother speaking Dutch. Ilse understood perfectly well he was asking Connie who she'd come with. She glanced away, noticing other uniformed German soldiers, smoking, drinking and laughing at tables with the locals. Connie seemed to know these people, from the way she nodded her head and raised a hand in greeting. Ilse was shocked. Why hadn't Connie said any of this to her before they came? She watched her friend gaze up at this German, offering her cheek for a kiss, before replying in Dutch, 'Let me introduce you to my best friend, Ilse.' She reached out her hand and drew Ilse close against her.

'*Enchanté*,' said the man confusingly, bowing his head, before switching to Dutch. 'My name is Jürgen.'

Ilse answered him politely, though her instincts warned her to be cautious. At that moment, her attention was drawn to a man walking towards them from the opposite side of the room. He was also in uniform and seemed a little older than Jürgen, but he looked less... German, Ilse thought, taking in his short dark hair, deep-brown eyes and lopsided smile.

Connie let out a little yelp of recognition and grabbed his hand, saying, 'Rudi, how lovely to see you and now we can make up a foursome. Meet my best friend, Ilse.'

Rudi bowed his head and shook her hand. 'Shall I get us all a drink? Tell me what you'd like,' he said, looking at Ilse.

Ilse felt herself redden and was unable to think what drink to have. Sherry had been her preferred tipple when she was at Leiden, but she hadn't touched a drop of alcohol in over two years. She glanced over at the array of bottles behind the bar and frowned.

'They do a passable red wine. Let's both have a glass,' said Connie, replying for her.

'I'll get a bottle,' said Rudi cheerfully, striding off to the bar.

Connie squeezed Ilse's hand and whispered in her ear, 'You're going to love these two. Just wait till the dancing starts. It's such fun.' She went over to Jürgen and threaded her arm through his and they walked over to an empty table for four. Ilse followed, feeling awkward and wishing she hadn't come. Connie hadn't mentioned anything about having a boyfriend and Ilse now wondered if her friend had set her up with Rudi for the evening. It was obvious to her that Connie and Jürgen were a couple from the way she was giggling and leaning into him. But Connie's behaviour didn't surprise her – she had always been the life and soul of parties in Leiden and hardly a week went by when she didn't have a new man in tow. It was seeing Connie with a German that unnerved her.

Rudi came back with a bottle of red wine, which he poured into four glasses. Together, Jürgen and he shouted, '*Prost!*', and they all chinked glasses. The men took a deep swig and chinked again.

Ilse took a sip of the dark-red wine. It was rough and sour, catching at the back of her throat and making her cough.

'Are you all right?' said Rudi with a look of concern, and patted her on the back. She nodded, feeling heat rise in her cheeks, knowing that all eyes were on her. Rudi jumped up and fetched her a glass of water, which she gratefully accepted. Connie and Jürgen were soon engrossed in their own private conversation and Ilse was left to make small talk with this stranger. He told her a little about himself, that he had been stationed in Holland for six months and could speak the language because he had a Dutch uncle, but he kept details of his work as a German SS officer to himself. Ilse was also careful to say very little about her own situation, just that she was a student of medicine in Leiden and hoped to resume her studies after the war. She was relieved when swing music started up with a crackle from a gramophone player behind the bar.

Chairs were scraped back, several tables lifted and moved to one side to clear a space in the middle of the room. Connie and Jürgen were the first ones to take to the floor. They were both light on their feet, moving and jumping back and forth in time to the music. One by one, other couples joined them, and the barman cranked up the music.

Rudi stood up, took off his jacket and held out his hand. 'Come and dance with me,' he said, laughter creasing the corners of his eyes.

Ilse hadn't realised how much she'd missed dancing till she was moving among people who were throwing themselves about in joyful abandon. When Rudi danced – and he was an excellent dancer – he seemed so happy and relaxed in her company. Ilse found herself smiling, then burst out laughing, as he made exaggerated gestures with his shoulders and writhed his body in time to the music. She knew she wasn't bad herself and was glad to have a dance partner who not only knew the moves, but taught her new ones. By the end of the record she was out of breath, but he kept hold of her hand as the next one started. He bent his head to her and said in a low voice, 'Don't go. I love dancing with you.' She felt his breath hot against her cheek, and knew she should stop right then, but the tune was a popular one and she couldn't resist carrying on.

Ilse and Rudi were still dancing together when a slow number started up. All around them couples were melting into each other's arms, including Connie and Jürgen. Ilse caught sight of Jürgen kissing Connie on the lips. She turned away.

'I need to sit down, I'm tired,' she said quickly, but Rudi was pulling her towards him, and placed his other hand gently on the small of her back.

'Just one more dance before you go,' he whispered into her hair. He remained close and rested his cheek against hers as he began to lead her round the dancefloor, his feet effortlessly tracing out the steps. Ilse could do nothing to prevent herself from being swept along. She felt as if she were flying.

'Where did you learn to dance like that?' she said.

'In the nightclubs of Berlin. I danced waltz, foxtrot, tango – everything,' he said with a sigh, and she wondered if he missed those days. 'But you've obviously danced a lot yourself,' he said, gazing into her eyes.

'Oh, it was nothing much, just student dances, and I haven't danced in a long time,' she said, feeling inadequate next to his prowess.

For a moment, his expression became serious and he looked as if he were about to say something more, but the music had come to an end. Everyone was applauding and whistling their approval. Rudi walked her back to their table and topped up her wine glass, handing it to her with a steady gaze. 'Thank you for being my dance partner.' He touched her glass with his. 'I haven't enjoyed myself so much in ages. Can we do this again?'

Ilse found it hard to look away. Her head was telling her to say no, that she was a fool even to consider mixing with a German – a Nazi – but she couldn't deny how joyous he'd made her feel. Not only was he charming and good-looking, but, boy, could he dance. That was all there was to it, she told herself. He was the perfect dance partner. 'I'd love to,' she found herself saying.

FOURTEEN

The following morning Ilse woke with a pounding headache and dry mouth. She screwed up her face, trying to remember how much she'd had to drink, even though she knew it couldn't have been that much. Maybe two glasses of wine? But after having so little to eat for months, she realised, her body could no longer tolerate alcohol. She swung her legs out of bed and found herself swaying a little. Then a wave of nausea swept through her. Clutching her middle, she staggered over to the sink to splash water on her face.

There was a knock at her door. 'Ilse? Are you up?' came Connie's muffled voice. The door opened and she rushed over to Ilse leaning over the sink and put an arm round her. 'Are you unwell?' she said.

Ilse straightened up with a pained expression.

'God, you look as white as a sheet,' said Connie. 'Come and sit down.' She filled a glass with water and pressed it into Ilse's hands, waiting till she'd taken several long sips. 'Better?'

Ilse nodded. 'I don't know what came over me. I was fine when I went to bed last night.'

'Don't you remember I nearly had to carry you up the stairs?' said Connie with a smile.

Ilse groaned and put her hands to the sides of her head to try to still the throbbing. 'I'm sorry. Was I that bad?'

'No need to apologise. You've done it enough times for me.'

Ilse's face brightened a little as she remembered the time she and a friend had had to support Connie back to their digs – she'd been so drunk she'd hardly been able to stand up straight. And it wasn't the only time. Connie never was able to resist the offer of alcohol. After a few, Ilse recalled, Connie could be rather amusing and would captivate a whole room with her crazy anecdotes, while swigging brandy and pulling on a long slim cigarette. But things were different now there was a war on, and she felt she must warn her friend about the company she kept. 'I think you should be careful befriending Germans. And careful you don't say anything that could land you in trouble.'

'I'm not stupid. I know what I'm doing. But I am entitled to have some fun. And so are you. Don't tell me you didn't enjoy yourself last night.' Connie threw her a challenging look. 'Come on. Let's go and drink tea in the garden,' she said, and for now the conversation was closed.

They sat on the wooden bench beneath the arbour. It was sheltered from the brisk easterly wind, and when the sun broke through it was almost springlike. Ilse felt better as she sipped her tea and enjoyed the sun on her face.

'How's Willem? Have you heard from him recently?' Connie asked.

Ilse sighed. 'The last letter I had was some weeks ago. He didn't say much. He never does. Either because his letters are vetted or because he's too exhausted to put pen to paper at the end of a long shift. They work them hard in the factories building machine parts for weapons from dawn till dusk with hardly a break. He mentioned there's been an outbreak of typhus in the camp, but he never complains. I hope he's fine. I know I should care more, but weeks go by when I barely think of him. Do you think that's bad?'

Connie shrugged and said, 'You've had a lot on your mind. I'm sure things will be different when the war's over and he returns home.'

'That's what I'm worried about. I've never thought of Willem as my boyfriend, just as a friend, but I don't think he sees it that way. I expect he'll want us to get married.' Ilse shook her head wearily. The last thing she wanted was to hurt Willem, and even the thought of letting him down was painful. 'But let's not talk about me. I want to know more about you and Jürgen. Are you a couple?'

'He's good company, and he can dance too, but that's all there is to it. What's your impression of him?' Connie often asked Ilse's opinion on her choice of men, as if she didn't quite trust her own judgement. But this time, Ilse thought she detected a note of anxiety in her voice.

'My impression? I find it hard to see past the fact that he's German and that he's a member of the Nazi Party. The *moffen* have done nothing but inflict misery on us ever since they took over our country. Put a German in Nazi uniform and it seems to give them the right to behave badly. Come on, you must have seen them out on the street, intimidating ordinary people just because they can. And I should know. Every time I go out on my bike I'm in fear of being stopped, and it's happened numerous times, even though it's obvious I'm doing nothing wrong. One time, a nasty piece of work ordered me to hand over my bike, but he rejected it when he saw what a wreck it was. I was terrified, thinking that he'd confiscate the few knobbly turnips I'd managed to barter earlier that day. That's how bad it was. And, Connie, I don't think we even know the extent of what goes on behind closed doors and over the fences in those awful labour camps. All I'm saying is that Jürgen may come across as friendly, but I really think you should be cautious.' Ilse pulled the sides of her cardigan together across her chest. She looked Connie in the eye and wondered if she'd gone too far. Losing her friendship was the last thing she wanted when Connie had been so kind and supportive towards her. 'I'm sorry, I didn't mean to...'

'No, it's fine. You're absolutely right and I admit I do get carried away when we go dancing. Enjoyment is in such short supply these days. But that doesn't mean I have feelings for him.'

Relieved that Connie wasn't taking Jürgen too seriously, Ilse still had a doubt niggling at her. It seemed strange the way Connie was able to carry on and enjoy life as if there was no war going on. 'You asked me my impression of him – what I didn't say was that I think he's really keen on you. You should be careful of encouraging him. I see the way he looks at you.'

Connie nodded slowly, as if she'd only just come that conclusion herself. 'Thanks for being so honest with me, and you're right, I should be on my guard.'

FIFTEEN

ANNA

From inside the house, she could hear the hum of a vacuum cleaner being switched off, followed by footsteps and the fuzzy shape of a person appearing through the opaque glass panel in the door. Anna took a step back as she prepared herself for coming face to face with the woman she'd built up in her mind. Though instead of the elderly grey-haired person from her imagination, the door opened on a youngish woman in blue jeans and a loose man's shirt, her curly hair secured in a jazzy headscarf.

'*Kan ik u helpen?*' the woman said questioningly. She stood with her hand on the half-open door.

Anna understood that the woman was asking if she could help, but didn't have any Dutch words in reply. 'I'm sorry to bother you. Do you speak English?'

'Ah, *Engels*. I speak a little,' said the woman, opening the door a little further. 'Who do you want?'

'I'm looking for someone called Ilse Meijer. This is the address I have for her. Does she live here?' Anna half expected Ilse Meijer to appear behind her.

'No. I'm sorry. You have the wrong address. A couple live here, no elderly lady. I am the help,' she said with a shrug.

Anna nodded, but was at a loss for what to do next. Disappointment must have shown on her face, for the woman appeared to soften, and volunteered a little more information.

'I work for the Smit family for two months. Are you sure you have the right address?'

Anna reached into her bag for her diary and checked the entry for today's date. 'Yes, I've written it down here,' she said, pointing at the words she'd written in strong black capital letters.

'The Smits might know her. Can you come back later?' said the woman.

Even though Rijswijk was only a ten-minute bus journey from Delft and it would be easy to return later, Anna had a strong feeling that coming back wouldn't lead to anything.

'Thank you. Perhaps I'll do that,' she said politely, and glanced past the woman into the hallway with its dark wood panelling and scuffed black-and-terracotta-tiled floor. She caught a whiff of something very Dutch – was it polish, or the smell of antique wood so familiar to her from her grandparents' house in Friesland? She took in a sharp breath, momentarily overcome by the thought that her real grandmother might have walked across this hallway. What would her father have done if he'd turned up on this doorstep? He, at least, had been able to speak Dutch and would probably have handled the situation more efficiently. Anna suddenly felt very alone, as if she had already failed him.

'Are you OK?' said the woman with a look of concern.

'Yes. Of course. I'll knock on some other doors and see if anyone remembers her.' Anna smiled.

'Good luck. I hope you find her,' said the woman kindly, before stepping back inside and shutting the door.

It wasn't the outcome Anna had been hoping for, but it was

a relief to have taken the first step towards solving this mystery. She walked back onto the street and took a long look at the row of terraced houses. They were all similar, with enormous picture windows filled with tall and luscious houseplants. She wondered if the neighbours all competed against one another for the most beautiful display. The thought brought a smile to her face. She decided to walk the length of the street and back again so that she could gather her thoughts.

The Emmastraat was a long, pleasant, tree-lined street, quiet at that time of day, and with only a few people about. Apart from an electrical shop and bakery, whose windows were filled with baskets heaped with different varieties of loaf and bread rolls, the houses were all residential, well maintained and with an air of affluence.

Anna found herself back outside number four again and decided to try the neighbours on either side. A tabby cat regarded her lazily from the window of number two, where it sat in between two large houseplants, like a tiger surveying its domain. Anna walked up the short path and pressed the bell, waited, but there was no answer. It was the same at number four and number six. Everyone must be out at work, she thought, partly relieved she wouldn't have to go through the rigmarole of making herself understood. At number ten, the last in the row of terraces, she heard footsteps approaching the door. A small man with sparse grey hair, who looked to be in his seventies, opened the door a crack. Anna was ready with a Dutch greeting, then asked if they could speak English.

A broad grin spread across the man's face. 'Of course. I like to practise English. Is there something I can help you with?'

'I hope so,' said Anna with relief. 'I'm searching for a relative who used to live at number four. I wonder if you knew her. Ilse Meijer?'

The man screwed up his forehead and took his time answering. 'Ilse... what did you say?'

'Meijer. She lived at number four until recently.' Anna looked at him expectantly, but he shook his head.

'I'm afraid I don't know the name, but I do remember when the couple and their children moved in at number four. Their removal van was outside my house all day and I had to park in the next street.' He frowned at the memory.

'And you didn't know the elderly woman who was there before them?' Anna persisted. 'She must be in her early eighties.'

The man paused to ponder again. 'Ah, yes, I do remember. We would say good day to one another, but nothing more. She walked with a stick and was always smartly dressed. I'm afraid I can't tell you any more than that. Did you ask the new owners?'

'I tried, but they're at work. But thank you, you've been most helpful.'

It was the first positive sighting of someone who might have been her grandmother. Although it wasn't much to go on, Anna's mood lifted. Glancing at her watch, she decided she had done all she could for now, for it was time to go and meet Kersten and Luuk.

SIXTEEN

ILSE

Any preconception Ilse might have had that the sanatorium was a place for the seriously ill and dying was swiftly dismissed the moment she walked through the doors of the modern airy building constructed from concrete, steel and glass. It felt more like a hotel, with its large open spaces filled with comfortable seating and vases brimming with flowers placed on low coffee tables. Patients were wheeled in and out, given cups of tea and reading matter, or simply left alone to enjoy the views of the grounds. From Mevrouw de Vries, the senior nurse in charge, she learnt that the patients had private rooms with their own balcony overlooking tall pine trees. At every opportunity, beds were wheeled onto the balconies so patients could breathe in the restorative scent of pine and recuperate in the open air and sunshine.

'We are so glad you've come to join us,' said the nurse, after showing Ilse round one of the patient wings. 'I hope you see that this place is nothing like a hospital, even though incoming patients are quite weak and need medical attention. Tuberculosis is an unpleasant disease if untreated, and it can take many months of recovery. We find that rest, nutritious food and access to nature are all essential and do our best to provide all three, though it's been very trying during this time of war. Fortunately, we aren't bothered by the Germans this far out of town. They're too scared about catching the disease, so they leave us well alone. That suits us fine. Come, let me show you round the garden.' She led the way out through open glass doors down onto the lawn and made for a small wooden gate that led to a sizeable vegetable patch where several young men were at work. 'Recuperation isn't only about rest and gardening is one of the activities we offer to patients before they return to their normal life.'

They walked up and down the neat rows of sprouting cabbages and creamy white leeks with fresh green tops poking through the soil. Ilse had never seen such abundance in all the time she'd been foraging for food. She thought of the tiny knobbly specimens she had dug from the frozen soil, that had never had a chance to flourish. The two women stopped beside a man hunched over his work and Ilse asked what he was planting. He rose to his feet and stretched, placing his hands in the small of his back. He had ruddy cheeks and a big smile. 'Spring cabbages in this row and then I'll be replenishing the spinach, which is running low. We grow the vegetables for the kitchen and any surplus is given away,' he explained.

'You have surplus?' Ilse said in surprise.

'Of course. We plant more than we need so we can give back to the community,' he said with a note of pride in his voice.

On their way back to the main building, Ilse asked how long he had been working in the garden. 'It's coming up to a year,' Mevrouw de Vries told her. 'Piet was terribly frail when he first came to us, but he's an example of how with the right treatment, people can get better, even thrive. He really should be going home, but he wants to stay, and we're happy to let him.'

. . .

Ilse was encouraged by what she'd seen and settled happily into her new job, caring for a group of patients who were making good progress in their treatment, but were still bedridden. Although her duties were light, she was often tired at the end of her morning shift and grateful it wasn't far to walk back to the house. She looked forward to stopping by the vegetable patch for a chat with Piet, who liked to show her how his crops were coming on. Sometimes he'd be waiting with a cabbage, or a handful of carrots, which he'd press on her with a kindly smile, saying he always had plenty to spare. The first time it happened, his gesture brought tears to her eyes that anyone could be so generous.

After so many months of gnawing hunger, she still felt guilt that she had proper food on her plate while her parents had so little; she often fretted about whether she'd collected enough tulip bulbs to last till she returned home. If the bulbs ran out, would her mother have the strength to leave the house to go in search of food herself? Ilse had lived by her wits, avoiding confrontation with German soldiers, and had relied on her network of contacts to direct her to the best, and sometimes only, available food source. She doubted her mother would be able to do the same.

One day, to Ilse's relief, she received a letter in which her mother sounded much brighter, saying that she and Pa had decided to take in a lodger called Mr Polman. He was homeless, after his apartment in The Hague had been bombed in a failed attempt by the Allies to hit Nazi targets.

'Imagine my surprise when he drew up to the house in a car!' her mother wrote.

It turns out he's an executive for the Shell company, who make sure their employees are well-provided-for with petrol and other luxuries the rest of us can only dream of. Would you believe, the day after he arrived, he came home with a

sack of potatoes! It was so heavy that he was barely able to lift
the sack out of the back of the car. He had to drag it along the
path, through the back gate and into the kitchen. He's such a
nice man and insisted we take as many potatoes as we need in
return for allowing him to store them in the cellar.

Ilse was gladdened by this news. Even if they had little else,
she knew that potatoes were nutritious and her parents
wouldn't starve – but only as long as the war didn't drag on too
much longer.

Little by little Ilse regained her strength. Life was less
stressful and she was surprised to find herself sometimes getting
bored. Her morning shifts ended at twelve and there was little
to do in the afternoons. Clara and Hans were always run off
their feet with home visits to patients, and Connie was out at
work all day, not returning till after six at the earliest. Some
days, she didn't return until well after curfew. She was always
vague about where she'd been, leading Ilse to wonder if she was
more keen on Jürgen than she was letting on.

One evening Ilse was in her room preparing to write a letter
to Willem when she thought she heard a faint thump coming
from the attic. Thinking she must have imagined it, she carried
on, until she heard another noise, as if a piece of furniture was
being dragged across the floor. There had to be someone up
there; but surely she would have heard footsteps on the attic
stairs? But who? Connie's parents were out and she hadn't seen
Connie since the morning. Suddenly, Ilse felt afraid that
whoever it was must have been up there the whole time she was
alone in the house. Then she remembered the time she'd heard
a movement from the attic and that Connie had dismissed her
concern, saying it was probably her mother moving around up
there. *It has to be someone else*, Ilse thought nervously.

After a little longer, she braced herself to go and investigate.
Opening her door quietly, she listened out for anything

unusual, before walking over to the steep wooden staircase leading to the attic. Gingerly she put her foot on the first tread, and it made an enormous cracking sound that seemed to reverberate through the empty house. Undeterred, she carried on, cursing inwardly at the sound her shoes made on the wooden boards, however quietly she tried to move. By the time she reached the top, her heart was thumping fast. She hesitated before turning the door handle. What or who did she imagine could be up there? But it was too late to give it any thought; she pushed open the door and took a step into the unlit room.

'Hello? Is anyone in here?'

No one answered.

Fumbling for the light switch on the wall, she found it, snapped it on.

The sparsely furnished room was empty and there were no signs of life. Uncertain what to do next, Ilse looked quickly from the wooden chair to the divan bed under the small sloped window, to a cupboard, hardly big enough to conceal anyone even if they had been trying to hide.

I must have been mistaken, she thought with a rush of relief. She turned back to the door and closed it with a soft click, before descending the staircase and returning to her room. She didn't hear another sound till the Van Dongens' return home at ten o'clock, when she was finally able to calm down.

SEVENTEEN

ANNA

Anna's nerves set in as she turned the corner of the street that matched the address she held in her hand. It was the realisation that Kersten was the only tangible link she had to her father's past; but apart from knowing her father from the holidays they'd spent together, what help could she possibly be? Still, Anna had nothing more to go on now she'd established her grandmother wasn't living nearby.

Anna pulled her concentration back to the ordinary-looking houses leading to identical multistorey apartment blocks lining the street. From the address, she guessed that Kersten's was a top-floor flat, but the numbers were confusing; it took several attempts before she found Kersten's surname among the name-plates. She pressed the top button. After a second, there was a long buzz and the door gave a click. Stepping into the cool hall-way, she went over to the lift and nervously waited for it to descend to the ground floor. Everything had happened so fast – she'd only arrived in Holland that morning – that there'd been no time to process it all. It was only then that it dawned on her – Kersten might actually be the person to hold the key to her father's secrets.

The lift doors opened at the top floor and Anna came face to face with Kersten – tall and willowy with clear blue eyes and long fair hair tied loosely back in a messy ponytail. She was wearing a pale-blue knitted top over cream palazzo pants that showed off slim tanned ankles.

'Anna! I'm so happy to see you. And how you've grown into a beautiful woman, but that doesn't surprise me one bit with those blue eyes and auburn hair of yours. Now tell me, did you have a good journey?' She spoke in a sing-song voice with only the trace of a Dutch accent. Beaming, she swept Anna into a warm welcoming hug. 'Come inside and we can relax over a glass of wine, or would you prefer coffee? Or tea?'

Anna laughed and felt herself relax. Kersten, so radiant and effervescent, was just as she remembered from all those years ago. 'A glass of wine would be lovely. It's been a long day already. They throw you off the ship really early.'

Kersten clapped her hands and laughed her throaty laugh. 'Well, I'm so glad you made it. And after everything you've been through – how are you?'

'I'm fine. It feels good to be doing something positive for my dad, though I'm trying not to build up my hopes too much. So far, I've drawn a blank about my grandmother and I'm not even sure if she ever lived at the address Dad had for her.'

'Don't be discouraged. We'll look into it together. But first, we'll have a nice glass of wine and after, we can have lunch. Nothing much, just a *broodmaaltijd*. Bread, cheese, a bit of salad, that kind of thing.' She did a skip as she led the way into her airy apartment, which had large abstract paintings on white walls, and enormous picture windows overlooking the leafy trees in the park. Sunlight glinted off the pond, just visible in the distance. A wide balcony wrapped around two sides of the building and was filled with plants of all shapes and sizes that took up every available inch of space – on the floor, on stainless steel shelving, and climbers in enormous containers that wove their tendrils around the balcony railings. A wrought-iron table and three chairs completed the outdoor scene.

'Come through and let me show you the view.' Kersten waved her hand in an expansive gesture towards the open balcony door and gazed admiringly into the distance. 'I can never get enough of looking at it,' she sighed, turning back to Anna.

'You have a beautiful home.' Anna couldn't fail to be impressed. She took in the surroundings, imagining her father having the same reaction if he'd been here. 'Have you lived here long?' she asked.

'I moved here after Markus and I were divorced, so that must be five... no, six years ago. It's smaller than my last place, but so well located for the office and the airport – I travel a lot for business, you see.'

'And that's when you bumped into Dad,' concluded Anna.

Kersten's blue eyes shone as she smiled. 'Yes, a chance meeting at a conference in Lisbon. It was quite incredible to meet him after all this time. We'd lost touch, you see, and life got in the way. Luuk was growing up and he'd stopped coming on holiday with us by the time he was sixteen. He was more interested in spending time with his own friends, so Markus and I started travelling around Europe, visiting countries we'd always wanted to. I don't know where the years have gone. Now, do take a seat while I fetch the wine.' She moved off to the kitchen, leaving Anna to settle herself out on the balcony.

Kersten returned holding three glasses by their stems and a bottle of chilled white wine, which she placed on the table. She filled two glasses, handing one to Anna. 'Cheers,' she said, holding hers up for a toast. 'Here's to unravelling the mystery of your grandparents.'

'Cheers. I do hope so,' said Anna with a smile. She gazed at Kersten and was about to ask how her family came to know her own father's when there was a shrill ring at the door.

'That'll be Luuk,' said Kersten, jumping up. 'He's so looking forward to seeing you.'

Feeling somewhat apprehensive about meeting Luuk again after so long, Anna picked up her glass and took a large sip of wine. She remembered those holidays well, and especially Luuk, the tall skinny boy with floppy fair hair and charming smile. He spoke good English, and had been keen to teach her Dutch words and phrases, not always suitable for adult ears. Smiling, Anna turned her head to take a look. He stood in the open doorway and somehow managed to tower over Kersten, who was already a good few inches taller than herself. His fair hair still fell over his forehead, though it wasn't quite the white-blond shade she remembered. She watched as Luuk and Kersten hugged one another.

'Come and see Anna,' said Kersten, leading Luuk over to the balcony, and then padded away to the kitchen to make lunch.

'It's nice to see you again. How long has it been?' said Luuk with a smile, helping himself to a glass of wine.

Their eyes met as he chinked his glass against hers.

Anna felt herself blush, but she was ready with an answer. 'It was the summer you took me out on Opa's boat and we had a picnic on the riverbank. We must have been fifteen.'

Smiling, Luuk slowly nodded. 'I had a crush on you but I was too young and foolish to do anything about it. I don't suppose you knew that, did you?' He regarded her with an amused expression and with such intense blue eyes that Anna felt herself blush all over again.

'No, I don't think I did,' she said, as she recalled how he'd held out her hand to help her back onto the boat. His strong grip had taken her by surprise, but she'd thought no more of it at the time.

Luuk laughed and sat back in his chair with his wine glass, stretching out his long legs. He turned to glance back at her, his expression now serious. 'It must have been such a shock for you to hear that your dad was adopted. Did you have no idea?'

Anna looked across at him, struck anew by how intensely blue and kind his eyes were. His good looks were disarming, but he was still so like the Luuk she'd known as a teenager that she had no trouble opening up to him. 'Never. I only found out after he'd died. Nor had I any idea he was looking for his real mother till I found he'd bought a ferry ticket. It was obvious he was intending to meet her. So that's why I came here – to find my grandmother... and for Dad's sake too. But I was naïve thinking it would be easy and that she would welcome me with open arms. You see, it looks like Dad was mistaken. The woman I spoke to at the address I had clearly had no idea who I was talking about.' Anna hadn't realised that tears had begun to leak onto her face as she spoke. It was the first time she'd spoken openly to anyone about her father's past and all she'd done was convince herself that she'd failed him.

Catching her breath in a sob, she felt a gentle nudge to her arm. Luuk was holding out a handkerchief. 'It's clean,' he said quietly. When she didn't take it, he leant towards her and dabbed her face with it. 'It's OK to cry. Tell me what you know about this woman who might be your grandmother. What's her name?'

Anna smiled through her tears, feeling foolish. Luuk nodded at her to continue.

'Her name's Ilse Meijer. She must be eighty. I'm afraid I don't know any more than that.' Anna now had the hanky in her hand. She blew her nose into it. She was feeling slightly better, though still wobbly.

Kersten came in from the kitchen holding a platter of food. 'Anna, Luuk now works at the university in Leiden and is writing a paper on the role of women in the Dutch resistance during the war. Perhaps he can help.'

'I'm a historian, not a detective,' he said with a dismissive click of the tongue. 'I don't see how my research into famous women Dutch resistance fighters can help you track down your grandparents.'

Kersten said, 'I didn't mean that exactly. I meant that through the university you have access to a lot of research on the Second World War. You may discover something of interest.'

'Well,' Luuk said, looking thoughtful. 'You've made a start and it's not the result you were looking for, so you need to work out what to do next. I don't mind giving you a hand with some research online. That's if you'd like me to.' He tilted his head to one side.

Anna realised how much she did want his help. For if she didn't accept, she would return home with nothing to show for her efforts. And there was another reason, one she was reluctant to admit to herself: although she'd only met Luuk again a few short minutes ago, she was curious to get to know him better.

'Maybe,' she said, darting him a shy smile. 'But I would like to hear what Kersten has to say about my dad first.'

'Fair enough. But it would be my pleasure to assist you. Why don't we enjoy lunch and talk about it later?'

EIGHTEEN

Lunch was much more than the scratch meal Kersten had suggested. She'd been busy in the kitchen preparing a large niçoise salad and copious amounts of *huzarensla* – a Dutch version of potato salad with added chopped cold meat and gherkins – which she served along with crusty French bread and an enormous wedge of mature Gouda cheese. All washed down with more wine, amid convivial chat and laughter. Anna warmed to the general bonhomie and listened spellbound as, glass in hand, Kersten recounted her childhood memories of visits to her father's house in Friesland.

'We went to visit Paul and his parents for as long as I can remember. Because they had a house on the lakes it was the perfect holiday for us. I was a little older than Paul and we always had such a wonderful time messing about together. While the grown-ups chatted over coffee, Paul and I roamed around the lanes on our bikes, often with his friends. Sometimes Paul's father let the two of us accompany him on his skiff, which he kept on the water behind the house. One time, he took us on a longer trip, along the waterways over to one of the main lakes.

It was such a thrill when he let us steer the boat across the lake to the other side.'

'It's so nice to hear about Dad as a boy,' said Anna. 'I remember looking at Opa's boat from the kitchen window, bobbing up and down on the water when other boats passed by, but he was too old to sail it then.'

'Though we did take it out by ourselves, didn't we?' said Luuk, exchanging a knowing smile with Anna.

'Did you? I don't remember that,' said Kersten, looking from one to the other.

'Tell me, how did you know my father's family?' said Anna, keen to steer the subject away from her and Luuk.

'Hannie and Steffan Dekker were friends of my grandmother. I don't remember when we first started visiting, because I was so very young. But those holidays became a family tradition. First it was my grandparents, my parents and me; then when Paul and I both married and had children of our own, we just carried on.'

'All that time you never knew that my dad was adopted?'

'No, of course not. I would have said so if I'd known.'

Anna nodded. 'It's just so strange that his parents never told him. I wish I'd had the chance to talk about it with him. All I have to go on is a scribbled note I found in his papers after he died. On it he'd written Ilse Meijer's name, the address I now know isn't where she lives, and a mention of a degree awarded from Leiden University after the war. It wasn't much to go on, but I hoped it might tell us something.' Anna swallowed hard, relieved to have recounted her predicament without breaking down in tears again. 'Wouldn't my grandmother have been the same age as your mother? Do you think they knew each other?'

Kersten shook her head sadly. 'It's possible, but my mother's no longer alive to tell us. She died eighteen months ago of a stroke.'

'I'm sorry. That was insensitive of me to ask.'

'You weren't to know. She was an old lady and hadn't been well for a while, so it wasn't unexpected. She never said anything about Paul being adopted, but then why would she? If it's any help, I can look through the old photo albums and see if there's any clue there. Unfortunately, I never got round to sorting through her things and they're still in storage boxes down in the cellar.' She finished with a sigh.

'Why don't I take a look? said Luuk, with a quick smile at Anna. 'You know how much I enjoy sifting through archive material. It may even throw up some interesting stuff on what she got up to in the war.'

'You're welcome to, but it'll take you a while. They were dumped down there by the removal people after we cleared out her flat, and they're still in rather a muddle. I should have paid more attention when we were clearing her flat, but it all happened so quickly that I can't have been thinking straight.'

'You can't blame yourself. You stayed with her right to the end,' said Luuk, reaching out to stroke his mother's hand.

A look of sadness swept over Kersten's face. 'You've reminded me of something she said in the weeks before she died. It may not be relevant, but she talked about a friend called Else. At least, that's what it sounded like, but her speech was quite slurred by then. She could have been trying to say Ilse.'

'Can you remember if she said anything about this friend?' said Anna, eager to know more.

'Let me think. She said they'd always been good friends but they hadn't always seen eye to eye. I can well understand that as my mother was unafraid to speak her mind, especially over matters of the war. Their generation had a tough time during the five years we were occupied by the Germans. I knew she had real hatred for the Germans and the damage they'd done to this country and the lasting effects on its people. I got the impression it must have been personal for her, because she refused to be drawn on it. In a more lucid moment, she said she was grateful for the friendship she had with Else during the dark days of the war. I detected there had been a tenderness between them. I'm afraid that's all I know.'

Anna felt a stab of disappointment. It seemed far-fetched to think that Else and Ilse were the same person. Yet, for all this talk she was still none the wiser about her grandmother's whereabouts and hadn't even begun to question how her grandfather fitted into it all. Suddenly, she was overcome with tiredness. She longed to be on her own so that she could process her thoughts.

'I really appreciate everything you've said. You've both been so kind, but I'd better be going back to my hotel. And thank you so much for the delicious lunch.'

She began to get to her feet, but Kersten stretched out her hand to stop her. 'You mustn't be downhearted that you haven't found what you came looking for yet. Luuk and I will dig around for any other clues. And if I find I remember anything more, perhaps I can call you.'

'I'd appreciate that. I'm staying in Delft for a couple of nights,' said Anna, and gave her the name of the hotel she was staying at, before leaning in for a hug.

Luuk stood up and began fishing in his trouser pocket for his keys. 'Anna, can I drive you back? It's hardly any distance and it's on my way home.'

NINETEEN

ILSE

'There's a new jazz trio starting at the dance club tonight and Jürgen's inviting us both to make up a foursome. Everyone's going and it'll be so much fun. Do say you'll come,' Connie said excitedly. She was back home from work early and had come straight upstairs, to find Ilse propped up on her bed reading a book.

Ilse shut the book and put it to one side. 'Tonight? I'm not sure. I did a long shift today and I'm quite tired...'

'Come on. You know you'll enjoy it,' said Connie, taking Ilse's hands in both of hers. 'We haven't been dancing for weeks and we could both do with a night out. I tell you what, you can borrow my blue satin dress – you know, the one with the full skirt. It'll look wonderful on you.'

'What will you wear?' said Ilse, laughing, forgetting how tired she'd been feeling only moments earlier.

'Remember the dark-brown dress with big polka dots I wore to the last summer ball we went to in Leiden? No one here has seen it, except you of course. It's as good as new. Wait here while I go and see if it still fits me.'

Connie's happy-go-lucky nature was so infectious that it

made Ilse realise just how much she'd missed socialising with her friend. Everyone was so serious these days that she'd forgotten what it was like to be young and carefree. When they'd been at university, they'd had a wide group of friends and there was always someone throwing a party at their digs or inviting a crowd out for drinks and dancing. Hardly an evening went by when they weren't out enjoying themselves. It wasn't surprising that Connie, always the more sociable of the two, was so keen on letting her hair down. Despite Ilse's earlier misgivings about Jürgen, Connie insisted there was nothing between them, and Ilse was relieved she was keeping him at arm's-length. But even she had to admit that Jürgen and Rudi were good company for an evening out, and as hard as she tried to find fault with Rudi, he was always the perfect gentleman, a wonderful dance partner and attentive companion.

Connie came back into the room wearing the polka-dot dress. It fitted her tall physique perfectly in all the right places. 'What do you think?' she said, smoothing the fabric that skimmed her slender hips. She caught her reflection in the round mirror on Ilse's dressing table and wiggled into a posture that brought a smile to her face. 'Now it's your turn. Let's see how you look in the blue satin.'

The dress, which at first sight looked so promising, was all wrong on Ilse. She was a good five inches shorter than Connie, as well as being more skinny. She looked with dismay at the waistline that sagged round her hips and the hemline that hung halfway down her calves.

'Oh,' said Connie, then laughed. 'Nothing that can't be fixed with a few pins and a belt.'

By the time she'd finished, Ilse looked presentable, though she knew that Connie would have carried it off better than she was ever able to. But it would have to do. She could hardly complain, as she had no going-out clothes of her own.

'You look fine. Lovely, in fact,' said Connie, as she peered into the mirror and outlined her lips with a crimson lipstick. Smacking her lips together, she held the lipstick out to Ilse, who shook her head. The last thing she wanted to do was to give Rudi any ideas by wearing anything that could be construed as provocative.

Connie shrugged as she twisted the lipstick back into its golden case. 'If you change your mind, just let me know. Are you ready? Now let's go and enjoy ourselves.'

The jazz trio lived up to expectations and was already in full swing when they arrived at the club. Jürgen was waiting for them at the bar, and shouted above a lively saxophone solo that Rudi had been held up at work but wouldn't be long. Ilse said she was happy to sit out the first few dances, and watched Connie and Jürgen whirl around the dancefloor and in and out of each other's arms. They weren't the only ones. The dance-floor was literally filled with men in uniform, whose partners were dressed up to the nines, all intent on having the time of their lives. She dropped her eyes and slowly stirred the olive around her dry martini.

She felt a gentle touch to her shoulder and there was Rudi, slipping into the seat beside her. She smiled at him, relieved she wouldn't have to keep sitting out the dances on her own.

'Sorry I'm late. You look lovely.' He bent down and his mouth brushed against her hair. 'I was on a late shift over at the Amersfoort camp.' He snapped his fingers at the waiter for a drink.

Ilse felt herself tense up at his words. Had she heard him correctly? She knew little about this place a few miles away, other than it used to be a prison camp that had been taken over by the Nazis; she'd heard it was now a transit camp for prisoners before they were transported to the death camps in Germany and Poland. Just then it dawned on her how little she knew about the work Rudi did. 'You were at Kamp Amersfoort?' she said, trying to keep the shock out of her voice.

Rudi glanced quickly at her and made light of it. 'Only for today. I was helping out with an administrative issue, but everything has been sorted out.' He nodded his thanks to the waiter, who had placed a glass of whisky down in front of him. Rudi picked it up, drained it, and unsmilingly held it up for another.

Ilse was about to ask a question about what it was he did but, on noticing the thin set of his mouth and severe expression, thought better of it.

The number came to an end and the crowd erupted with cheers, whistles and applause. As the noise died down, the piano player started up with the first bars of a slow waltz. Rudi's face lit up and he took hold of her hands. 'Shall we dance?'

Ilse let Rudi lead her round the dancefloor, but her mind wasn't on the dance. She tried but failed to stop thinking about Rudi going inside that terrible place without the slightest concern for the plight of the prisoners incarcerated for the flimsiest of reasons – why else would he be here dancing with her and acting as if everything was perfectly normal? She waited till the dance ended before making an excuse to sit back down again.

'Are you quite well, Ilse?' Rudi said, dropping down beside her. He seemed irritated with her.

'Yes, I'm perfectly fine. Just a little dizzy,' she said. 'But I'd prefer to sit this one out, if you don't mind. Perhaps you can dance with someone else?'

'I wouldn't dream of it,' he said, looking affronted. 'I came here to dance with you and if you don't feel like it, I am quite happy to sit with you.'

Ilse wished she didn't feel guilty about rejecting his offer to dance. Rudi was always so kind and considerate towards her – but at the same time she was unable to reconcile this man beside her with the monsters who were doing so much harm to her country and people. But with this newfound knowledge about him, she knew she must try to distance herself from him in future.

Rudi ordered more whisky for himself and another martini for her. The alcohol seemed to relax him and the conversation moved to less controversial topics than his work.

When the tempo of the music increased once again, Ilse couldn't resist getting back up on the dancefloor. By now, she was feeling more than a little tipsy, and was determined to forget about their earlier conversation as the beat of the music reverberated through her entire body. How she loved dancing, she thought, as Rudi swung her into a series of fast jive moves. It was the only time she truly felt alive.

TWENTY

Ilse woke in the early hours of the morning to the unmistakeable sound of footsteps creaking up the attic stairs, followed by the click of a door opening. After a few minutes of shuffling above her head, all fell silent. Still tired from the night before, she lay listening for voices, but the only sound came from the steady tick of her bedside clock. Had she been imagining things again? Her eyelids grew heavy and she was drifting back to sleep when she heard another sound – this time it was footsteps descending the stairs. Suddenly wide awake, she dashed to the door and came face to face with Connie. In the half-light, the expression on her face confirmed everything she'd suspected.

'I think you'd better come in and tell me what's going on,' she said, pursing her lips. 'And who it is you've been hiding in the attic.' She stood aside for Connie to come in.

'I didn't mean to wake you.' Connie spoke softly, her pale face drawn.

'What *is* going on?' Ilse repeated.

Connie sat down on the bed with a long sigh. 'What I'm about to tell you, you mustn't repeat to anyone, not even my parents. Promise?'

Ilse gave Connie a searching look as she pondered her request. What if Connie was mixed up in something so serious that Ilse had no choice but to confide in her parents? She hesitated, knowing that if she refused to promise, she might never discover the truth about what was happening under their roof. 'You know you can trust me,' she whispered, as her heart began to pound in her chest.

'Upstairs is a young Jewish man. His name is Levi Abel,' Connie began. 'He's on the run from the Germans and his life is in danger. He managed to escape the Nazis who were targeting his street in Amsterdam, systematically arresting and deporting all the Jews living there. At first, friends in another part of town took him in, but they were worried when a neighbour came knocking and asked after the man she'd seen entering their house. They denied it, of course. But from that moment on, they were scared that Levi had been found out and was about to be arrested. They were fearful for their own lives too. Straight away they contacted someone they knew in the resistance, who agreed to get him out of Amsterdam. That's how he ended up here. You'll be wondering how I got involved.' A look of wariness briefly crossed Connie's face, and Ilse wondered if she was having second thoughts about confiding in her.

'Go on,' Ilse said softly, willing her to continue.

'Well, that is the part I shouldn't be telling you, even though you're my best friend. I've been working for a resistance group for some months. They swore me to secrecy, which is why I've never been able to say where I go in the evenings. I can't tell you much, but you can probably guess it's about helping people in need flee the Germans. And a lot more besides. Not even my parents know the full extent of what I do. Of course they know about Levi, they had to as he's living under their roof, but I don't let on about the other work I do. Frankly, they'd try to stop me if they knew. They think I'm just helping out a friend, not that I'm a member of the LO. Have you heard of this organisation?'

Although she did know about the LO, she wanted to hear it from Connie, whose eyes shone as she described the founder, Helena Theodora Kuipers-Rietberg, whom she clearly admired. 'Helena began by find hiding places for people needing to hide, but it became increasingly difficult. It wasn't just Jews who needed to disappear, but students, men who refused to work for the Germans, members of the resistance wanting to cover their tracks and many others. She had the brilliant idea of creating an umbrella group combining lots of smaller groups. As the organisation grew in size, the LO began to do so much more, such as forging papers and ration coupons and other things to support the families of those in hiding.'

Ilse's head reeled at what she was hearing. All this time Connie had been keeping a secret, even lying to her, because if anyone found out about her resistance activities she would be arrested – or even deported to a death camp. Ilse admired her courageousness.

'I just wish you'd told me sooner,' she said. 'But now I know this much, can you tell me how long this man has been upstairs? Will it be for long?' Ilse had heard about young men going underground to avoid conscription by the Germans, but hiding Jews was a whole different level of risk. That this young man hiding under their roof could be discovered made her shudder; the whole family, including herself, would be in grave danger.

'I'll tell you what I can. Everything was arranged by Rik, one of the leaders in our group. He's had a lot of success finding safe places for fugitives. I told him our house is spacious and next to the sanatorium. We've never been visited by the Germans as they're too scared even to set foot in the grounds for fear of catching tuberculosis.'

'Yes, I've heard it said that the sanatorium is one of the safest places around. Do you think your parents might want to take in more *onderduikers* for that reason?'

Connie shook her head vehemently. 'Not a chance. It's not

that they don't want to help but, being doctors, they worry one of their patients might catch wind of what they're doing and report them to the authorities. It took all my powers of persuasion to get them to agree to take in Levi. The problem is that he was only meant to be here for a short time.'

They both looked up at the sound of a soft thud above them, then looked at each other and smiled. Even if Connie hadn't told her everything, Ilse was grateful she'd brought her into her confidence.

'I should have told you sooner, shouldn't I?' said Connie sheepishly.

'I wish you had. I went up to investigate the other evening, thinking someone had broken in, but the place was in darkness and no one was there. How was that possible?'

'There's a small hiding place in the eaves, where he's been told to go if he hears anything suspicious. I'm sorry I put you through that.'

'Forget it. At least I know now. But how much longer will he be up there?'

'We're still waiting until Rik can find somewhere else for him, but he's decided this is the safest place for him right now. And it should be fine, as long as he doesn't come downstairs. My parents are right – we can't afford to let slip we are hiding a Jew.'

'Connie, don't you worry about Jürgen and Rudi finding out?' said Ilse, as her old worries resurfaced. 'It would be disastrous if they did.'

'We are the only ones who know about Levi, so there's no reason for them to find out. We must carry on as before, as long as we don't arouse their suspicion. I need you to support me in this, Ilse. And trust me that I'm doing the right thing.' Connie spoke abruptly, and Ilse thought she could detect a different, harder side to her, that brooked no further argument.

'Of course I do.'

'Good. Well, I think it's time you met Levi, don't you?'

TWENTY-ONE

He was standing with his back to the room, peering intently out of the tiny window that faced the vast lawn belonging to the sanatorium. He couldn't have heard Ilse enter the room for he kept on standing there, till she cleared her throat, causing him to swing round. Instantly, she saw panic written all over his face, and his eyes darted round the room as if he were searching for a means of escape.

'It's all right,' she stuttered, and took a step back towards the door. 'I'm so sorry if I disturbed you.' She could hear him trying to control his breath, which came out in shaky bursts, and noticed that beads of sweat had broken out on his brow. She felt awful that she had caused him such distress.

'Please don't go. I just wasn't expecting anyone. Are you... you must be Connie's friend.' He was obviously trying to regain his composure, but his hands were shaking.

Ilse tried to reassure him with a smile. 'Yes, that's right. We're best friends and have been since we were children. I'm staying while I help out at the sanatorium – that place you can see over there.'

The young man still looked nervous as he quickly followed her gaze out of the window and back again. 'Are you a nurse?'

'Not exactly. I hope to be a doctor eventually, once I get back to my studies. But it's useful practical experience working there.'

He dropped his eyes to the tray she'd forgotten she was holding. It had been Connie's idea she should bring him breakfast.

'Let me take it,' he said, making a move to take the tray. His hands, still shaking, fumbled as he took hold of the handles, and briefly their hands touched. Flustered, she dropped her gaze to his long slender fingers and an image came to her of hands flying across the keys of a piano – her father's hands. This inter-action all happened in an instant, before he turned away to find somewhere to put the tray down. Apart from the bed, an armchair and a wardrobe in one corner, there was no other furniture. He settled on the edge of the bed, balancing the tray on his knees. Ilse stood by awkwardly, unsure what to do next.

'Will you stay and keep me company for a little while?' he said, gesturing for her to sit down in the armchair beside the bed. 'I've hardly spoken to a soul this past week.'

Ilse's heart went out to this polite young man, wrenched from his home, who must be feeling so anxious about his future while doing his best not to show it.

'I'm Levi. I'm pleased to meet you,' he went on with a slight bow of the head, as she took a seat.

'I'm Ilse.' She met his dark-blue eyes and was captivated by them. All at once, she felt heat rise to her face. 'I'm afraid it's not much, just tea, bread and margarine,' she said in a rush. 'One of Mevrouw van Dongen's patients is bringing eggs today, so I'll make sure I bring you one later.'

'Thank you. I don't want to cause you all any more trouble than I have already.'

'You mustn't think that. It's no trouble. It can't be easy for you being stuck up here. How are you coping?'

'I try not to think about it too much, otherwise I'd go mad.' He studied the tray for a moment, before lifting the cup to his lips and taking a sip of the tea. He seemed finally to have calmed down. 'I don't suppose you've been told much about what brought me here.'

'No, but do tell me. If you want to, that is.'

He nodded and began his story, tentatively at first, then letting it all out as if he'd been waiting a long time to do so. 'I've lived in Amsterdam my whole life – that's where my family come from. We're a big family and many of us are in the jewellery business started by my great-grandfather over a hundred years ago. I joined my father as an apprentice silver-smith eighteen months ago, but it's been hard learning a trade when the Nazis have been hell-bent on stopping us. After my uncle and family fled to England in 1939, it was just my father and me running the business. My uncle's doing well, appar-ently, living and working in the jewellery quarter of Birm-ingham making buckles, buttons and other metal trinkets that people need, rather than the high-class silver bangles and bracelets he was once famous for. He wanted us to follow him, but my father refused. Amsterdam is where we made our name and he was adamant he wanted to stay. Although he knew the Nazis were a threat, I don't think he ever believed they'd come for him. My mother was more realistic and kept trying to change his mind. By then it was too late. Along with many others with jewellery shops in Amsterdam, the Nazis forced us to close, though my father kept his workshop going in secret. But shutting up shop was only the beginning. We were singled out and repeatedly forced to report to the authorities and to wear the yellow star. That meant we were refused entry to shops, places of worship, theatres, cinemas... in fact, just about everywhere. Life became very difficult.' Levi stopped for a moment and turned his sorrowful blue eyes to Ilse. 'My father was stubborn and did all he could to resist so he could carry on the business he'd dedicated his life to,' he went on with a sigh. 'This meant we had to become invisible and never draw attention to ourselves. But the Nazis had information on who we were and where we were living.'

Levi paused to take a sip of tea. The cup rattled as he replaced it on the saucer. 'I was out visiting a neighbour when they came and it was the only reason I wasn't arrested. When I came home through the alleys behind our house, I saw the back door open, swinging on its hinges. Inside, the evidence of what had just happened was there for all to see – tables upturned, drawers pulled out and their contents strewn over the floor. And there was no sign of my parents or my younger sister, Rebecca. Not even a note. I can only have missed them by minutes. And now, I can't stop thinking about what might have happened if I'd been there too. Would I have been able to convince the *moffen* to leave my family in peace? Or would they have taken me too?'

He wasn't looking to Ilse to provide answers as he gazed into space, grappling with these imponderables.

'Have you any idea what happened to your parents and your sister?' asked Ilse, though she was dreading the answer.

Levi slowly shook his head. 'I wish I did, though I can only guess that they were forcibly arrested and transported away to a concentration camp in Germany or Poland. Rebecca was only nineteen.' He paused to steady himself and took in a long breath. 'I lie awake wondering if, by some miracle, they returned and found I'd gone too. But how could I stay knowing those thugs could turn up any time and arrest me too? I had no choice but to leave my home where I'd lived all my life. I miss it so much, but I suppose it's too late to worry about all that now.' He gave a forlorn smile. 'All I can do is pray that they will be spared.' He glanced round his surroundings as if observing them for the first time. 'At least I have somewhere safe to stay. I'm so thankful to your friends for helping me.'

Ilse gave him a small smile, but found she could offer him little in the way of comfort. She simply couldn't imagine how desperate he must be feeling, losing his family in such tragic circumstances.

'You said you came here to offer medical assistance at the sanatorium. Where are you from?' He tilted his head as he regarded her. 'That's if you don't mind me asking.'

No, she didn't mind. Far from it. Having listened to Levi open up about himself made her want to share her own story. She'd told so few people about what she'd had to endure before coming to Hilversum, let alone the guilt she felt leaving her parents to fend for themselves. Not even Connie knew all the details of what she had done to keep her family from starvation.

'I live in Rijswijk with my parents and we were coping quite well up until Christmas. But we never imagined *moffen* could be so cruel, just when winter arrived with such force – within weeks they'd cut off the electricity and stopped food getting to the shops. At first, we made do with what we'd managed to stockpile, but it soon ran out. When we were given coupons for food we were elated, until we discovered the choice was one bowl of watery soup or a few measly potatoes. My mother said potatoes were the better option because they were more nutritious, but it turned out to be a bad decision. The greengrocer never received any deliveries and we never saw one potato.' Ilse quickly reached into her pocket for her handkerchief and blew her nose.

Without saying a word, Levi reached over and gently placed his hand on her arm. It was such a tiny gesture, but his touch radiated warmth and gave her the confidence to open up about her desperate searches for scraps of food in the biting cold, and the state of her father's deteriorating health.

'We ended up eating tulip bulbs.'

'Can you eat them?' Levi looked incredulous.

'Only if there's nothing else to put on the table. None of us wanted to at first, but we soon realised if we didn't we would starve. Then a letter came from Clara, Connie's mother, asking for my help at the sanatorium. I was reluctant to leave my parents, but I realised that by me leaving, the tulip bulbs would go further. At first it was hard being here and I worried that they wouldn't be able to cope, until my mother wrote that she'd taken in a lodger who arrived with a sack of potatoes.' She gave a short laugh at how absurd this must sound, but Levi's expression was deadly serious. 'She sounds so much happier now they have proper food, as she calls it. And I've stopped worrying about them as much.'

'That's for the best. There's no point dwelling on what you can't change.' Levi squeezed her hand gently.

From the hallway, three flights down, the clock struck the hour. It was eight o'clock. Ilse realised they'd been talking for over an hour and that she would need to hurry if she was to get to work in time. 'I need to go, but can I bring you anything else to eat?' she said.

They both looked at the untouched bread and margarine.

'I'm sorry, I got distracted. Leave the tray with me. Will you come and fetch it later, Ilse?' he said hopefully, getting to his feet and placing the tray on the bed.

She got up too, and was struck by much taller he was than her. For some reason, this made her feel safe.

'Thank you for listening to me,' he said. 'It's done me the world of good.'

TWENTY-TWO

ANNA

Switching on her mobile for the first time since she'd arrived in Holland, Anna discovered that Hugo had left two voice and five text messages. She frowned. Hadn't he read her text saying she'd be away for a few days? Clearly not, she thought in irritation, scrolling through his increasingly frantic messages demanding to know where she was. Frowning, she wondered what on earth he was even doing back home when he should be in Boston. He'd only been gone two days. But what really upset her was his assumption she'd be at the flat, ready to welcome him the moment he walked through the door, preferably with a hot meal ready for him in the oven. *Because that's what you always do*, a small voice whispered inside her head.

Anna groaned and threw her mobile onto the bed before heading to the bathroom to run herself a hot bath. She knew she would only behave irrationally if she rang him back now, and the truth of the matter was that she simply didn't want to. She was exhausted and wrung out after the past twenty-four hours, not only through lack of sleep, but by the surprise turn of events that had taken place that day. After she'd drawn a blank on meeting her grandmother, she could so easily have given up, but she was glad she hadn't. Discovering the connection between Kersten and her father had been intriguing, even if it did seem unlikely that Kersten's mother had known her own grandmother. And then there was Luuk, the boy she'd last seen fifteen years ago, who had grown into the tall, good-looking man she couldn't deny being attracted to. She could think of no good reason to turn down his offer to help her look into her family background further.

Tipping the complementary rose-scented bath foam into the steaming water, she took a deep calming breath and lowered herself into the fragrant bubbles. Finally, she could switch off and relax.

Moments later, a buzzing sound came from the bedroom, more specifically from the bed where her mobile lay. Anna eyed up the distance between the bathtub and the door, reached a hand out and pushed the door shut. But as she lay back and swished the bubbles over her body, a niggling thought came to her. Had Hugo been so persistent in trying to reach her because something terrible had happened? Could it have been her mother – who hated using a mobile phone – begging Hugo to call her?

Hurriedly wrapping a large white bath sheet around her, she slid her feet into the towelling slippers supplied by the hotel and went to investigate. But it wasn't Hugo's name that came up on her mobile screen. Still convinced the call must have something to do with her mother, she returned it. Immediately there was a click and a man's voice said 'Hello' in a brisk voice.

'Who is this?' she asked warily.

'Anna! It's Luuk. I hope I didn't disturb you, but I've found out something about Ilse Meijer. I wanted to tell you right away.'

Anna's heart began to thump in her chest. She pushed back her hair, which was dripping down her face, and put the phone to her ear. 'Was it something Kersten remembered?' She sat down on the edge of the bed and waited for him to continue.

'No, I haven't spoken to her. But I am hopeful we'll find something in the boxes when I get a chance to go through them. After you said Ilse Meijer had been to Leiden, I've been doing some searches online. Her name came up in an old article about students returning to Leiden University after the war to finish their studies. It's dated September 1945. It was a big story at the time with pictures of the celebrations and processions in the streets of Leiden to welcome back the students. Then I spotted a blurry photograph of a crowd of young people at the reopening of one of the student societies and her name listed below the picture, along with about a dozen others. It doesn't say who is who, but it's something.'

It definitely felt like progress. She found herself smiling at Luuk's enthusiasm, but then a dark thought crowded in on her. 'Wait a minute – Dad wasn't born until later that year, so that meant Ilse would have been about five months pregnant in September 1945. Why would she be restarting university when she was about to have a baby? This surely means she had already made up her mind to give him up.'

Anna felt herself harden against the woman she knew so little about. Going to university was a big decision for anyone, and Ilse must have made it willingly and in the knowledge that she'd be unencumbered by a young child. What could possibly have been her reasons? Anna's heart clenched at the memory of her darling father who had done nothing to deserve any of this. Perhaps it was for the best he had never discovered the truth.

'We can't be sure it's her.' Luuk's voice interrupted her thoughts. 'It's just one newspaper article and it might not even be the Ilse Meijer we're looking for.'

'Hmm. How many Ilse Meijers can there be?' Anna said wearily. 'But what if it is her, and something terrible happened for her to give her baby away? I simply can't imagine how difficult a decision that must have been for her. Luuk, I wonder whether I should stop looking for her. It'll only end in tears.' *My tears*, she thought sorrowfully.

There was a pause on the end of the line. Anna realised she was probably overreacting, and blamed it on her tiredness. 'Luuk, I appreciate your help, but this has been a lot to take in. I've been on the go since six this morning and I need a good night's sleep. Can we talk about it in the morning?'

'Of course. And I didn't mean to upset you. Why don't I come to your hotel at ten and we can go for coffee. Then I can show you round Delft. It would be a shame for you not to see this beautiful place before you go.'

Anna smiled to herself, secretly pleased at his offer. 'I'd like that, Luuk. And thanks for all you've done.'

'It's my pleasure. Really it is.'

As soon as she came off the phone, Anna thought about Hugo and knew she couldn't put off ringing him any longer. She wasn't expecting him to pick up – he rarely did – but to her surprise he answered at the first ring. When he heard it was her, he launched straight into a reproach her for not being at home.

'Where are you?' he said, a little too brusquely for her liking.

'I sent you a message before I set off. Didn't you see it?'

'No, I didn't. Where are you, for God's sake?'

'I'm in Delft. Holland. I've come to find out about my grandmother. We did talk about it,' she said, unable to keep the irritation out of her voice.

There was a slight pause, before he said, 'Oh. Yes, of course. But I didn't think you'd actually go. When are you coming back?'

Anna huffed a sigh, still irritated at his apparent lack of

interest, but she didn't have the energy to argue. 'Monday. But why are you back so soon? Is everything all right?'

'Not really,' Hugo said in a sullen voice. 'As soon as I got to Boston, my boss called me in to his office to tell me they're making cuts and they're letting me go. I was stunned. I still don't understand why. My only consolation is that I'm not the only one – but can you believe they let me go all that way only to tell me they're making me redundant?'

Anna heard him take a shaky breath and her heart went out to him. All these months of travelling back and forth to Boston, only to find he was dispensable. She knew how hard he'd worked for his position in the firm; he'd been expecting a promotion to associate partner with a pay rise to match, not this. She was angry on his behalf, and felt guilty that she'd only been thinking of herself and wasn't at home to support him.

'I'm so sorry, really I am. Let's go to the Italian when I'm back – we can have a bottle of wine and a plate of spaghetti and talk about it then.'

'OK,' Hugo said in a tired voice. 'And you can tell me what you've been up to. I love you, hon,' he said, his voice now softer, pleading.

'Love you too.'

Anna hung up, her tiredness gone, replaced by a feeling of shock and mounting unease. How would they cope on her unpredictable income if Hugo was unable to get another job? Suddenly, her attempts to go chasing after the family she hadn't even known existed seemed insignificant. She needed to get back home to support Hugo, back to real life, and forget about chasing her dreams. The only problem was, why did the idea so fill her with dread?

TWENTY-THREE

ILSE

Ilse's bedroom was directly below the attic. At night she lay awake straining to hear every small movement through the floorboards. It would start with a minuscule creak, as she imagined Levi, unable to sleep, getting out of bed and trying not to make a noise as he moved over to the door, across to the window and back again – over and over. What emotions was he experiencing as he paced up and down? Did he do so out of boredom, fear, sadness, or because he was lonely? She felt so sorry for him, but she didn't think she knew him well enough to ask. Whenever she went up with a tray of food, he was always so happy to see her, and she didn't want to spoil the mood between them. She could only hope there would come a time when he felt able to confide in her.

Connie was out most evenings. Ilse could only guess at the seriousness of her assignments; she knew better than to ask her where she went and what she did. But she wanted to know more about the resistance, so began reading the illegal newspaper *Vrij Nederland,* where she picked up information about the success various resistance groups were having in dispelling German propaganda.

One evening Connie came home early, and Ilse saw her opportunity to talk about what she'd been reading, but Connie became irritated, saying Ilse shouldn't believe everything she read.

'Look what happened last September when the whole country believed the Allies had succeeded in pushing back the Germans at Arnhem. Whoever wrote that rubbish was deliberately misreporting the facts and attempting to shape public opinion. I don't read that stuff any more because they publish as much propaganda as the Germans themselves.'

Ilse was astounded at Connie's outburst. 'But I thought *Vrij Nederland* was the voice of the resistance. If I shouldn't read the newspapers and you can't tell me what's going on, then where else am I to find out the truth?'

'I'm afraid I can't answer that,' Connie countered.

'I know you can't, but I feel powerless to do anything myself,' Ilse went on, feeling upset. 'And powerless to boost Levi's morale. I'm the only one he ever sees and I can tell he's just putting a brave face on it. He's effectively locked away up there without any prospect of escape.' Ilse knew she was being dramatic, but she couldn't think of any other way of getting through to Connie.

'Nowhere is safe these days. Believe me, we're monitoring Levi's situation all the time and we know it's a risk having him here, despite being next door to the sanatorium. Rik is trying to find a way to move Levi to the countryside where he'll have more freedom, but it's getting harder to find anyone prepared to take in Jews these days.'

Of course Ilse understood, but that didn't stop hot tears pricking her eyelids. It seemed so unfair that Levi had no part to play in where he went, and that his fate lay in the hands of people who didn't even know him. 'I'm just worried about him up there by himself. At night, I hear him pace up and down. I can tell he's troubled.'

Finally, Connie seemed to listen. 'I hadn't realised it was that bad. I wish I could do more, but I'm simply not around to. Perhaps you could spend more time with him?'

Ilse was more than happy to oblige, even though she was working longer hours herself. In addition to her shifts at the sanatorium, she covered the reception desk for Clara and Hans when one or the other was out on call. Her job was to open the door to patients, checking their details and keeping the appointments diary up to date. When she was the only one in charge, she tried not to allow herself to dwell on the fact that it was just her downstairs and Levi hiding in the attic. She dreaded the ring at the door from a Nazi demanding to make a search of the property, knowing she'd be helpless to prevent it.

During the following days, she did what she could to make Levi's living space more comfortable by bringing up pieces of furniture from her own bedroom: a small oval coffee table where they could place their cups and plates and a small book-case, which she filled with books borrowed from the extensive collection around the Van Dongens' house to keep Levi occupied during the long days and evenings when he was alone.

One evening, she managed to struggle up the stairs with a second armchair. Levi sprang up to help her.

'It doesn't seem right that I always take the only chair,' she said with a laugh, as they pushed it across the floor into position. She stood up straight and, both smiling, they looked into each other's eyes. It was the happiest she'd seen him and she was pleased to be the cause of it.

Now they could sit in comfort, Ilse often came up to chat. She looked forward to finding him sitting in his armchair reading one of the books she'd brought up for him, and often teased him that he would run out of reading matter the rate he was getting through them. For his part, he always greeted her with a smile, and he liked to read out passages he thought she'd find particularly interesting or simply funny. Sometimes they both collapsed in giggles.

But sometimes his mood was sombre. 'Don't feel you have to come up and keep me company. I'm sure you have better things to do with your time,' he said one evening.

They'd been sitting quietly together without the need to fill in the silences with conversation. At least that was what Ilse had thought, and she was surprised by his comment. The light was fading and she wasn't able to make out his expression. 'I'd only be reading in my own room, so please don't think that,' she said.

He shut his book and put it down on the table. 'I thought you might want to spend time with Connie, go out and meet her friends. I'm sure they are more entertaining than being here with me.'

'I've been dancing a couple of times and yes, it was fun, but I can't say I'm too keen on the company she keeps. Wherever you go, there are Germans who want to meet the local women, but that's not for me.'

'And Connie? She strikes me as someone who wouldn't let that bother her.'

Ilse laughed. 'She was always the life and soul at parties when we were at university and she likes going out and having a good time. Connie still goes dancing on Tuesday evenings. She keeps asking me to make up a foursome with a couple of German men she knows, but I don't want to. It feels all wrong. This war has changed everything. And believe it or not, I look forward to being here with you.' The words came out before she could stop herself, and she felt herself blush. She was relieved it was too dark for Levi to see.

'So do I, Ilse.' Levi's voice was almost a murmur and she had to strain to hear him. 'Seeing you is the only thing I look forward to. I know I'm not the most exciting company, stuck up here on my own. But I'm pleased you want to spend time with me. Really I am.'

Ilse watched him get up and go over to the window to close the blackout blind before turning on the lamp in the corner. She waited, hoping he might carry on the conversation, even pull his chair closer, but he sat back down with a sigh and resumed reading his book.

TWENTY-FOUR

Ilse realised the effort it must have taken for Levi to admit to liking her company. The fact that he'd returned to his book without another word seemed like a confirmation that something had shifted in their friendship. Sometimes, she felt they were like an old married couple who were content to be in one another's company without the need for constant conversation. This made her sad and she wished they could be so much more, but she couldn't be sure he felt the same way about her.

It was rare for Levi to receive a letter, so when a blue envelope came through the network, his name written in neat capital letters, Ilse felt her heart lurch. The thought that Levi had a girlfriend and had never mentioned it was simply too painful to contemplate.

Levi turned pale and his hand trembled as he took the letter from her. She hadn't seen his hands shake so much since the first time she'd met him.

'Do you know who it's from?' she made herself ask.

Levi gave a single shake of his head. 'Would you mind giving me a minute?' And he turned away to open the letter in private.

It was then she realised how wrong she had been to jump to the conclusion that this was a love letter. How could she have forgotten what Levi was going through and that he would be waiting day in day out for news of his lost family? She moved quietly to the door, ashamed at her selfish assumption.

'Don't go,' she heard him say.

She stopped and looked back, but was unable to read his expression. Holding up the letter, he took a step towards her. 'It's from a friend of the family. Rebecca is alive! My little sister... I can't believe it.' Levi looked at the letter again for confirmation, and read out loud how Rebecca had been out of the house when the Germans were making their arrests and had fled through the streets to the house of her Christian friend who lived a mile away. By some miracle, and at great danger to herself, the friend's Swiss mother had managed to arrange for Rebecca to travel to relatives who lived in a small village outside Bern, where she was now in safe hands.

Levi looked up, his eyes glistening. Ilse couldn't stop herself from flinging her arms round his waist, delighted to share in his good fortune. 'That's wonderful news,' she said, and kissed him warmly on the cheek. 'Oh, Ilse,' he murmured, cupping her face and gazing into her eyes, before suddenly dropping his hands to his sides.

Ilse felt her cheeks burn with embarrassment. 'I'm sorry,' she stuttered, realising she'd misread him twice now.

Levi shook his head. 'There's no need. I was thinking about my dear sister. I miss her so much and I don't know if we'll ever see each other again. She'll always be my little sister. I always tried to look out for her, but I failed on this occasion.' He let out a long sigh.

'You mustn't blame yourself,' said Ilse, wanting to make things better, but knowing she couldn't. 'It's hard for me to know what it must be like for you losing your family. I hope you don't think I'm unsympathetic.'

'Not at all. I should perhaps have spoken about them sooner. Stay a while, will you, and I can tell you more. If you'd like.' Levi looked at her anxiously.

'I would,' said Ilse, relieved that she hadn't spoiled everything between them.

From that moment, there seemed to be a change between them and they started to talk properly. Levi told Ilse there had been a Jewish girl back home his parents had been expecting him to marry.

'Did you love her?' said Ilse, her heart beating a little faster. Just when she'd been so sure of her feelings, now this.

'I wouldn't be truthful if I didn't say I really liked her. She was sweet and dependable. I knew I'd be pleasing my mother if I agreed to marry her.' Levi shrugged. 'But no, I didn't love her.' He held Ilse's gaze as she waited for him to say the words she so wanted to hear. Instead he looked away. 'She disappeared six months ago and I never heard anything more.'

'That's awful,' said Ilse, and meant it. What was the point of worrying about someone from Levi's past when the future seemed so uncertain?

But it was time for Ilse to talk about Willem, the boy back home who wanted so much more from their friendship than she was able to give. Each letter she received, she was torn between worry about his situation and dread that he was about to come home and expect her to marry him. 'I haven't the heart to tell him I can't reciprocate his feelings.'

Levi didn't comment at first. Instead, he stroked her hand and they remained silent for a long moment.

'What this war is doing to us all... it's such a mess,' he said at last, shaking his head. He said nothing more. He didn't need to.

* * *

It was after ten one evening and Ilse was reluctant to leave. She could barely make out Levi's features in the dim light cast by the lamp on the bookcase. Sinking back into her chair, she allowed herself to be lulled by Levi's quiet deep voice and his stories of life in Amsterdam before the war. This evening, he was telling her about his father's jewellery business and the craftmanship needed to fashion bespoke pieces for clients as far afield as America. The Abel brand was evidently well regarded in high-society circles, given the number of actors, singers, even royalty who regularly made visits to the small workshop to discuss their commissions. Levi spoke admiringly of his father's work, but he admitted that he thought his designs were too traditional for his own liking. He had begun to explore the versatility of precious metals and glass in the creation of abstract, more modern designs.

'I'd like to show you some concepts I've been putting down on paper. I've no idea if they will work, or even if anyone would like them. They're just doodles really,' he said modestly. 'I haven't shown them to anyone yet.'

'I'd love to see them,' said Ilse, with a bubble of happiness that he wanted to share his private ideas with her. In the low light, she watched him as he stood up and went to the bookcase, where he stood for several minutes, searching for whatever it was he was looking for.

'Ah, I thought I'd mislaid it,' he said, retrieving a slim leather folder inserted between two books. He turned to Ilse and his face lit up, as he walked back towards her.

She would always remember that moment, the look of pure joy as Levi caught sight of the smile on her face. Their eyes met and she was about to say something back when a tremendous roar erupted above their heads. In that split second, Ilse felt her world fall apart.

The shock caused Levi to drop the folder to the floor, loose papers scattering at his feet. Instinctively, he lunged forward and tugged Ilse to him, covering her head protectively.

The unmistakeable thunder of planes passing overhead kept on, one after another, until finally the deep throb of the engines receded into the distance.

Ilse lifted her head, her eyes wide with terror, as she searched Levi's face. 'It's enemy planes, isn't it? They've never been this close before.' Her voice was barely audible as a fresh wave of planes came roaring overhead.

'I don't think it can be,' Levi whispered, drawing her close to him again. 'From the direction they're travelling, they must be Allied planes. They're heading east and that probably means their target is somewhere over the border. Let's go and look.'

He took Ilse by the hand with a look of hope on his face. But it was too soon for optimism, she thought.

'Wait. If it's the *moffen*, we'll be seen up here.' She hurriedly switched off the lamp on the bookcase before going to open the blackout blind a notch. Levi came and stood behind her, wrapping his arms round her waist. They stood pressed against each other, peering out at the dark night sky through the crack, but there was nothing to see. The procession of planes had finally passed over and for a long moment it was deathly quiet.

They were about to turn away when they heard the high-pitched whine of an engine starting up from the west, intensifying to a deafening scream as it drew closer.

'It's burning up!' Levi gasped in horror, as the force of an explosion reverberated right through them and shook the floor below their feet.

Terrified, they clasped one another anew as they followed the trajectory of an enormous orange fireball that came hurtling across the sky at speed, shedding fragments of burning fuselage, falling like giant hailstones onto the lawn of the sanatorium.

'No!' gasped Ilse, turning from the terrible spectacle into

the safety of Levi's arms. Tears cascaded down her cheeks at the realisation that the pilot and maybe more people had lost their lives right in front of their eyes.

Levi held her tightly and she felt his body tremble against her own. She closed her eyes, but that did nothing to block out the searing image of flames etched onto the backs of her eyelids. After what seemed like an age, they pulled apart and dared to look again. Down below, the lawn looked like someone had lit bonfires all over it. Not big ones, but small clumps glowing, smouldering in the blackness. Even with the window closed, the sharp acrid smell of engine fuel and burning filled their nostrils. All at once people came running from the sanatorium building, visible only by its indistinct black outline against the still faintly glowing sky. There were voices, some raised, as they ran from spot to spot, using shovels to beat out the flames of burning debris, then attempting to cover them with soil.

Levi turned to Ilse, his face so close she could feel his warm breath on her. 'What is there over the tops of those houses? More houses?' he whispered.

Ilse had to think a moment. 'A school, and a playing field. That's probably where the pilot was aiming for.'

'I hope you're right. If the plane came down there, he would have avoided an even bigger catastrophe. But I don't think anyone could have survived that.' He squeezed Ilse tight again, as if needing to comfort himself against the thought. But she noticed he was still trembling.

'It's all right, Levi. You're safe up here.' She reached up and kissed him gently on the cheek.

'But what if they come looking for survivors? And if they find me? It's you I worry about.' He held the sides of her face so he could look into her eyes.

Ilse's heart pounded. She knew they were both at risk, but she had to be strong for him.

'I should go downstairs and see if everyone is all right,' she murmured, and pressed her cheek into his shirt.

Levi took her shoulders so he could look at her again. 'Come back to me tonight, Ilse. After all that's happened, I want to be with you.'

'I will.' She understood what he was asking, that he was frightened of what the future might bring. In the darkness, she tilted her face and yielded to him as he kissed her for the very first time. She didn't want it to end and sensed that neither did he.

Tonight, they had witnessed something momentous, but she was afraid it was a portent of far worse things to come.

TWENTY-FIVE

Ilse's shoes clattered on the wooden treads as she hurried down the attic stairs, along the landing and down another flight. Where was everyone? In her panic, she almost lost her footing. Then, as she prepared to turn to descend the last three steps into the hallway, she saw him standing right in front of her. He was unmistakeable – tall and upright, short fair hair, wide forehead. Her heart leapt in fright. What on earth was he doing inside their house?

She turned at the sound of the flushing toilet in the cloakroom to her left. Connie emerged, looking slightly dishevelled. Her normally neat hairstyle was a mess, with strands of hair escaping from their tortoiseshell clips. When she caught sight of Ilse staring, she quickly smoothed the errant wisps of hair back into place. Ilse looked from one to the other and felt a wave of disgust. How could Connie be so careless, turning up with him after all they'd said about the danger of mixing with Nazi officers? But it was Jürgen's presence that upset her the most.

'What do you think you're doing coming into our house?' she said, panic surging through her as it occurred to her that Jürgen wasn't here for Connie but to search the attic.

'Well, Ilse, it's a while since we last met. Rudi was saying only tonight how much he misses you. Don't you like to go dancing any more?' he said.

Ilse chose to ignore his comment – all she could think was that his presence here meant that Levi was now in more danger than he'd ever been. Instead, she addressed Connie. 'What's going on? Why have you brought him here?' She was desperate for her friend to come up with a better reason than the one careening through her head.

'It's all right, Ilse. Jürgen was seeing me home and we were just turning in to the street when the explosion happened. But when burning debris came down, it was obvious a plane was falling out of the sky. We had to run for shelter. Jürgen was about to head off home, but I asked him in as I didn't want him to be caught up in the chaos.' Connie's expression was serious as she turned to him. 'It's best you go now.'

'If you say so. Connie's safety was my priority and I had no intention of intruding,' said Jürgen, shooting Ilse an annoyed look. 'Will you be all right now, *liebchen*?' He moved to Connie so he could lift her chin in a show of tenderness. Ilse couldn't bear to watch. She just wanted him to leave. She went to open the front door, letting in the sound of distant sirens and sharp smell of smoke. 'I apologise if I was rude, but it's been such a dreadful evening. Ever since the explosion I've been jittery. It was such a shock to find you here.'

'Apology accepted,' said Jürgen, with a curt nod of the head. 'I think we're all a little shaken up. By the morning, I'm sure we will have forgotten all about it.'

As she pushed the door shut on Jürgen, Ilse closed her eyes in relief. She was right to get him out of the house. He couldn't be trusted. He was German and, worse than that, he was a Nazi.

Turning to Connie, she said, 'What were you thinking letting him in? And if he'd insisted on searching the house?'

Connie looked uncomfortable, but seemed determined to justify her actions. 'I can see why you're worried, but if I'd refused, he would have become suspicious that I was hiding something from him. I couldn't let that happen. I knowingly took that risk by bringing him in. I was actually trying to protect you and Levi.'

Ilse frowned, unconvinced by this explanation. 'You shouldn't be taking risks in the first place. Why keep spending time with Jürgen knowing what his people get up to? It just doesn't make sense.' She wondered if Connie was losing her mind. Being brave was one thing, but consciously carrying on with a German was reckless. She watched Connie intently and was sure she saw a flicker of uncertainty cross her face.

'I know I should break it off, but it's not that simple.'

'I don't understand. What do you mean?'

Connie gave Ilse an odd look, then went on, 'Come into the sitting room. It's time I told you some truths.'

Once they were seated, Connie spoke in a low voice about how she had met Jürgen and her need to keep their acquaintance going. It wasn't at all what Ilse had been expecting and she was shocked that Connie had managed to keep it quiet all this time.

Connie began by saying how eager she'd been to please Rik when she'd joined his resistance group, but that he had wanted to test out her loyalty before giving her more responsibility. At first, she did administrative jobs and organised anti-propaganda leaflets for distribution. 'But I wanted to do so much more. So when the Germans cut off all telephone connections, I asked Rik if I could work on the illegal exchanges that facilitate the transfer of sensitive information to help the Allies in their advance into the Netherlands. And when I heard about the plight of Jews needing to hide, I knew I had to help by offering space in our big house. Since Levi's arrival, working to find safe houses has been my main focus. It's been such a fraught time and Rik and I have grown close. I suppose it's the intensity of working under pressure and in dangerous situations. Then he came up with the idea of befriending Jürgen to extract information useful to the resistance. All I had to do was to pretend to hit it off with him, so I agreed to go dancing. It was a huge risk, but the information Jürgen's passed on to me has helped save many innocent lives. It's true Rik has found it hard seeing me stepping out with a German officer, and at times I've been very conflicted about my subterfuge, but I hope you can see how necessary it's been. Though I admit it was a mistake to bring Jürgen here, particularly tonight of all nights. I wasn't intending to, and regretted it as soon as we stepped through the door. I asked him to wait a moment while I went to splash water on my face and gather my thoughts. And then you turned up. It was a shock. I guessed by your face what you were thinking, and now I see you were right. But when we were running through the streets not knowing what was happening, I really feared for my life. I've never experienced that before and it's made me think... all those people I've helped and now Levi... I can't imagine what it must be like living with fear all the time.'

'No, I don't think I can either,' said Ilse, her mind on Levi. 'Connie, there's something you should know too. I took up your suggestion of getting to know Levi. At first, I felt sorry for him and just wanted to keep him company, but the more I've got to know him, the more I want to be with him, and I'm sure he feels the same way about me. I know it's mad and can't possibly lead anywhere, but I don't think I can stop myself.' She took a deep breath before continuing. 'When the explosion happened, we watched from the attic window. It was so close and the noise so deafening I was sure it would hit the house. I was terrified, but I couldn't just stand by and do nothing. That's why I came running through the house like a madwoman looking for you and your parents. And when I saw Jürgen, I panicked.'

'I'm sorry I put you through that. And I'm so pleased for

you and Levi. What you both have is a wonderful thing. Make the most of the time you have with him, and don't worry about what's coming next. And remember, whatever happens I'll be here for you.'

Ilse took comfort in her friend's words, but wished she could be as optimistic about the future. Everything with Levi had happened so fast and she was scared it would abruptly come to an end.

They both gave a start at the crunch of footsteps on the gravel drive. At the sound of a key in the lock, Connie stood up. 'It's my parents. They will have gone to give medical help.' She waited for the door to close, and the sound of the hall light switch being turned on, before both of them went to see if she was right.

'No survivors,' said Connie's father, dumping his medical bag on the tiled hall floor. He looked exhausted, his face grey in the weak lamplight; his hair was a mess.

'Worse than that. There are body parts scattered all around. I've never seen anything like it,' said Connie's mother, heading for the chair under the clock and lowering herself down with a deep sigh. 'In fact, we weren't much use at all. That poor pilot.'

They had been among the first ones on the crash scene where the fighter plane had broken up, she went on. The impact had been so severe that there was little left of the school playing field. Several windows in the buildings facing the field had been blown out.

'I knew it was bad. I was upstairs when I heard it come down, and saw it break up even before it hit the ground. It was a miracle it didn't hit the house,' said Ilse. 'Do you have any idea what nationality the pilot was?'

'British,' said Hans. 'He was flying a Spitfire and was obviously trying to avoid crashing into any buildings. He did a good job, not that it helped him. He didn't stand a chance.'

'Will they be able to identify him?' asked Connie, who had been listening quietly.

Her mother shook her head. 'Unless they can find any papers, but that's unlikely. It'll be hard to identify anything among the wreckage. It's all been blown to smithereens.'

The little group stood lost for words, unable to find anything more to say. 'Well,' said Hans at last. 'We've done all we can for now and I suggest we all go to bed.' He went to each of them to give them a hug, and was the first to trudge up the stairs.

TWENTY-SIX

The sweet fluting of a blackbird roused Ilse from her sleep. As she gently came to, the cascading trills of its song floated over her. It was early, though she knew she wouldn't manage to fall back to sleep. She rolled onto her side and laid her head on the crook of her arm so she could look at Levi, so peaceful in sleep. She didn't want to disturb him. Instead, she gazed at the tangle of hair that fell across his forehead, his dark lashes that brushed his cheeks and the suggestion of a soft smile at the corner of his lips. *This is how I want to remember you*, she mouthed silently to herself, as his eyes fluttered open.

'I was dreaming that you were next to me. And I find it's true.'

She laughed as he wriggled closer so he could wrap his arms round her and kiss her. She had never felt this happy.

'I have an idea,' she said. She was suddenly gripped by an irresistible urge to go and investigate, but she knew she didn't want to do it alone. 'No one will be about this early on a Sunday morning. Will you come and help me look for something that might identify the pilot so at least his family will know what happened to him?'

Levi frowned as he thought about it. 'What time is it?'

'The clock downstairs struck five a few minutes ago. If you don't want to, just say.'

'No, it's just that it's so long since I've been up here, I've forgotten what freedom is like. We should go.'

Levi stood rooted by the open back door. He lifted his head to the sky and breathed in the clean spring air, then sighed it out.

Ilse watched him for a moment, her heart overflowing with a mixture of love and sadness. She took his hand, anxious to get on before anyone was up. 'Come on, we don't want to be seen.'

Together, they walked along the driveway leading to the vast lawn in front of the sanatorium. But up close, it no longer resembled a lawn. What little grass was left was either flattened or scorched black. There were small craters and pockmarked indentations all over, the result of pieces of burning metal hurtling from the sky. All over were fragments of metal, and things she could not put a name to.

They kept their eyes fixed to the ground as they picked their way across the devastation, stooping here and there to pick up an object, before laying it back where they'd found it. It was hard to make out what they were looking at, so mangled, twisted and sharp were the shapes that had sheared off in the impact.

Then Ilse's eye was caught by something different, not metal. She went to investigate and saw it was a leather flying helmet with the chin strap hanging free of its buckle. Unbelievably, apart from a few scuff marks, it had escaped unscathed. Ilse bent down, but as she lifted it to show Levi she caught sight of something that made her drop it with a cry. For nestling in the leather folds lay something strange, curved like a pale-pink shell. Instantly, she knew what it was. Levi came rushing over to see what had upset her.

She stared at the severed ear, her hand covering her mouth.

'It's... horrible.' Her voice came out hoarsely. 'But how did that happen when the impact was over by the school?'

'The pilot must have had a passenger who bailed out. He probably ordered him to, thinking he'd save his life. Poor fellow.'

Ilse shook her head. 'I can't do this,' she said with a strangled cry, stumbling backwards.

'Let's go back inside,' said Levi, scanning the lawn. 'There may be more things like that.' He put an arm round her shoulders and they walked away towards the house. Ilse began to sob.

Suddenly, he stopped. 'Wait. What's this?' He dropped to his knees.

'Please, Levi. Let's go. I can't take any more.'

But Levi wasn't listening. He picked up something small and round from the dirt and rubbed the soil away until it glinted in the sunlight. Turning it over and over between his long fingers, he peered closely at it. 'It must have dropped out of the airman's pocket when he bailed out. It's been badly damaged by the impact.'

He'd got Ilse's attention and she leant in for a closer look. The silver coin was bent almost double, but the marks and lettering were still perfectly legible.

'I've seen one of these before. It's a sixpence coin... and it's English.' Levi pointed to the letters 'Sixp', but the rest of the word disappeared into the crease where the coin had been bent over. 'I suppose we now know they were British airmen on their way to bomb Germany. But what a terrible way to die.'

Still holding the coin, he stood up and helped Ilse to her feet. She fought back tears at the thought of this young serviceman who had died along with his co-pilot in such a tragic failed attempt to free her country.

'I don't want to leave it here,' said Levi, looking closely at the coin again. 'I think I can straighten it out and polish it up. And it will be beautiful again.' He gazed deep into her eyes.

Her heart gave a jolt. Something significant had happened

today, something both terrible and wonderful, and she knew the memory of what they'd both experienced would stay with her for ever.

TWENTY-SEVEN

ANNA

Anna was checking out of her hotel when Luuk appeared at her shoulder.

'Anna, are you leaving so soon?' he said, staring at the suitcase by her side.

'Oh... hello. Just give me a minute and I'll explain.' Anna felt herself redden as she turned away.

After she finished checking out, she went to find Luuk, who had retired to the lobby and was sitting cross-legged in a leather armchair, leafing through a design magazine. Anna noticed how stylish he looked, in dark denim jeans and a shirt that matched the blue of his eyes. Catching sight of her approaching, he immediately put down the magazine and stood up.

'I need a coffee. There's a very nice café round the corner,' he said, and before she had a chance to utter a word, Anna found herself being steered out through the glass door and into the warm spring sunshine, where Delft was coming to life. From the square rang the distinctive bells of a carillon striking out the hour, as people criss-crossed the open space, coffee cups in hand and mobiles pressed against their ears. Outside the surrounding cafés, waiters dusted down chairs and rearranged menus on the tables. She wanted to pause and enjoy the scene but Luuk didn't stop. He strode quickly, as if on an urgent mission; Anna was forced to run to keep up.

'Here we are,' he said, stopping outside a tall building with intricate gabling and enormous picture windows. 'This is where they do the best coffee in Delft.' His face suddenly relaxed into a smile. He ushered Anna into the dark panelled room filled with people standing around at the counter drinking little cups of coffee, or sitting in twos and threes at small round tables or in the booths that lined the walls. The place was positively humming.

They sat opposite one another in a booth, both with cups of strong black coffee, a tiny sweet Dutch biscuit on the saucers. Anna was aware of Luuk's gaze on her, earnest and questioning. She wished she didn't have to let him down after all he'd already done for her. Briefly, she regretted her impulse to leave so soon, before reminding herself that she must stick to her promise to Hugo and return home. She should tell Luuk. But as she lifted her eyes to meet his, she saw something written there – such intensity, such expectation that it made her falter. Taking in a sharp breath, she concentrated on stirring a sachet of sugar into her coffee.

'If it's something I said last night, then I'm sorry.' Luuk sat back and pushed a hand through his thick fair hair. 'Perhaps I was a little too eager to help. When it became clear our grandmothers might have been friends, that made me want to find out more. I admit I may be jumping to conclusions over the article online, but what if it was your biological grand-mother? And what if they'd been at Leiden together? Wouldn't it just be the most amazing coincidence?' As the questions tumbled out, his blue eyes shone brightly. It wasn't the first time she'd noticed this endearing trait, and she couldn't help but smile.

'Yes, it would,' she said with a little laugh, 'but let's not get

ahead of ourselves. Wouldn't Kersten have had a stronger
memory if the two of them had been friends?'

'Not necessarily. Maybe they'd been friends in the war and
lost touch afterwards. It must have been chaotic for people
trying to return to normal life. And war can do terrible things to
people.'

Deflated, Anna stared into her cooling coffee, resigned to
this whole thing not going anywhere. 'I suppose you're right.
But it doesn't look as if we have much else to go on,' she said,
looking back at him. 'You've already done so much for me. I
don't expect you to keep delving into my family history.'

Luuk made a dismissive gesture with his hand. 'So that's
why you're going back home early?'

Anna knew that if she were to mention Hugo now, the
mood between them would be spoilt, and she wasn't ready for
that. She looked up as a couple walked past their booth – he
whispering in her ear in some private joke and she laughing –
and was relieved to have the brief distraction. It was time now to
be more honest with him; but she stopped short of telling the
real reason she was leaving. 'I expected coming all this way
would be easy, but I was wrong. I imagined my grandmother
would be living at the address Dad had written down. When
she wasn't, it felt like losing Dad all over again.' She bit down on
her lip.

'I'm sorry. It must be tough,' he said, keeping his eyes
on her.

Anna regarded him and found herself comparing him to
Hugo – Hugo would never have shown her such sympathy.
And then, as if to reprimand herself for having such a thought,
an unwelcome image of Hugo came into her head, begging her
to come home. Realising she'd become lost in thought, she
noticed Luuk reach across the table and take her hand. It was
warm and reassuring and she didn't want to pull away.

'My grandfather died when I was young and I remember

how much I missed him after he'd gone,' he said. 'He was such a quiet, kind man, it came as such a surprise when I came across his name in a research document describing him as an active member of a resistance group during the war. So when I heard you'd come looking for your grandmother, it made me think about him all over again. I wish I'd had the chance to talk to him about it.' He sighed and looked wistful.

Anna nodded, but all she could think of was that he was still holding her hand across the table and she didn't want him to let go. This physical connection was starting to mean much more to her and she knew she should stop it now... Luuk moved his thumb over the top of her hand and, as he did so, her heart seemed to lurch sideways in her chest. *Stop this*, she scolded herself. *It means nothing.*

'Luuk,' she began, and her heart thumped harder. She reluctantly withdrew her hand and reached down to her bag, feeling inside for the soft blue scarf in which she'd wrapped the necklace. 'This is what brought me here,' she said, smoothing the scarf open on the table. She took hold of the necklace by the catch and held it up for him to see. 'After Dad died, I found this hidden away in an old Dutch biscuit tin. I've a gut feeling it's important, but can't work out why. Along with his train and boat ticket, it's all I have to go on, but I believe it must be connected to his search for his mother.' She paused a moment, studying Luuk's expression for clues as he looked intently at the coin.

'Maybe it's something to do with your grandfather. What nationality was he?'

She sighed. 'I don't know anything about him. Why do you ask?'

'It's an English coin. If he gave it to your grandmother, perhaps he was English.'

'That's what I need to find out. Something happened between my grandparents to make them give up the baby, or at least make my grandmother want to give him up. I thought it could be because she'd been in a relationship with a German.'

'Or maybe he was an Englishman she'd met when the Allies came over and he gave her the necklace as a keepsake.' Luuk kept turning the coin over and over between his fingers. 'It's odd, though. Why give something that's damaged unless it meant something?'

'Like what?'

'I don't know. But if we can find your grandmother, perhaps she can tell you.' A broad smile spread across Luuk's face. Anna returned his smile, reassured she didn't have to go about this on her own. As she gazed into Luuk's blue eyes, she felt a pang of regret that she'd made the decision to leave so soon, and realised she couldn't avoid telling him the reason any longer.

'I wish I could stay, but I can't,' she began. 'I spoke to my boyfriend, Hugo, last night. He called me to tell me he's lost his job. He's been working for a consulting firm and thought he was in line for promotion, not the sack. Unsurprisingly, he's in a state of shock. As soon as he told me, I realised I shouldn't be here and needed to go straight back home. I'm sorry, I should have told you about him sooner.'

Luuk sat back in his seat. She wondered if he'd already guessed. 'It's no problem. Of course you must go,' he said. 'These things happen and you can always come back another time, can't you?'

Anna nodded sadly, knowing that it would be far harder to return once she was back with Hugo, who clearly needed her support. And by then, the whole idea of finding her grand-mother would be no more than a distant dream.

'Well, let's make the most of the time you have left,' Luuk went on, in an attempt at cheeriness. 'Do you still have time to look around Delft?'

TWENTY-EIGHT

After a refill of hot coffee, they left the café to wend their way back to the main square, where Luuk showed her around the beautiful Renaissance town hall building that stood across from the enormous Nieuwe Kerk. They emerged into the bright sunshine just as the tuneful bells of the church tower chimed out the half hour. From there, they walked along the quaint cobbled streets lining the canals.

'The name Delft comes from the old Dutch word *delvan*, which means to dig. The city's original name, Delf, meaning ditch, is still the name of the town's main canal. Tourists often call Delft Little Amsterdam,' Luuk said, turning to Anna, who was feeling like a proper tourist. They were approaching one of the many humpbacked bridges crossing the canals. 'I prefer Delft myself. It's not as frenetic,' he said. No sooner were the words out of his mouth than a group of cyclists came flying over the bridge, loudly ringing their bells. Luuk reached out to pull Anna out of harm's way and put a protective arm around her shoulder. 'Well, perhaps not all the time,' he said, laughing.

They kept on walking along the canals, stopping here and there for Luuk to point out an interesting feature or view. 'Look to the side of that building,' he instructed Anna, as they drew level with two step-gabled buildings in red brick linked by a paved alleyway. 'It's the scene that inspired Vermeer to paint *The Little Street*... so they say.'

'You don't sound as if you believe it,' said Anna, peering towards where he was pointing.

'This might be the place, but it's not proven. In the seventeenth century, Delft was full of little streets with houses lining narrow canals like this one.'

Anna was charmed by what she saw: a slightly peeling, white-painted door stood open, affording a view onto a cobbled yard where a small boy was playing with a plastic toy car. He looked up and waved at them. 'I suppose he must be used to people coming to look,' Anna said with a wave back, but she was embarrassed that they had intruded; she had to pull Luuk away by the sleeve to stop his gawping. She'd noticed this about the Dutch, how they didn't think it rude to stare, but she was willing to forgive Luuk.

They carried on meandering over bridges, past rows of bicycles left propped up against trees coming into leaf along the canals, while Luuk spoke of his love of history and art and how it was encouraged by his father, who was passionate about old Dutch masters and took his son to museums and art galleries throughout his teens. 'Most teenagers would be bored by the idea of being dragged round exhibitions, but fortunately for my dad, I loved it. He always wanted me to go to Leiden, but I didn't pass the entrance exam and went to my second choice, Utrecht. It wasn't such a bad choice – I've now ended up working in Leiden.'

'Your English was always good, but where did you learn to speak it so fluently?' said Anna. They had stopped to admire the view from one of the bridges.

'Do you think so?' Luuk, said, glancing sideways at her as he leant against the iron railing. 'We Dutch have to speak good

English if we're to get anywhere in our jobs. After my degree, I spent a year as an assistant lecturer in Cambridge, which helped. I sometimes have to lecture in English now, but it's much harder than doing it in my mother tongue. How's your Dutch these days?'

'I'm getting better and can understand a lot more than I can speak. You'd think having a Dutch father I would be able to, but we've always lived in England. Dad moved to England for work, met Mum and settled in Oxford. We only ever spoke English at home, though I did pick up a few phrases from Dad.'

'And from me, if I remember rightly. Though nothing useful unless you need a suitable swear word,' said Luuk with a wry grin that made Anna laugh.

Suddenly, she wanted to tell Luuk about her own work, what it was like being a freelance journalist, the deadlines that always seemed to pile up one after another, followed by lengthy periods when she worried if she'd be commissioned to write another piece. 'I know I'm only as good as my last piece of writing. But it's not all bad. If I had a boss, I wouldn't be able to take off at a moment's notice to go chasing after my crazy dreams.' She waited for Luuk to speak, but he was staring straight ahead at the water. She was wondering if he'd actually been listening when he slowly turned his head to look at her.

'It's good to have dreams, however crazy they might seem. You'll regret it if you don't see through what you've started. Don't turn your back on them now.' His words seemed to hang between them as he kept looking at her.

Anna felt her insides tighten, knowing full well he wasn't referring only to her search for her grandmother. And she wasn't sure it was just her dreams he was alluding to; maybe it was his own too. With a slight shake of the head, she was reluctant to say anything that might betray her emotions. She was so perilously close to changing her mind and staying, but then she stopped herself. She had made up her mind to go back to Hugo, who was so desperate for her to return, and nothing must stand in her way.

Across the rooftops, the church clock struck the quarter-hour. All morning as they'd walked through the Delft streets, glimpses of the tall tower and the regular pealing of the chimes had been a constant reminder of how little time they had left together. *And now it's nearly over*, Anna thought as she checked her watch. 'I'd better pick up my suitcase and head off. I really shouldn't miss the ferry,' she said.

'Will you let me take you back to the hotel?' Luuk offered his arm, and she was relieved to see that smile of his again. She took it – it would have been churlish not to – and they set off in companionable silence, stopping briefly by a street seller for a *broodje haring*, which Luuk insisted she tried because it was so typically Dutch. He laughed as she nervously bit into the soft white roll containing chunks of raw herring, onions and gherkins. She was surprised at how delicious it tasted and laughed with him, enjoying the moment and wishing all this didn't have to end so soon.

Luuk insisted on accompanying her to the station and carrying her case. For the last time they crossed the square, and he continued to tell her little anecdotes about Delft's history, peppering them with stories of his own childhood memories of his old school in the centre of town, which he'd obviously loved.

All too soon they arrived at the station concourse, which was thronging with people. Loud train announcements crackled from the tannoy every few seconds. Luuk located Anna's plat-form easily, giving her instructions on where to change for the Hook of Holland.

'Seven minutes till your train is due. And it's on time,' he said, looking up at the sign above the barrier. 'You'd better go through so you get a seat. Will you be OK?' he went on, frowning a little.

'Of course I will, Luuk. And thanks for all you've done. I'd probably have gone straight back home if you hadn't offered to show me round.' Anna swallowed hard. She'd always hated goodbyes, especially in noisy public places. That was why she never went to see Hugo off at the airport; she knew she would end up in tears.

'Well, I'm glad you didn't, even if we didn't get very far in our investigations. I'm sure I can get to the bottom of who your grandmother is, if you allow me to.'

A group of teenagers turned up at the barrier, laughing and jostling their backpacks against each other, and Anna was forced to take a step back to get out of their way.

Luuk caught her by the arms. 'Anna, please say you'll come back,' he breathed as he stared down at her. He bent to kiss her on each cheek, before pulling her into a clumsy hug. Anna leant her cheek against his shoulder. Briefly closing her eyes, she inhaled his warm scent that was both thrillingly different yet familiar. Her eyes began to prick with tears and she tried hard to blink them away. She glanced up at the departure board.

'I'm going to miss it if I don't go now,' she said, her voice breaking, and reached out for her suitcase at the same time that Luuk did.

'Come back soon,' he said, his hand covering hers.

Anna could only nod in response as she lifted her suitcase away to concentrate on squeezing through the barrier. Without a backwards glance, she sprinted along the platform, her suitcase banging against her leg, unable to hold back her tears.

TWENTY-NINE

ILSE

Monday mornings were always busy in the surgery. Patients who had held back from telephoning to discuss their ailments at the weekend came streaming in to see a doctor in person. No sooner had Ilse shown the next person into the waiting room and returned to her desk to log their arrival in the appointments book than the insistent buzz of the doorbell would start up again. And today, in addition to the usual greetings on the doorstep, it seemed that everyone wanted to chat about the plane that had come down. Was it a Canadian fighter plane, or British, or even German? Had Ilse actually seen it burst into flames from the house... did the Van Dongens' house suffer any damage... was anyone hurt... did she know if there were any survivors? Ilse was careful not to say too much. She had a job to do and Clara, aware as she was of how her patients gossiped, had warned her not to engage in any tittle-tattle of her own.

Moments after Ilse had sat down at her desk, the doorbell went again. She glanced through the diary to see if it could be the next patient arriving for their appointment, but no one was due for another half an hour. Suppressing her irritation at another interruption so soon after sitting down, she closed the appointments book, just as the doorbell rang out again. 'For heaven's sake,' she muttered under her breath and hurried across the hall. She swung the door open, composing her features into a smile. For a split second, she didn't recognise the man standing before her, because he was out of uniform and dressed in a plain dark jacket, trousers and matching trilby hat that cast a long shadow over his face. Then he opened his mouth and greeted her in heavily accented Dutch. Her expression hardened as she realised who it was, and her mind descended into turmoil.

'It's you. Why are you here?' She spoke in an urgent whisper, in case anyone inside the house could hear her.

Smiling, Rudi removed his hat; he seemed pleased to see her. 'Good morning, Ilse. I came because I was worried about you when I heard about the plane crashing near to your house. I wanted to come sooner but was detained on official matters.'

'Did Jürgen send you?' Ilse said suspiciously.

Rudi shook his head and frowned. She could tell he was put out by her response. 'No. Of course not. Why would he?' He spoke curtly. 'Didn't you know everyone's talking about the crash? And then there are the rumours.' His eyes narrowed as he watched her.

'What rumours?' Ilse found herself tensing up.

'There have been sightings of a man, possibly a survivor, who was in the crash area. We believe the man is hurt and that someone has taken him in. We would need to know, if that is true. Did you see anyone?' he said, examining her face closely.

'No, I haven't,' she said, growing suspicious of his probing. Was this an excuse for him to search the house? 'It's not possible,' she went on. 'I saw the plane come down with my own eyes, from an upstairs window, and no one would have survived that.' She wanted nothing more than to shut the door on him, certain that someone, probably Jürgen, must have known that a

Jew was sheltering under her roof. They had sent Rudi, the Nazi officer who was sweet on Ilse, imagining she'd be only too pleased to receive him into her home. She was desperate for him to leave. With one hand on the door, she said, 'I'm afraid I can't talk to you right now. I'm busy.'

Rudi stepped forward and held up his hand. 'Ilse, wait. Seeing such a thing up close must have been very frightening for you.' He cleared his throat. 'I admit I needed an excuse to come and see you. I've missed you so much. It hasn't been the same since you stopped coming dancing with me.'

His tone was wheedling, which made her even more suspicious. She stared back at him, trying to work out what his real motives were. Could his feelings be genuine?

But before she could answer, she heard someone cough violently, and turned to see one of the patients, leaving after their consultation.

'Mevrouw van der Daal. Did the doctor give you something to help that cough of yours?' she said, relieved to have someone to distract her from this unsettling conversation.

'Yes, thank you,' said the woman in a croaky voice. 'Dr van Dongen says I should go home and stay indoors in case I'm still infectious.'

'That sounds like good advice, but do telephone the surgery if your cough gets any worse. And look after yourself.' Ilse stepped aside to let the woman through. 'Goodbye.'

'Thank you, dear. Goodbye.' The woman pulled a scarf over her mouth, coughing into it as she crunched away down the path. Ilse noticed how Rudi twitched and took a step back as the woman walked past him. He'd gone quite pale. Ilse almost felt sorry for him, but not enough to make her agree to see him again.

'Rudi, I didn't mean to be rude, but I've been a bit jumpy lately. It's not a good time now and I need to get back to work.'

'Before you go.' Rudi appeared to have resumed his composure, and was gazing intently at her. 'It's my birthday tomorrow and it would make me very happy if you would come dancing with me.'

Ilse blinked hard. She would love nothing more than to forget the horrors of that night for just one evening and lose herself in the enjoyment of live music and dance. And she had to admit that Rudi was a very good dancer... but there was nothing that could persuade her to change her mind.

Her attention was diverted by the sound of a door slamming upstairs. Had Levi crept down from the attic to listen? Resolving not to give Rudi any cause to suspect, she continued addressing him. 'I'm sorry, Rudi. I want you to understand that I can't be seen with you, as much as I've enjoyed our Tuesday evenings together. It's best we say goodbye and forget about everything.' As soon as the words were out of her mouth, she regretted saying them. Rudi's expression shifted to something hard and unforgiving, sending a cold shiver right through her.

'I did not expect this of you.' Rudi spoke in a clipped voice Ilse didn't recognise. 'If that is what you want, then I will respect your wishes. But...' He paused, pressing his lips into a hard line. 'I have one question for you. Who was the man you were with the morning of the plane crash?'

Ilse managed to keep her face very still. She was petrified that he might be able to read the shock written on her face. 'I have no idea what you mean,' she whispered.

Rudi barked a short laugh. 'Come, Ilse. Don't play games with me. You were seen wandering around the grounds of the sanatorium with a man who could not in any way have been the survivor of a plane crash. Unless I'm mistaken. Hmm?'

Ilse knew she had to stand her ground and must not look away. 'Yes, Rudi. You are mistaken. Now, goodbye.' She began to push the door shut.

'Don't imagine you can fool me,' Rudi said, before raising a stiff hand to the side of his head. 'Heil Hitler!' he barked, swivelled on his heel and strode away.

Safely inside, Ilse leant with her back against the door, taking shallow breaths to calm the pounding in her chest. He's gone and that's all that matters, she kept telling herself, though she was unable to ignore the panic racing through her. With a sense of foreboding, she knew that he was finally showing his true colours. What if he came back, next time with his colleagues, and forced entry to the house?

Trembling, she tried to shake away her troubling thoughts and hurried back to her desk, where a queue of people, some grumbling among themselves, were awaiting her return. She'd only been away a few minutes, but she shouldn't have allowed herself to be distracted. Apologising, she dealt with their complaints and restored order. Slowly, the waiting room emptied out, and the rest of the morning passed by uneventfully, though her mind was still in turmoil. She was itching to find out if Levi had heard any of her conversation, and desperate to warn him of the dangers that lay ahead.

At last the hall clock struck twelve and the last of the patients left. Clara came out of her consulting room and peeled off her white coat. 'I'm glad that's over,' she said with a sigh as she threw it over the back of a chair. 'I'm afraid this plane crash is bringing us a lot of unwanted attention. It's unnerving how people expect us to know the details just because it was so close. I hope they didn't give you too much trouble. How did you cope out here?' She picked up a pile of patient folders from Ilse's desk and began flicking through them.

'There's something you should know.' Ilse rose nervously to her feet and waited till she'd got Clara's attention. 'I had a visit today from someone who could put our lives in danger.

Someone I met a few weeks ago when Connie and I went dancing. It meant nothing as far as I was concerned, but I'm afraid he's become obsessed with me. I only went a couple of times, then stopped... because he's German. The trouble is he's friendly with the boy Connie is seeing, and I'm afraid they'll come searching for survivors of the crash.' She spoke quickly, stopping short of saying she'd been seen standing with Levi outside, something she now deeply regretted.

Clara replaced the folders and sat down on the arm of the armchair nearest Ilse's desk. 'I thought it might come to this. I warned Connie that it's not wise to be seen mixing with German officers while Levi is hidden under our roof, but there's no point arguing with her.'

Ilse felt uncomfortable that she couldn't tell Clara how much she knew about Connie's dealings with the resistance. But Connie had sworn her to secrecy and Ilse knew she must respect her wishes.

'Tell me what his friend said to make you so worried,' said Clara.

Ilse realised she had no choice other than to be truthful. 'Rudi was friendly at first, saying he was worried about me with the plane crash being so close. I wanted him to go, but when I refused to accept his invitation to go dancing again, this change came over him. I could tell he was really angry. And then he accused me of being seen outside with a man on the morning after the crash. I denied it of course, but the thing is, it's true. It was Levi.'

Clara pursed her lips and shook her head. 'I'm sure I don't need to say how foolish you've been. This is serious and you're right to be worried. In fact, we all should be. I've turned a blind eye to Connie's association with that German because she assured me it was just a dalliance that meant nothing to her, but now I fear she's gone too far. One or two people have been asking questions about Connie after seeing her with a man in

German uniform. I've managed to deal with it, but that's how suspicions grow. We simply can't take any more risks. I'm afraid Levi will have to go. We'll discuss the matter later and work out how to move him safely. In the meantime, you know Levi better than any of us, Ilse. Will you tell him?'

THIRTY

Straight after her conversation with Clara, Ilse rushed up to see Levi, who threw open the attic door before she even had a chance to knock. His hair was all over the place, as if he'd been thrusting his hands through it, and his face was pinched. 'Ilse!' he cried, and pulled her inside, pushing the door firmly shut. He crushed her against him and she held him tight around his waist. Pressing her cheek against his chest, she felt momentarily comforted by the warmth of his body.

'Something terrible has happened, hasn't it?' Levi let her go and lifted her chin so he could look into her eyes. She gave a weak nod as he went on, 'I knew it. I heard your voice from downstairs and could tell something wasn't right from your tone. I had to do something, so I crept down the attic stairs and crouched down to listen, but I forgot I'd left the attic window ajar for some air. A gust of wind slammed the door shut. I saw you look round. I was convinced I'd be found out, so I crept away as quietly as I could. I've been cowering inside that low cupboard under the eaves, expecting the worst. But nobody came. I've only just come out. Oh, Ilse, I've been out of my mind with worry.'

'I came as quickly as I could, but I had to wait till the end of surgery.' She could hardly bring herself to look at him as she rapidly described the conversation with Rudi on the doorstep, and her horror on discovering that he knew about Levi. 'I can't believe I put you in such danger.'

Levi looked grave as he said, 'Slow down and tell me why you think that.' He took her by the hand and sat her down on the bed next to him. Still holding her hand, he said again, 'Please tell me.'

'It's all my fault. I should never have made you go outside with me. Someone saw us together – I have no idea who but I can only think it was someone who was looking out of the windows of the sanatorium when we were on the lawn. It's hard to believe but whoever it was must have passed information on to the Germans close by – that's how Rudi came to know. I was so stupid to think we wouldn't be seen.'

'Now listen to me. I knew as well you about the dangers of being seen outside. It was barely light, so I thought there'd be no risk. And I didn't want you to witness the crash site alone because I guessed it would be upsetting. So you mustn't blame yourself.'

'No,' said Ilse unhappily. 'But Rudi now knows, and he's bound to come for you. When Connie comes back from work she's going to have to move fast to help you get away. It's over, Levi, we both know that.'

With tears in her eyes, Ilse lifted her hand and traced the contours of his face. Levi cupped his own hand over hers and gently removed it so he could wipe away her tears. Then he kissed her, first gently and then with increasing passion. He lifted her onto the bed so they could lie facing one another, and they talked about their concerns and fears, interrupting each other's words with caresses and kisses. Eventually they ceased talking and Ilse succumbed to the desire welling up inside of her, stronger than she'd ever experienced. She knew this would be the last time.

Later, a soft breeze from the open window nudged Ilse from sleep, but she didn't stir. She continued to lie there, letting her eyes wander around the room as she savoured the intense memory of the past few hours. As she took in a deep breath, she felt a slight movement as Levi shifted and pulled her towards him. *Soon he'll be gone*, she thought, and a tear escaped from the corner of her eye. She hastily brushed it away. Blocking out any thoughts of what lay ahead, she twisted her body to face him.

'Hello, my darling,' he whispered in a lazy voice, and allowed his lips to melt against hers once again. She had never been as happy or sad as she was in that precise moment, and refused to let go of the delicious bittersweet feeling. Then Levi murmured against her hair that he had something for her. Ilse propped herself up so she could take a good look at him, and tried to guess what it could be. Her heart was full as she lifted her hand and touched the soft tangle of dark hair that curled in the nape of his neck, committing it to memory.

'Close your eyes and hold out your hand,' ordered Levi with a teasing smile.

Ilse obeyed and listened to his breathing and the faint rustle of paper. Then something light dropped into the palm of her hand. 'Can I look now?' she said impatiently.

'Go on.' He laughed.

'How did you do it? It's beautiful,' she said with a gasp. The coin that Levi had discovered half buried in the lawn was now attached to a delicate silver chain. Holding it up, she examined the small medallion that glinted and twirled in a shaft of sunlight falling across the bed. The sixpence was still slightly bent, but she could now make out the raised script around the outside surrounding a royal crest above the letters 'GRH'.

Levi watched her face with a smile. 'The only thing of any value I took with me when I fled was my little bag of jewellery tools. As soon as I saw it was a coin I knew what I wanted to do with it. You don't think I was wrong to take it?'

Ilse was still staring at the coin, remembering the moment when, suffused with the horror of what they'd both witnessed, she'd experienced an indescribable closeness to Levi as with heads touching they'd examined their discovery. In that moment, she'd known she would never feel that way about anyone ever again. And to think that someone had been watching, judging and preparing to betray them, she now thought with a tremor. 'If you hadn't picked it up, it would only have lain in the mud, perhaps never to be discovered,' she said quietly. 'No, you did the right thing.'

Levi looked relieved. 'Here, let me put it on.' Taking the chain in one hand, he raised her thick hair with the other and fastened it round her neck. 'Think of me when you wear this,' he said, gazing deep into her eyes.

'I promise I won't take it off till until the next time I see you,' she said earnestly, fingering the smooth roundness of the coin. She was acutely aware that time was running out and that everything they needed to say to one another had to be said now. That they may never see one another again was a distinct possibility neither dared acknowledge.

As if reading her thoughts, Levi said he would write to her as soon as it were safe to do so, but warned her that she may not hear from him for some time. 'If I can, I'll pass on a message through the network, but any communication via couriers is likely to be circuitous and tortuous. No one wants to take risks for fear of information leaking out on the whereabouts of people in hiding like me and falling into the wrong hands.'

'How will I know if you're safe?' Ilse said, letting her mind run away with visions of brutal Nazi soldiers roughly manhandling Levi into one of the unmarked vans so often seen on the streets, whose purpose was to round up Jews and take them away to live in intolerable conditions in camps far from home. The thought made her sick, and she clung more tightly to him. She couldn't bear losing her soulmate so soon after they'd found each other.

'You have to trust me,' said Levi, gently stroking her hair. 'But you'll put yourself in even more danger if you try to contact me. Promise me you won't.'

Ilse nodded her assent, though she felt her heart was breaking. They resolved to stop talking about the inevitable and speak only of a time when they hoped to be reunited.

THIRTY-ONE

'What's happened?' said Connie, panic straining her voice, as she walked through the door to find her parents and Ilse in heated conversation.

'You may well ask.' Her father regarded her gravely. 'It appears that the game is up. Our *onderduiker* was seen outside the house with Ilse the morning after the plane came down. And this information was passed on to the German officers the two of you have been associating with, who no doubt will be back with their cronies to flush him out. Your mother and I have repeatedly warned you about this...' He wagged a finger at Connie, whose face had turned very pale.

'Hans, this isn't the time for recriminations,' said Clara, trying to placate him. 'We have to act fast to get Levi away to safety. You know Connie is the only one who can arrange that.' She shot her daughter a look of sympathy.

'I thought it would come to this,' her father went on. 'You know how much I was against the idea of providing a hiding place for someone on the run. Any one of our patients could have betrayed him.'

Connie kept her gaze steady as she addressed her father.

'Can you please stop overreacting? You don't know if any of that's true. I need to find out the facts before anything can be done. Ilse, come with me.' She took Ilse by the arm and steered her towards the sitting room. 'I'm guessing it was Rudi who told you,' she said in a low whisper.

Ilse was unnerved by the conversation between the three Van Dongens and was unable to shake off the feeling that she had endangered them all through her carelessness. It was obvious Hans was too polite to blame her and was taking it out on Connie. She needed to convince Connie that she could rely on her, Ilse's, support. But before she could reply, the telephone in the hall rang out, loud and shrill. Hans strode over to answer it.

'Hans van Dongen,' he said curtly. 'Yes.' He caught Clara's eye. There was a pause. 'And where is this?' Another pause.

The three women eyed him silently, waiting to hear who it was and if it had anything to do with the grave situation they were facing.

'We'll be there as soon as we can,' Hans said, then replaced the handset in its cradle. 'Clara, get your coat and bag. There's been a collision between two trains a mile or so from the main station. It's not known how many casualties there are, but urgent medical assistance is needed. Both of us must go.' He paused to frown at Connie. 'What are you going to do?'

'Go,' Connie said firmly. 'Don't worry about me. I know what I must do and by the time you come back, Levi will have been moved to safety.'

'I trust you,' said her mother, briefly hugging Connie to her, then reaching over to squeeze Ilse's hand. 'Be careful, both of you.'

The only thing that mattered was getting Levi out of the house and as far away as possible. The urgency of the situation became clear as Connie laid out her plan for Levi's escape.

'I'll cycle straight over to Rik and get his contacts to stand ready to receive Levi at short notice. The best solution is for him to stay no more than a day, maybe even less, at each safe house, while we work out how to get him away from Hilversum. I shouldn't be too long. I'll be back within the hour. Will you be all right by yourself?'

'What if they come searching before you're back?' asked Ilse, terrified that the plan would backfire.

'They won't,' said Connie calmly.

There were so many more questions coursing through Ilse's head, but she realised that now wasn't the time to ask. She simply had to trust Connie's judgement.

Connie went on, 'I'm not saying the situation isn't serious, but I don't actually believe we'll get a visit. From what I've heard, and I have reason to believe the information I've received is accurate, they are still searching for survivors of the plane crash and are following leads over to the east of town. While I'm out, I want you to do this for me. You must erase all signs that anyone has been living up in the attic. Levi can help you. If I'm not back by the time you're finished, take him down to the cellar. It's not pleasant down there – it's a bit damp – but it's safe, and it's big. He can hide behind the shelves of preserved food at the back. After you've locked the door, take the key with you and put it in the drawer of the reception desk.'

As the enormity of the situation hit Ilse, she bit down hard on her lip. 'I won't let you down,' she said. 'Now please hurry.'

The two girls embraced fiercely. Without another word, Connie strode off to the scullery. Ilse stood by as Connie wheeled her bike out through the back door, then pushed it shut behind her. She waited till she could hear the grating sound of the key turning in the lock.

Now entirely on her own, she tried not to panic as she ran into the hallway and up the stairs, two at a time, arriving breathless at the top of the house. Hurriedly she explained the plan to Levi, who took it calmly. This wasn't the first time he'd been on the run, he told her, and he was confident they would succeed. He gave her a heartfelt hug, and together they set about returning the attic to how it was before it was his hiding place. They moved the table, two chairs, books and bookcase back downstairs. All that remained was the bed, now reinstated as a divan, which they covered with an old blanket and a flat red cushion that had seen better days. Before leaving the attic room, now stripped of all signs that Levi had ever lived there, they held on to one another tightly. Then gently Levi stroked his fingers against Ilse's throat, feeling the precious necklace she kept hidden under her collar and that nestled warm against her skin. 'We'll be together soon. I'm sure of it,' he murmured.

Ilse nodded, though she wasn't as convinced as he was. 'Please stay safe,' she replied, as he leant in for one last tender kiss.

THIRTY-TWO

The only sound in the empty house came from the persistent ticking of the hall clock. Ilse kept vigil beside it, nervously counting the minutes till Connie returned and straining for any unusual sounds. Then her ears pricked up at the faint scraping of the key in the back door. Jumping to her feet, she ran to the scullery, relief flooding through her when she saw Connie lifting her bike over the doorstep.

'Thank God you're home,' she said, exhaling an enormous breath. 'Did you manage to arrange everything?'

'Yes. Rik is coming with a car and will park a little way up the road.' Connie looked tense as she pushed the door shut behind her and placed her bike back in its place against the wall in-between a mop and bucket and pile of shoes. 'It's cold out here. Let's not stand around.' She removed her coat and hat and hung them on a peg behind the door.

'The attic's clear and Levi is in the cellar. How long till Rik comes?' Ilse trailed after Connie, wishing she'd tell her more.

'It depends. He's still arranging a safe house for Levi. All we can do is wait and hope he'll be here soon.'

But Ilse could tell she was distracted, and wondered

anxiously if the plan was about to fall apart. She watched as Connie reached into her coat pocket for a wad of papers and began flicking through them.

'I'll go and make us some tea,' said Ilse, casting her an anxious glance. Connie looked up briefly, smiled and nodded her thanks.

Shivering, Ilse went into the kitchen, put the kettle on and took a teapot and tea caddy out of the cupboard above the sink. It was a relief to have something to take her mind off Levi holed up in that dark cellar. It was unimaginable what he must be going through. Soon the water began to rattle loudly against the sides of the kettle as it came to the boil. So loudly, in fact, that she didn't hear the creak of the back door opening and the clicking of boots crossing the tiled floor.

'Well, well. If it isn't Ilse, all by herself.'

Ilse swung round, and gasped in panic. The figure standing before her was dishevelled, his uniform jacket was unbuttoned and he swayed a little as he came towards her, before stopping to hold on to the back of a kitchen chair for support. His eyes were puffy and he had a nasty sneer on his face. It was obvious he was drunk.

'Rudi... why are you here?' she said, backing away. To her alarm, she realised that Connie must have forgotten to lock the back door.

He was facing her, so was unaware that Connie had appeared behind him in the doorway. Connie lifted a finger to her lips and shook her head before moving soundlessly away. From this gesture, Ilse guessed she wanted her to deal with Rudi on her own. She prayed that Connie would be able to get Levi out of the house before Rudi suspected anything. But what was she to do? Desperate to distract him, she said quickly, 'I'm boiling myself water for some tea. Would you like a cup?'

He seemed momentarily caught off guard and frowned, before the cruel sneer returned to his face. 'Tea? I didn't come to drink tea. Surely you must know that? I'm here for another much more important reason.' He let go of the chair and unsteadily circled the table while Ilse edged further away. Rudi advanced towards her till she was cornered at the far end of the kitchen, with her back almost up against the stove. Steam was rising from the kettle in a fast upward plume.

'Turn that thing off!' ordered Rudi. He was so close that Ilse caught the smell of stale alcohol on his breath.

Her hands trembled as she fiddled with the knob on the stove. The kettle ceased its frantic boiling.

'And now you will show me where you are hiding your precious Jew.' Rudi spat out the word 'Jew' with a hatred that made Ilse flinch.

'I... I don't know what you're talking about. There's nobody hiding in this house.' She tried to speak calmly, although her voice shook.

'*Ach*, Ilse,' he said, staring at her as if a thought had just occurred to him. 'Why do you refuse to come dancing with me on my birthday? Now I have no partner. And we make such a good couple on the dancefloor... don't you agree?' He held a hand out to her in a familiar gesture that she recognised from the first time she'd met him at the club. His smile was less sneering now, more conciliatory, but Ilse was repulsed. She felt herself harden against this man. How dare he break in and behave like this?

As he leant forward, arms outstretched to embrace her, she deftly stepped aside. Her mind was racing. She needed to get him away from the kitchen so Connie had time to get Levi out of the house. Edging towards the kitchen door, Ilse put her hand on the doorframe, and spoke loudly for Connie's benefit. 'Come with me and you can see for yourself there is no one hiding here.' Her heart pounded and she hoped she wasn't making a terrible mistake. But it was too late for that now.

'Sensible girl. I was thinking you would never ask,' Rudi said with a leer.

Concealing her fear, she hurriedly crossed the hall and began to climb the stairs, alert to Rudi's heavy breathing as he followed on behind. When they reached the landing, she turned to face him and, to her dismay, caught sight of his hard expression. Rudi wasn't swaying now. In fact, he appeared quite sober.

'Which room is yours?' he demanded, grabbing her wrist. Wincing under his grip, she led him to the door she'd left ajar and, glancing quickly at the items of furniture she and Levi had moved there less than an hour before, was relieved to see that nothing was out of place.

'Come. I don't want you running off.' Rudi yanked her rudely into the room with him. 'Sit here and wait,' he ordered, pushing her onto a stool. He made a show of searching the room, looking under the bed and behind the curtains, though the only possible hiding place was the small wardrobe, hardly big enough for a child, let alone for a grown man.

Ilse kept perfectly still, barely daring to breathe. But the less he could find, the more angry he became.

'*Verdammt!* Where did you hide him?' he shouted, pulling her clothes out of the wardrobe in a frenzy – her blouses, skirts and the blue satin dress she'd worn the last time she'd been dancing with him – and dumping them all over the floor.

'Nothing, nothing,' he kept repeating. 'You're mocking me, aren't you?' He swung round to face her.

Ilse gave the tiniest shake of her head, not risking meeting his eye.

'You're mocking me, aren't you?' he repeated. He was now standing in front of her, and yanked her by the arms to standing.

'No, Rudi, no,' she gasped. He slapped her hard across the face. Stunned, she stumbled forward, clutching her cheek with both hands. He caught her roughly and hauled her out of the room.

'Where is he?' he growled in a menacing low voice.

Ilse dared not answer. She braced herself for another blow. But something must have distracted him, for she stole a glance at his face and saw that his black eyes were fixed on the attic staircase. 'Of course. The attic,' he said, a triumphant tone to his voice.

Not relinquishing his grasp, he pulled Ilse up the stairs until they reached the top. Kicking the door open, he dragged her in, threw her onto the divan bed and ordered her not to move.

Resigned to her fate, Ilse sobbed quietly as Rudi strode around the room, ending up by the small window, where he craned his neck to get a good look out at the grounds, then turned his attention to the sparsely furnished room. His eyes alighted on the built-in cupboard under the eaves. The door jammed as he tried to yank it open, causing him to erupt in a torrent of German expletives. One last tug and it flew open and he got on his hands and knees, peering into the gloomy interior. Ilse watched, wishing she had the strength to shove him inside and lock the door. As this thought came to her, he hauled himself up to standing, fury etched on his face. He towered over her. 'The Jew isn't here, but you knew that, of course. Where is he? Tell me!'

Ilse refused to look at him. 'There's no one hiding in this house. Surely you believe me now?' she pleaded, defeated after all she'd done to try to deflect him. She screwed up her eyes, waiting for him to strike her again. But he didn't. When he didn't speak, she dared open her eyes a crack, and saw he was kneeling beside her.

'Ilse, did I ever tell you how beautiful you are?' His tone was needling. His mood had switched once again. Did he really think he could win her round with insincere words of flattery?

'Ilse,' he said again, now sounding as if he were trying to win round a naughty child. He stroked the cheek he'd struck only minutes before. He was on the bed next to her now, grasping her round the waist as he leant in to kiss her.

'Rudi, please stop!' she cried, as she fought to push him away, but he was too strong for her, and her efforts to resist only made things worse. But all she could think of was buying time to allow Connie to get Levi out of the house before Rudi realised what was going on. So she relented a little, tears running down her face, allowing Rudi to caress her back and pretending she didn't mind when she felt his hand touch her leg and move under her skirt. She prayed for this whole nightmare to be over.

THIRTY-THREE

Up in the attic, Ilse waited till she could be sure Rudi wasn't about to return.

The hall clock struck eleven. As the chimes died away, she craned for any sound that would indicate that he was still in the house, but it was completely quiet.

Tiptoeing to the door, she placed a foot on the top step, then tentatively descended. With every step there was a creak that sounded like gunfire. The hall was in darkness as she felt her way towards the cellar door, which gave slightly. She hesitated, knowing she must turn on the light switch if she was to climb down the cold stone steps, but terrified that she might find Rudi holding Levi hostage in the dark. It was an irrational thought, but she had to know if Levi had made it out of there. She pushed the switch on and the cellar stairs were instantly flooded with light. Her heart in her mouth, she descended to the bottom, but there was no sign of him.

'Levi?' she whispered urgently, but there was no response as she moved around the cellar, peering behind shelves and into the dark spaces. After a tense moment, tears of relief mixed with grief spilled from her eyes, as it dawned on her that Connie had kept her promise and managed to get Levi out.

There was nothing more do. She turned to climb back up the steep staircase into the hallway, then heard the sound of a door closing. She froze. Was Rudi leaving, or had Connie been waiting till she was sure it was safe to leave? Ilse didn't think twice – maybe this was her chance to see Levi and say one last goodbye.

Heart pounding, she took the steps two at a time, crossed the tiled hallway and rushed towards the back door. Careful not to draw attention to herself, she opened it a crack, listened, then crept out into the night.

It was cold and a pale mist hung low over the lawn. Ilse shivered as she skirted along the side of the house, avoiding the gravel path that led in one direction to the sanatorium and the other to the road.

She heard it then: the noise of a car idling. Angry shouts. Scuffles. A sickening thud. And Connie's voice, loud and shrill.

'Rudi, Jürgen, leave him alone. He's done nothing wrong!'

'Stay out of this, you bitch!' Jürgen had Connie pinned against a wall. 'I trusted you. And all this time you were leading me on so you could betray me. You Dutch whore!'

Horrified, Ilse stood from behind a tree witnessing the scene unfolding before her eyes. Then, she caught sight of someone being dragged along the ground. It could only mean one thing...

Rudi suddenly let go of Levi and began aiming kicks at his body. From his whimpering, Ilse could tell he was trying not to scream. His hands were curled over his head in self-defence.

'Don't think you'll survive this. I'll make you pay, you dirty Jew,' growled Rudi, towering over Levi, raining repeated blows on him.

Out of the corner of her eye, she saw Connie break free and make a dash to help Levi. But Jürgen was quicker and grabbed her viciously by the hair, tossing her to the ground. She scrabbled to get up, but Jürgen deflected her with a blow to the head.

Ilse couldn't stand it any longer. She had to do something. Surging from her hiding place, she made a run for Levi, flinging herself across his body. 'I won't let them do this to you,' she said, a desperate cry.

'Ilse, no... please leave me... you must go...' Levi could barely utter the words.

Ilse felt two hands grip her shoulders and was forced to loosen her grip on Levi. Rudi pulled her up to standing and struck her hard across the face, as he had only minutes earlier. Her head reeling from the blow, she watched helplessly as Rudi and Jürgen dragged Levi towards the road and the idling car.

'When we've seen to him, we'll be back,' shouted Rudi in a menacing voice over his shoulder. The two Germans exchanged words she couldn't understand, but their laughter was enough for her to grasp what they had in mind.

Ilse turned swiftly to Connie, who touched her shoulder and asked if she was hurt.

'I'm... fine. And you?' Ilse said, darting a nervous look towards the road in case Rudi and Jürgen reappeared. The sound of a car pulling away confirmed that they were safe for now.

'I'm fine too. But we don't have much time before they come back. Neither of us can stay here. You understand that, don't you?'

'What are you saying?'

'We can't be seen out here. Come back to the house and I'll tell you what you need to do.' Connie's face was in shadow, making it impossible to read her expression.

Ilse's heart pounded as she followed Connie back in. Connie secured the door. When she turned, Ilse saw her eyes were bright with tears.

'You must leave now while it's still dark. Go home to your

parents. Take my bike. It's a bit rusty but it'll get you there. Once you're out of the town, you should be able to see by the light of the moon.'

Ilse stared at her as she took in the enormity of the situation. 'What will you do?'

Connie flicked away her tears with the back of her hand, but her voice was breaking. 'I'll go and find Rik and we'll work out where to go next. Nowhere round here is safe any more.'

'Oh, Connie. I'm so scared,' said Ilse, tears spilling from her eyes.

Connie held her by the shoulders. 'Don't be. You must be strong.'

Tears flowing freely, they clung to one another, knowing this was probably the last time they would ever see one another.

Connie was the first to pull away. 'When you get home, call my mother and explain everything. She'll understand.'

'I will,' whispered Ilse.

She watched as Connie turned her attention to the bike to make sure it was in working order. Connie then untied her blue scarf from around her neck and insisted Ilse wear it against the cold night air. Ilse wanted to protest, but was silenced by Connie's fierce stare.

Together they left the house, Ilse wheeling the bike to the road, where they anxiously looked for any signs of life. The only sound was the hoot of an owl somewhere up in the trees.

'Now go, quickly. And take care, Ilse.'

Connie kissed her briefly on the cheek, then ran quickly towards the cycle path that led deep into the woods.

Oh, Connie. I hope you know what you're doing, Ilse prayed. Now completely alone, she knew she must hurry herself before Rudi and Jürgen returned. She mounted the bike, wobbling slightly as she gained her balance, and pedalled away as fast as she could into the night.

THIRTY-FOUR

ANNA

Anna pushed the front door open with her foot and dumped her suitcase in the small hallway before kicking off her shoes. She was exhausted and wanted nothing more than a long hot bath and a glass of chilled wine to put her into a better state of mind before facing Hugo. Sighing, she supposed he'd be in no mood to listen to her tale of woe – about how the boat had been delayed, resulting in her missing her train connection and a long wait on a windy platform, and how when the packed tube train finally did arrive, she was forced to stand, pressed up against homeward-bound commuters and people dressed up for an evening out chatting loudly above the noise of the train as it thundered through the tunnels. Knowing Hugo, he wouldn't even ask how she was and would just be expecting Anna to show him compassion for his predicament. And loads of it.

'Hello? Where are you?' Anna padded over to the living room, expecting to find Hugo hunched over his laptop. But there was no one there. 'Typical,' she sighed, annoyed with herself for rushing back early and believing him when he'd said he needed her by his side. She wouldn't put it past him to be out drinking with his mates having forgotten she'd said she'd be back today.

Then she heard a low moan coming from the bedroom. But instead of relief that he was home, she felt exasperation at the prospect of having to minister to his needs. Investigating, she found the curtains drawn. From the doorway, she surveyed the unmoving bulge under the duvet. 'What's the matter?' She walked over and cautiously lowered herself onto the edge of the bed.

Hugo's messy dark hair emerged from the depths of the duvet. He looked terrible – red-rimmed eyes, shiny nose – and when he spoke his voice came out as a hoarse whisper.

'Where did you put the paracetamol? I feel dreadful.'

Anna leant across to open the drawer of the bedside cabinet, where they kept several packets of painkillers. Taking an open packet, she went off to the kitchen to run him a glass of water. To her dismay, she found the place in a mess, with unwashed bowls and plates in the sink, a splash of milk on the counter next to a half-empty carton and an assortment of cereal and biscuit packets littering the counter. She hated seeing the kitchen in such a state. She set about clearing the packets, mopping up the spilt milk and liberally squirting the work surfaces with the cleaning spray she kept under the sink.

'Hon... where are you?' came Hugo's pitiful voice from the bedroom.

Heaving a sigh, she surveyed her efforts, relieved to have restored at least some semblance of order. 'Coming,' she called out, putting down her spray and cloth before returning to the bedroom with the tablets and a glass of water. 'Sit up and take these,' she ordered.

Hugo gave another groan, shuffled himself into a sitting position and accepted the tablets and water she held out. 'Must have caught it off someone on the plane,' he managed to say, before tossing his head back so he could swallow the pills down.

'I'm so glad you're home,' he croaked, then erupted into a sneezing fit. Anna managed to grab a handful of tissues from a box that lay on the pillow and thrust them at him before he could spray her with too many of his germs. He slumped back down, clutching a wad of tissues to his nose, and rolled over to face the wall.

Relieved she wasn't required to do anything more for him at that moment, Anna tiptoed out of the room and went in search of a bottle of wine. She longed to relax in front of the television with a drink till she could get her mind straight. Pleased to find a half-empty bottle of Sauvignon in the fridge, she poured most of it into one of the big wine glasses she and Hugo had bought when they'd first moved in together. Taking a large sip, she walked over to the sofa and settled herself down. She checked her phone for messages, but was disappointed to find there were none. Was she really expecting to hear so soon from Luuk? Sighing, she flicked through the channels, before eventually opting for an undemanding nature programme.

She hadn't realised she'd fallen asleep, but she woke with a start to find Hugo, wrapped in the tartan dressing gown and leather slippers she'd given him for Christmas, sitting next to her on the settee. He was looking better than he had earlier and was smiling at her. 'I'm sorry, hon, I should have asked you how your trip went. Was it worth it?'

Anna stretched her arms above her head and yawned. It wasn't a question she'd been expecting, but she was pleased to be asked. 'I'm not sure, really. I went all that way expecting to find my grandmother living at the address I had for her, but the only person there was a cleaner, and she said a couple lived there.'

'Sounds like a waste of time,' said Hugo, fishing a tissue from the pocket of his dressing gown and noisily blowing his nose.

Anna turned her head away, irritated at him for dismissing

her efforts with such a throwaway remark. 'I'm not going to give up that easily. In fact, I met up with some old family friends and they're keen to help.'

Hugo didn't seem to be listening. Anna noticed that he was staring at the silver medallion nestling in the hollow at the base of her throat.

'I don't remember seeing that before. Is it new?' Hugo's voice was still husky, but not as croaky as before.

She'd forgotten she'd unwrapped it from the scarf during the long sea crossing, wanting to feel the silky fabric and the solidity of the coin while she tried to fathom its significance to her father. She'd been lost in thought as she'd peered closely at the 1942 date, believing it must offer some clue as to its provenance. Did Dad used to sit in his study and take it out of the battered old tin, feeling its weight and connection to the family he never knew? Or was there some other reason he kept it hidden away without telling Mum or her about it? Anna didn't want to entertain that idea. But when Luuk had speculated that the coin could have once belonged to an Englishman who might possibly have been her relative, Anna hadn't wanted to believe that either. For if it were true, why did Dad think his father had been German? There must have been some other reason.

As she'd sat on the bench in the passenger lounge of the ferry, Anna had given up trying to guess. Toying with the medallion, she'd noticed how it gleamed as it lay in the palm of her hand, looking quite beautiful. Holding it up, she'd fastened the chain by the tiny clasp, intending to leave it on for just a moment, but had been distracted by a family with young children and an assortment of carrier bags and backpacks who had parked themselves on the bench opposite. By the time they'd settled down, the eldest child with a comic and all three with bags of sweets, Anna had quite forgotten she had put it on.

Aware of Hugo's eyes still on her, she automatically put her hand to her throat and ran her finger over the familiar bump where the coin didn't quite sit flat. 'I found this among Dad's things when I was staying with Mum. I thought it must have been precious to him as he kept it in an old tin with Dutch writing on it. So I decided to take it with me. I'd hoped to ask my grandmother about it when I found her. Except of course things didn't work out that way.' She let out a sigh. Suddenly an image of Luuk taking her hand in the café swam into view and she quickly blinked it away.

'Well, there you are. You did your best, hon,' said Hugo, looking relieved at her explanation. He leant towards her for a kiss, but she stopped him by holding on to his forearms. She told herself it was because she didn't want to catch his germs, though it was becoming clear to her that wasn't the reason at all. She was tired of his lack of interest in her quest to find out about her family; and she struggled to remember a time that he'd been any different. *Why did everything always have to be about him,* she thought, *and why had it taken her father's death and the decision to search for her family to realise it?*

She felt a sudden wave of sadness. She saw little point in saying anything more about the matter. Instead, she gave him a thin smile and said, 'Let's not talk about all that. Tell me about Boston.'

THIRTY-FIVE

'Anna?' Hugo called from somewhere in the flat. Anna frowned, glancing towards the door of her study. *Not now*, she thought with an exasperated sigh. She stared at the sentence she'd just written, part of an article that she was on a deadline to finish that day.

Her sympathy towards Hugo was wearing thin. It was some days since he'd been made redundant, but he was in no hurry to get himself on to recruiters' books. Most of his time was spent browsing auction room websites on his laptop in the hope of bidding for artworks he must surely realise they couldn't afford. When he was bored with this, he would hang around Anna's study, distracting her with idle chit-chat, oblivious to the fact that she was hard at work.

Anxious to finish her article, Anna ignored him, hoping he wouldn't interrupt her again. No such luck; moments later, she glanced up to see him standing in the door of her office. He looked remarkably pulled together in his smart chinos, black polo sweater and tan brogues. More like his old self, she thought with a jolt of nostalgia, remembering the days when she couldn't wait to finish work so they could be together.

Anna switched her computer to standby. 'Are you going somewhere?' she asked, trying to keep the irritation out of her voice.

'Yeah,' Hugo said, leaning his arm against the doorframe. 'I'm meeting a recruiter who's taking me for lunch. He called and said he had some interesting opportunities for someone of my calibre.' He beamed at her, and she had to admit she felt pleased for him.

'That's great news. Let's hope it leads to something. Be yourself and I'm sure you'll impress them.' She got up to plant a kiss on his cheek, hoping it was the break he needed to get him back into corporate life where he belonged.

Anna listened for the click of the door closing before reaching for her phone and tapping out a text to Caro asking when she'd be free to chat. In her mind's eye, Caro was in her buzzy Paris office, surrounded by colleagues, united in working to a deadline for a client presentation.

Caro immediately rang back. 'Anna! It's so great to hear from you. I'm in-between meetings, so let's chat now.'

Anna could hear the clack-clack of Caro's high heels walking down the street and the sound of traffic in the background. 'Where are you exactly?' said Anna, laughing.

'I've just come out of Printemps on the Boulevard Haussmann.'

'That doesn't sound like work to me.' Anna laughed again, imagining Caro walking down the street with a clutch of designer shopping bags swinging on her arm.

'I did say I was in-between meetings. Listen, can I call you back in five?' Caro hung up without waiting for a reply.

Smiling, Anna shook her head as she stared at her phone.

Minutes later, Caro was back. 'Sorry about that. I just dived into a café where it's quieter. I've been dying to hear how you got on. Why didn't you call me earlier?' she rebuked, even before Anna could ask how she was.

'I'm sorry, but I haven't had a chance. Hugo's lost his job, then he was unwell, plus I got behind with my work. Today's the first day I've been on my own, which is why I'm calling you now.'

'That's bad luck for Hugo. What'll he do now?'

Anna sighed. 'Hopefully find another job quickly. He's been mooching around the flat and getting in the way. He's seeing a recruiter today.'

'Well, that's positive. Tell me how your search for your grandmother went.'

'She wasn't at the address I had, which was disappointing. If you remember, before I left I called Kersten, a family friend we used to go on holiday with, and she invited me over. And her son, Luuk, came for lunch and... we haven't seen each other since we were both fifteen.'

'Interesting. What's he like now?'

'Really good-looking,' said Anna, with a short laugh. 'Very tall, like a lot of Dutch men, gorgeous thick fair hair and very blue eyes. He works as a historian at Leiden University. You know, he was so interested to hear that Dad was adopted. He even thinks his grandmother might have known mine. Long story. Anyway, later on he drove me back to my hotel. He insisted on doing some digging online and called me later. I didn't want to get my hopes up when he told me he'd found a newspaper article mentioning my grandmother's name. It could, of course, be a complete coincidence. Luuk was so excited about his discovery, though I'm not sure it was her. He then asked if I'd meet him the next day so he could show me round Delft. So I agreed.'

'This is so exciting,' Caro said breathlessly. 'What happened then?'

'Well, it got a bit complicated after that. What I didn't know was that Hugo had been trying to reach me to tell me he'd been made redundant. I couldn't very well stay.'

'That's really bad luck. But also tough on Hugo,' Caro seemed to add as an afterthought.

Suddenly, Anna realised she wasn't ready to share details of how magical the day with Luuk had been, so she tried to steer the conversation back to Caro and her new job. But Caro wasn't taken in.

'I bet you didn't tell Luuk about Hugo,' Caro said mischievously.

'Of course I did,' said Anna unhappily. 'But Hugo needed me and that's why I came rushing back.'

'Or ran away from Luuk, because you didn't want to face up to your feelings?'

Caro had guessed right, but Anna wasn't ready to confront what she secretly knew to be true.

THIRTY-SIX

Over supper one evening, Anna casually dropped into the conversation that she was going to visit her mother for a few days to keep her company. The truth was she wanted some space, as Hugo's constant presence around the flat was getting on her nerves. She knew she was being unfair on him. Maybe it was just her, but more than ever she felt that they were drifting apart. On top of everything else, he still wasn't making any real effort to find a job.

'Perhaps you can chase that recruiter while I'm away and see if anything has cropped up?' she asked hopefully.

'I've told you, hon, he'll get back in touch when he's got anything. It won't help me ringing him every five minutes,' Hugo said, sounding exasperated.

'Surely he's not the only one? I thought these people were falling over themselves to get people on to their books,' she kept on.

'It's not like that. The market's flat right now, so there's no point hassling him.'

'Fine. But it might have slipped his mind. Please say you'll try?' she said.

Hugo leant over and stroked her cheek. 'OK... I promise I'll do some chasing up in the next day or two. You go off to your mum's and stop worrying about me.'

Relieved to be parting on good terms, Anna took the train to Oxford, arriving in time for lunch. Her mother had specially baked a quiche and prepared a tossed rocket and spinach salad; she was delighted to see her daughter.

'Mum, you shouldn't have,' said Anna, smiling, as her mother brought their lunch out onto the sunlit patio.

'It's lovely to have you here. Just the two of us.' Her mother poured her a glass of elderflower fizz from a tall green bottle. 'I'm afraid it's not the real thing, but cheers anyway.'

'Cheers,' echoed Anna, clinking glasses. 'How have you been, Mum?'

'Not so bad now that the worst of the admin is over. Aunty Jane's been such a help getting your father's affairs in order, but there's still such a lot to do.' She let her gaze sweep over the house. 'This place is too big for me on my own. Jane thinks I should move close to her, but I know you're quite attached to this house. Would you be upset if I were to sell?'

Anna shook her head, pleased to hear her mother making plans for her future. 'No, of course not. I don't live here anymore. If living close to Aunty Jane is what you want, you should do it.'

Anna's mother reached for her daughter's hand. 'Thank you, darling. I hoped you'd agree. I've left it to Jane to look into and I'll keep you posted of any developments.'

She began slicing up the quiche. 'Shall we eat? Help yourself, then tell me how you got on with Kersten. I must say it was a comfort to hear that you'd gone to see her. It brought back such fond memories of our Dutch holidays together – they were like family to us. Did you say you saw Luuk too? I bet he's changed.'

'He has,' said Anna, carefully lifting a slice of quiche onto her plate and doing the same for her mother. 'He's doing quite well for himself. He works as a historian at the university. I can't believe it's fifteen years since we last saw them.'

'Is it really? I've been thinking a lot about that last visit. Your grandparents were so normal and relaxed. You'd never have guessed it, would you?'

'No, but then, why would we? As far as Dad was concerned, they were his parents, and that's all that mattered to him.'

'But it is a pity he didn't have the chance to look into his birth family,' her mother said wistfully.

'I suppose so, but now I can. Luuk's got access to loads of archive material and Kersten says she'll sort through her mother's things to find anything that could throw light on Dad's real parents. I really hope there's a clue in there somewhere. I want to do more myself, so thought I could start by looking at Dad's photo album from when he was a child.'

'I thought you might want to,' said her mother with a smile. 'I got it out just before you came. Let's look at it after we've had coffee.'

'Here you are. This has pictures of your dad as a little boy.' Her mother placed a well-worn leather-bound album in front of Anna and turned to the front. 'Have we never shown you it before?'

'Yes, but not for a long time,' said Anna, examining the small square black-and-white photos stuck onto coal-black pages. The year was written below each photo in white pen. 'Look at Dad here – wasn't he sweet?' Anna pointed to a photo of a toddler on a wooden trike with a shock of dark hair. 'And this one's of him next to his birthday cake with one candle. Oma looks so proud. She looks as if she's about to blow it out for him.'

Anna turned the page and the photos began to include people she didn't recognise. Her mother didn't know them either, and said vaguely that they must have been friends of the family. But Anna's attention was caught by a tall fair woman, her face side-on to the camera, as she looked lovingly at the little boy on her lap. Looking up at her was a little girl, her fair hair tied up in two bunches with ribbon. Behind them stood a clean-shaven man with a cheerful smile, who was gazing directly into the camera. Anna recognised the little boy in the centre as her father.

'Do you know who these people are?' Anna asked, staring at the photo.

'I can't be sure, but the little girl is almost definitely Kersten. Those will be her parents. The date is 1948, which fits, as it would be about the time they started visiting your dad in Fries-land. He said they used to come every summer. And then Kersten kept up the tradition when she had her own family.'

'That reminds me. I asked Kersten whether she'd ever heard her mother mention a friend called Ilse. The name didn't ring a bell with her, but she's sure her mother was friendly with a girl called Else. It could be the same person.'

'What are you saying?' asked her mother.

'I'm not sure, but I have a hunch that the woman in the photo holding Dad must be connected to his real mother, Ilse Meijer. I'm probably wrong,' Anna said with a shake of her head. She put the thought from her mind as she continued looking at the photos of her father as a young boy.

THIRTY-SEVEN

ILSE

Exhausted from her long bike ride through the night, Ilse turned into her street as the sun broke through the trees. It was six thirty in the morning. She wheeled Connie's bike up the path and through the gate, where she leant it against the wall. Only as she fumbled with the key in the lock did she notice how much her hands were trembling. She simply couldn't believe she was out of danger. It wasn't until she was the other side of the kitchen door that she allowed herself to believe she had actually made it home.

The first thing she did was fill the kettle at the sink and find a match to light the stove. The clock above the dresser ticked quietly, as she savoured the quiet moments before she would have to tell her mother why she had come back home, and so early in the morning.

As she waited for the kettle to boil, she untied Connie's scarf and took a long look at it. It was a favourite of Connie's, a beautiful peacock blue. Folding it carefully, she vowed to keep it safe until she was able to give it back to her, convinced that Connie, of all people, would have made it to safety.

The kettle came to the boil and she jumped up to catch it before the whistle woke the household.

The tea was warm and comforting, but not enough to soothe her troubled thoughts. As she'd pedalled through the dark night along narrow lanes, past silent villages and out onto the polders, she'd been unable to erase the image of Levi being kicked and so brutally hauled away by Rudi and Jürgen. Where had they taken him? She'd heard of Jews being shot for no good reason, but she refused to believe they would have taken Levi away by car if they had been intending to shoot him. More likely, he was destined for hard labour in a work camp. Like Willem, she remembered, though the Germans were unlikely to treat Levi with any lenience. Her mind painfully circled back to their tearful goodbye in the attic before the start of this nightmare.

'Ilse, is it you?'

Ilse's mother appeared at the door to the kitchen, tying the cord of her dressing gown.

'Yes, it's me. I can't tell you how glad I am to see you. How are you? And how's Pa?'

'We're still alive,' said her mother, with a soft laugh. 'But what is all this? It's so early. Did someone drive you home?'

'Sit down, Mama. Let me pour you a cup of tea first.'

Her mother clicked her tongue and took the kettle from her. 'I should be doing that. You sit down and tell me what's going on.'

Ilse didn't want to worry her, so spared her the worst of the details of the night before, but she was desperate for her mother's sympathy. 'I suppose we all thought the house would be safe, being so close to the sanatorium. If it hadn't been for the plane crash, I doubt they would ever have come looking. Levi didn't deserve any of it, really he didn't. And all because he had the misfortune to be born Jewish.' Tears began to roll down her face, as the anguish of losing Levi hit her all over again.

'You really cared for him, didn't you, Ilse?'

'Yes, I did— I do really care for him. But I don't think I'll ever see him again,' she said despairingly.

'It's still early days. Try not to worry. I'm sure Clara will let us know if there's any news.'

* * *

Levi occupied Ilse's every waking moment with an intensity that caused her physical pain. Days went by, but there was no word on where Levi had been taken and if he had even survived. The only good news was that Connie had managed to get a message through to her mother: she and Rik were in hiding with friends some distance from Hilversum. She promised to keep in touch.

Ilse threw herself into caring for her ailing father, who lay listlessly upstairs in bed. His eyes brightened the first time Ilse walked into the room, and she sat on the side of the bed clasping his dry cool hands in her own. She forced herself not to cry, as she gazed down at the hands she knew would never fly across the piano keyboard and fill the house with joyous music again. She diligently administered his medicine and gradually saw an improvement: his hacking cough became less laboured and he was able to keep down the soup that Ilse insisted on preparing herself with the remains of the potatoes the lodger had left behind before he returned home to The Hague.

One Saturday evening in late April, Ilse was sitting with her mother, close to the illegal wireless set they'd brought out from its hiding place to listen to the crackly nightly broadcast on Radio Oranje. The Allies had made significant advances in pushing back the Germans. Food was finally on its way, with RAF drops scheduled for the following afternoon. No precise locations were given, but it was the first positive indication that the Allies had got the better of the Nazis after being repelled on so many occasions. The details were so unclear that Ilse refused to accept it was actually happening. With food supply lines so heartlessly cut off by the Germans, what hope was there of any the food shops reopening? She remembered the time when the Red Cross had distributed delicious loaves of bread made from flour shipped over from Sweden and baked locally, the likes of which the entire Dutch population hadn't tasted since before the war. People desperately wanted to believe that this fleeting act of kindness must surely mean the war would soon be over and life would return to normal, but she was more realistic: How could one loaf per family be expected to alleviate their gnawing hunger? It was impossible to imagine that life could ever return to normal.

At 2 p.m. the day after the Radio Oranje announcement, there was a rap at the door – not the menacing thud of a German rifle butt, but a cheerful rat-a-tat-tat. Ilse exchanged a nervous glance with her mother, who was peeling two small, shrivelled potatoes and slicing the remains of a wilted cabbage for their evening meal. She put her knife down and nodded assent to Ilse, who hurried to open the door. There stood young Piet van der Hoeven from number seventeen, red in the face from racing from door to door with the news that everyone was to go immediately up onto the roof where they could get the best view of the planes as they approached.

'Hurry! We're going to get food, tins of meat, packets of biscuits, chocolate, real food at last,' he sang out. 'It's going to be fantastic!' He was talking so quickly that the words tumbled out in a torrent of gibberish.

Ilse gave a short laugh at his enthusiasm and thanked him for letting her know, saying she'd be straight up. But as she turned to go back inside, she was floored by a wave of sickness and had to clutch hold of the doorframe to steady herself. Her mother rushed forward to help and led her to the kitchen table, where she pulled out a chair.

'I can't think what's come over me, but I suppose I wasn't expecting to hear that,' Ilse said. She tried to wave her mother away, but her head was spinning. 'It's nothing, Mama. Please don't worry.' She pressed her knuckles into her eyes.

Her mother peered at her, looking unconvinced. 'Sit still a minute. Let me fetch you a glass of water.'

As she sat back in her chair, Ilse thought back to the nausea that had washed over her on waking that morning. It was the fourth time that week. When it had first happened, she had mistaken it for hunger, but she now realised it had happened too often for that.

Shakily, she accepted the glass and swallowed down the cool water, which did make her feel a little better.

'How long have you been feeling this way?' Her mother watched her closely.

Their eyes met. Ilse knew she couldn't deceive herself any longer.

'You're expecting, aren't you?' Her mother's voice was so gentle that it set Ilse off crying. And then a new doubt crept into her mind. What if the baby wasn't Levi's, but Rudi's? The thought terrified her. Frantically, she tried to count the weeks since she and Levi had last lain together, but the spectre of Rudi forcing himself on her was all she could think of.

'I can't be... I mean I can't have a baby without Levi,' she sobbed. 'It wasn't meant to be like this. Honestly, Mama.' She accepted the handkerchief her mother held out, and buried her face in it. 'I never thought about the possibility of falling pregnant because I haven't had my monthly since last year,' she said through tears.

Her mother let out a sigh. 'You won't be the first woman to say that. But it's best you know, so you can start to plan for when the baby arrives. From the sounds of it, it'll be quite a while before it comes, and maybe your Levi will have turned up by then.'

Ilse glanced at her mother, knowing she was only trying to be helpful. 'And if he doesn't? What will I do then?' She dared not whisper her fear that the baby might not even be his.

'Don't think about that. You must try and stay positive, for your own sake and for the baby's. Now dry your tears and go and see what's happening up on the roof. This is the day we've all been waiting for.'

Ilse rose from her chair and gave her mother a gentle hug, catching her breath at how small and frail she felt in her arms. She seemed so fragile. *Like life itself*, she reflected sorrowfully, as she drew her mother close once more.

THIRTY-EIGHT

In the bright sunshine up on the roof there was a party atmosphere. A crowd of young people from the street had congregated, laughing and chatting with excitement. Ilse recognised one or two by sight, but not well enough to speak to, so she took up a position by herself in the shade of a chimney stack and watched the group engaging in joyful conversation. She looked on enviously at those happy, smiling faces, all united in their optimism for a better future they believed was just around the corner; it seemed as if no one had a care in the world. Turning away, all alone, she had never missed Levi as much as in that moment.

All at once the laughter faded, as everyone turned to listen to a young man in a rakish homburg hat who was talking in a raised voice.

'Did you hear that? They're coming!' Ilse heard him say as he pointed up at the sky.

There was a deafening hush, before a low rumble could be heard coming from the west. Faces upturned, everyone scanned the clear sky, but there was no sign of any planes. 'It's a false alarm,' someone murmured in a disappointed voice.

Ilse had begun to wonder if coming up here was a waste of time when she felt a light tap to her shoulder that made her jump. She turned to find Willem standing behind her. His jacket hung off his thin shoulders and his once-ruddy face was gaunt, yet his smile lifted her heart.

'You're back,' she cried out in surprise, and hugged him with all her might.

'Just yesterday,' he said breathlessly. 'Several of us managed to get away when the camp descended into chaos. We ran for our lives before we realised no one was coming after us. It was pure luck.' He grinned.

At that moment a cheer went up from the other people on the roof, and the rumble intensified to a roar. Suddenly, over the treetops, a squadron of British RAF grey-green Avro Lancaster bomber planes appeared, their propellers a blur and their bomb flaps open. A collective gasp went up as everyone saw that it wasn't bombs they were carrying, but piles and piles of canvas bags, stacked high in the hold. The pilots in their tiny cockpits waved furiously at the small crowd; everyone was jumping for joy, shouting, laughing and crying and frantically waving handkerchiefs in the air. Ilse joined in, hot tears of relief, sadness and joy streaming down her cheeks. Willem, standing behind her, slipped his arms round her waist and pressed her tight against him. But as she stared skywards through blurry tears, she was overcome by the thought that it should be Levi holding her close, that it should be the two of them witnessing the end of hostilities together. Blinking hard, she couldn't fail to remember how only a few short weeks ago, she and Levi had watched another plane, piloted by an Englishman who hadn't survived.

Everyone craned their necks to watch the planes pass over. The food parcels came tumbling like stones out of the holds and another raucous cheer erupted from the hysterical group on the roof. They cheered and whooped for joy as dozens and dozens of parcels fell from the perfectly blue sky – until the sudden realisation that they had missed their target and none had landed close by. In that moment, it became obvious that other people would reach them before they had a chance.

Ilse twisted round to look at Willem and saw his eyes were red with crying.

'I can't believe it. They could see us waving at them... why would they fly straight over?' Ilse said in despair.

Willem wiped a hand across his eyes. 'I don't know, Ilse. I wish I did.'

The celebratory mood quickly faded and everyone dispersed back into their houses. There was nothing more to keep them up there.

It was a bitter disappointment. Together, Ilse and Willem searched up and down the street, joining scores of people all desperate to get their hands on the food parcels they'd seen falling just out of their reach. No one spoke as they kept their eyes kept glued to the ground, scouring the pavements, before heading further afield into bare open spaces and the surrounding farmland; but there was nothing. It was as if all the parcels had been spirited away. Confusion hung heavy in the air as rumours spread that the Germans must have known about the drop and swooped in to steal all the food for themselves.

Despondently, Ilse and Willem returned home in silence. Ilse was tired with all the fruitless searching and wanted to be alone after all that had happened that day. When they arrived outside number four, she said, 'There's nothing more to be done. Go home, Willem. We'll hear soon enough if anything changes.'

'I'll be here to help. Don't hesitate to come and knock.' He looked anxious, hopeful even.

'Of course, Willem,' she said kindly. She thought briefly of asking him in, but then she stopped herself. She was in no mood for it. Instead she gave his arm a consoling squeeze. 'I'm glad you're back home.'

Later that evening, Ilse and her mother sat with heads bent over the wireless set, trying to catch snatches of information as it faded in and out. There were confirmed reports of numerous food drops across the region, including Rotterdam, The Hague and Gouda. The authorities had allocated collection points in schools and community halls, but it appeared that nobody was in charge of the distribution of the food. Crowds of starving people were turning up outside the designated places. The situation was descending into chaos, with fights breaking out when it became clear that the food drops had been a failure. Rumours were spreading that the food parcels been looted, although intelligence suggested that those lucky enough to be close by had grabbed whatever they could for themselves. *Keep calm. Be patient. Food is on the way*, the Radio Oranje newsreader instructed the nation.

The broadcast finished abruptly and a loud hissing filled the space left by the crackly voice. Ilse leant forward to switch off the wireless set, then turned to her mother, who was shaking her head. She looked like she was trying to hold back her tears. Ilse knew she had to be strong for her, but wasn't sure how to after an emotional day of such highs and lows.

The two women both looked up at a small scraping sound above their heads, followed by slow shuffling footsteps on the landing. Instantly, Ilse's face lit up, and she rushed into the hall, calling up, 'Pa, is that you?' She took the steps two at a time and found her father bent over the banister with an expression of grim determination on his face. 'Pa, let me help you,' she said, hooking her arm through his. 'Are you trying to come downstairs?'

'I heard voices. Have we visitors?' he said, lifting his grey head with a hopeful smile. It was the first smile he'd given her in weeks and it broke her heart.

'No, Pa,' Ilse said gently, reminding herself that the medicine must be working for him to want to get out of bed. 'Mama and I were just listening to the news on the wireless about the food drops. It shouldn't be long now,' she added with false cheeriness.

'So no visitors.' He breathed heavily and slumped against her, causing her to grab the banister. 'I won't come down then.'

Ilse tried to hide her disappointment that matched his own. 'Are you sure? We can light a fire for you in the living room. And I can make you a cup of coffee.'

'Tea. Bring me up a cup, will you?' He didn't look at her as he turned to shuffle back along the corridor to his bedroom.

* * *

A week after that ill-fated first food drop, Willem arrived at her door proudly bearing two packets of biscuits. 'Your dinner, madame, courtesy of our generous British allies,' he said to Ilse with a mock bow.

Ilse laughed, and invited him in. She took the packets, then realised he was being deadly serious. 'So there's nothing else?' she said, disappointed.

'I'm afraid not.' Willem sat down heavily with a sigh. 'I've come straight from the town hall. I was lucky to get anything, and I had to beg extra for you. The place is teeming with angry people who can't believe that's all that's being handed out. Nor can I, actually. People are refusing the biscuits and demanding to be given decent food, but those in charge say there's no more for now. It's a deliberate ploy on the part of the Allies – apparently if we were to eat rich food after so long we could fall seriously ill. Even die.' Willem raised a sceptical eyebrow. 'Aren't you going to open one?'

Ilse examined one of the packets, which had English words written in black on a plain white background. 'Energy biscuits fortified with vitamins,' she read, and translated it as best she could into Dutch for Willem. She slid one end of the packet open with her finger and shook out two biscuits, handing him one. The square, thick biscuits didn't look too appetising. They each bit down, looking one another in the eye.

'Not bad, but I would have preferred a *spekulaas koekje*,' said Willem with a grin.

'I don't think it's meant to taste good,' Ilse said in a resigned voice, but she kept on eating her biscuit and noticed that for the first time in days, she actually felt better for it. She secretly prayed that it would be the end of the sickness she'd suffered for so long.

THIRTY-NINE

Ilse looked forward to Willem's morning visits. They sat together at the kitchen table, pretending to like the sweet Camp coffee, a new addition to the foodstuffs that were starting to come through, and engaging in easy conversation and laughter.

Until one day the conversation took on a more serious tone.

As Ilse placed a cup of coffee in front of Willem, he didn't give her his usual cheerful smile, nor did he look up.

'Are you all right?' she ventured.

Willem slowly shook his head. 'I've just heard that a friend of mine has died of typhus. I suppose I was lucky to escape that.' His breath came out in a long shuddering sigh. 'Dirk and I were close in camp. He didn't actually fall ill till after we both left, but the terribly cramped and unhygienic conditions had weakened him. I thought he was recovering well when I went to visit him last week and we sat outside in the sunshine. He was so much brighter in himself. So enthusiastic about his plans to train as a civil engineer. I was delighted to see him on the mend. And now I can't believe he's gone.'

It was the first time Willem had spoken to Ilse about the

conditions in the camp and she was shocked to hear how bad they were. Willem had escaped with little outward signs of ill treatment, apart from loss of weight and the muscle weakness that still affected him, but it was obvious the mental scars would take much longer to heal. She listened as he described the punishing jobs he'd been forced to do, both inside and outside the camp, the long hours and lack of food and sleep. By the time he'd finished, his eyes glistened with emotion. He reached out and clasped Ilse's hand in both of his. 'I'm sorry to go on about it,' he said.

'No, I'm glad you told me, and I'm glad you made it out alive.' Ilse bit her lip, forcing herself not to dwell on the possibility that Levi might have experienced similar hardship at the hands of the Nazis. It was scant relief that the only news she'd received was inconclusive: days after Levi's arrest, a group of forty or so Jews had been sent to Kamp Amersfoort. Levi might or might not have been among them. Ilse shuddered at the very real possibility that he hadn't survived. But Willem had, so maybe Levi will too, she told herself firmly.

'Can I tell you about my time in Hilversum?' Ilse said, after they had sat in silence for a few minutes. 'The sanatorium where I worked seemed such a quiet, safe place, surrounded by tall trees in a private road – but I couldn't have been more wrong. I ended up losing my best friend... and the love of my life.' She took a deep breath and paused to gauge Willem's reaction. She wanted to be truthful, even if it meant hurting him. She'd long suspected Willem was in love with her, even though he'd never said as much, but she knew she could never feel the same way about him.

'I'm truly sorry to hear that.' Willem spoke in a flat voice, but he listened attentively as Ilse spoke of how meeting Levi had changed her life. She described the constant dread that he'd be discovered and how their friendship had developed into something much more, but then been so cruelly destroyed by the two Germans who had discovered he'd been hiding in the attic of Connie's house.

She took a deep breath before voicing her suspicions out loud. 'I think he was sent to Kamp Amersfoort. If that's the case, I don't believe he can have survived that. I've heard they kill Jewish prisoners there.'

'But you don't know for certain, do you?' said Willem.

'No, but it's over a month since he was arrested, and the war is at an end, and still I've had no definite news.'

Willem got to his feet and walked over to her side of the table so he could envelop her in a tight embrace.

'Thank you. You're a good friend,' was all Ilse could say. Briefly, she noticed the tiny fluttering sensation in her belly. *Please let it be Levi's*, she prayed, as the niggling doubt that it might not be resurfaced. Instinctively, her fingers went to the silver coin that always lay in the hollow of her throat and she was soothed by its smooth edges and dips.

They stood like that for a long moment, united, each in their own private grief, until Willem whispered, 'I will take care of you.'

* * *

Three weeks later Willem left to begin work in Rotterdam on the reconstruction of the city, which had been left in ruins by German bombardments right from the start of the war. Initially, he would be working long days clearing rubble from bombed-out buildings. Eventually, he wanted to train as a civil engineer, inspired by his friend Dirk's words before he died.

Before he left, Ilse had been intending to tell Willem she was expecting, but there never seemed to be the right moment. She felt she'd hurt him enough by telling him how much she'd loved Levi. And by the time he'd gone, she still wasn't showing, so she thought it best to let matters lie.

As the weeks went by, she agonised over what she should do about the baby after it was born. Although she couldn't be completely certain, she'd convinced herself that the baby had to be Levi's, but the longer she didn't have news of him, the more she knew she must give the baby up.

One morning, a letter dropped onto the doormat while Ilse and her parents were having breakfast. Her father was finally well enough to come downstairs, and they were tucking into boiled eggs, bread and margarine, still marvelling that fresh food was available again.

'I'll get it,' said Ilse, laying down her napkin and going to pick up the typewritten envelope, which was addressed to her. Her heart thudded as she ripped it open, fully expecting it to contain terrible news about Levi. But then she saw the Leiden University insignia at the top of the letter. Her knees went weak with relief as she walked back, reading it, into the kitchen.

'What is it?' asked her mother.

'The university is opening up and it's an invitation to resume my studies in September.'

'Is that wise in your condition?' said her father, frowning. Ilse had confided little to him about her pregnancy, but sensed his disapproval.

'Of course she must. It would be a waste not to continue her studies. I'm sure Ilse would make a fine doctor,' said her mother proudly.

'Hmm. And the baby? What will you do about that?' said her father, turning his gaze on Ilse.

But Ilse wasn't listening. If the letter had been confirmation of Levi's death, would that have made any difference to her future plans? With sadness, she realised it was time to move on with her life, and that she had to do so alone.

FORTY

ANNA

Anna was on her way home from a meeting in central London when her mobile rang. A light rain was falling and she struggled to put up her umbrella while trying not to drop the phone.

'Caro?' she said, without looking to see who it was, as she darted across the road in-between traffic. A white van came towards her, the impatient driver loudly honking his horn, missing her by inches. 'Oh God, what an idiot,' she said jumping onto the pavement, her mobile still clamped to her ear.

'Anna, are you there?' said a voice, familiar but definitely not Caro's.

'Yes, I'm here.' Anna's voice was shaking from the shock of almost being run over. She headed for a nearby shop doorway for shelter, and moved the phone to her other ear.

'Look, if it's a bad time, I can call back. It sounds like you're busy.'

'No, please don't. I mean, don't ring off. I was just surprised to hear from you.' She could hear herself getting flustered, but didn't seem to be able to help it. It had been weeks since she's last seen him, at the barrier in Delft train station, but suddenly

Luuk's was the only voice she wanted to hear. 'It's good to hear from you. How have you been?'

'I'm fine. I'm sorry if I surprised you. What happened just then?'

'Nothing. Just London traffic. A van tried to mow me down,' she said, trying to make light of the situation. She raised her head and noticed the shop owner glaring at her from the other side of the glass door. *Sorry*, she mouthed, and moved back out onto the street, where the rain was hammering down in earnest.

'It sounds alarming. What's that noise I can hear now?'

'Oh, that. It's suddenly come on to rain and it's pounding on my umbrella.' Anna laughed, suddenly feeling absurdly happy. She held out her hand to feel the raindrops that were splashing on the pavement all around her. 'Are you at home?' she said, imagining a cosy ground-floor flat with a patio window looking onto a small garden filled with beautifully maintained shrubs and pots overflowing with flowers.

'Yeah, I'm in front of my computer. That's why I'm calling. Remember I said I'd keep looking for information about your grandmother?'

I did and I've been waiting for this moment, she thought. 'Yes, of course. What have you found out?'

'I would have called you sooner, but I wanted to wait till I had something definite. And now...'

A bus roared past and Anna missed what he said. 'Luuk, can you hang on a moment till I find somewhere quieter? I'm coming up to a side street... just a minute.' She shook away an image of herself sitting close to Luuk, their arms touching as they pored over the computer, uncovering the secrets of her past. Her heart began to pound.

The pavement was crowded and everyone had put their umbrellas up against the torrential rain. She was just turning in to the street when there was an enormous clap of thunder overhead.

'Good God, what's that? It sounds like an earthquake.' Luuk's voice sounded far away.

Anna didn't answer as she breathlessly searched for shelter, eventually coming to a halt outside a pub where a crowd of people were congregating in the doorway, smoking, laughing and staring out at the summer storm. 'Luuk, I'm going to have to call you back. Sorry,' she said, and reluctantly switched off her phone. 'Sorry,' she said again as she pushed her way through the throng into the pub, where she found that everyone seemed to have had the same idea as her. The place was heaving with people who had come inside out of the rain and were enjoying an excuse for a drink. Alicia Keys's 'Fallin'' was belting out over the speakers, and it reminded her of when she first knew Hugo and how they used to joke that this song was playing wherever they went. Hearing it now seemed all wrong and she just wanted to get away. She headed back outside.

The rain stopped as suddenly as it had started and she was relieved to be on the street again. She inhaled the rain-cleansed air deeply, and the word 'petrichor' came into her head; a perfumer had once told her that was the name for the fresh clean scent you get after summer rain. Would Luuk know the word, she wondered, with a sudden urge to tell him.

She walked quickly through the maze of narrow streets till she came across a quiet public garden with a wooden shelter in its centre, housing several slatted seats. She could hear the cheerful chirping and fluttering of sparrows, but couldn't see them up in the foliage. Drops of rain, caught in the branches, pattered onto the wet paving stones.

Anna sat down in the shelter, took out her mobile and dialled Luuk's number. He picked up on the first ring.

'Anna! Thank goodness! Has your tropical storm passed over?'

Smiling at the sound of his voice, again she thought of him safely indoors, hunched over his computer. 'Yes, Luuk, it has. And I've found somewhere quiet to sit. Now, what was it you were trying to tell me?'

'Anna, listen. I've found your grandmother – it's really true. Ilse Meijer is alive and living in a retirement home in a town not far from here.'

Anna took a sharp intake of breath as she processed his words.

'Anna? Are you still there?'

'I'm still here. It's just such a shock. I really wasn't expecting this. How did you find her?'

'It wasn't me, it was Kersten. After you came, she was intrigued to find out whether Else and Ilse Meijer were one and the same person. She remembered she had a friend who works in the care sector and has contacts in retirement homes. That's how she came to find that Ilse's living not so far away. And Kersten's offered to take you over to meet her. Isn't that amazing?'

'Yes, I suppose it is,' replied Anna. For weeks there had been nothing, and now this. She was finding it hard to take it all in.

There was a pause on the line. 'Are you sure you still want to go through with this?' Luuk's voice sounded uncertain. She switched her mobile to her other ear.

'Of course I do. It's just all a bit sudden. I need some time to sort things out here before I come. Work and so forth,' she said, knowing this last bit was only partly true.

'I understand. There's no rush. Leave it with me to arrange with Kersten for you to come. By the way, she insists you stay at her apartment, so you don't need to worry about that.'

'That would be lovely,' Anna said, unable to stop herself from smiling at his eagerness to sort it all out.

'And, Anna...'

'Yes?'

'I can't wait to see you again.'

FORTY-ONE

The delicate scarf billowed up in a cloud of sapphire blue and Anna let it float down onto the mahogany coffee table. She lifted her thick auburn hair from the back of her neck so she could unclasp the necklace, saying, 'I was scared to wear it, thinking the catch might break and then I'd lose it... but once I put it on, I haven't wanted to take it off.' She looked fondly at the silver coin and chain cupped in her hand before letting it drop onto the scarf.

Her mother moved closer to examine it. 'He never mentioned it in all our years of marriage. Where did you say you found it?' As she ran a finger over the silver coin, her voice sounded wistful.

'It was wrapped in the scarf inside the old Dutch biscuit tin Dad kept up on the shelf in his study. I did feel a bit guilty taking it, thinking I'd stumbled on some secret he didn't want you to know about.' Her eyes were on her mother's face as she waited for her to ask why she hadn't mentioned it before.

'You know, I used to dust in there and it never crossed my mind to look inside that old tin. I just thought it was full of his junk that was best kept out of the way. I wonder if Paul would've said anything to me if I'd found it.'

Anna pressed her lips together as she mused over her words. She was still unable to work out if her father had deliberately kept it hidden because of some secret, or had simply forgotten about it. He'd never seemed the quiet secretive type, in fact quite the opposite – he was always cheerful, with a ready joke, and so at ease in company. Anna couldn't contemplate the idea that he'd been hiding an affair from them all these years; instead she wanted to believe this memento was a keepsake from his childhood and that it had simply slipped his mind.

'I'm sure he would have told you if it had been important,' she said with growing certainty. 'You know Dad – he probably put it in the tin rather than get rid of it and that was that. He wasn't the sentimental type, was he?'

'No, he most certainly wasn't that,' said her mother with a small smile. 'He was always on the go with this or that project, or off to play a round of golf with his friends. It's just strange how he suddenly wanted to go delving into his family background when he did. As if he had a premonition that he was going to die and wanted some kind of closure.'

Anna moved close to her mother so she could put an arm round her. 'Now, Mum, you mustn't think like that. It's quite natural he would have thought about his birth family. And maybe he just felt a bit superstitious with all the flying he did.'

Her mother managed a few quick nods and sniffed. 'Before he left... that last time... he said he was going to cut back on all the travel, that he didn't need the stress any more. I'd been telling him that for years, so I was relieved to hear it from him. He promised me this would be his last trip...' Her voice caught as if only just realising what she'd said.

'Oh, Mum,' said Anna, giving her a squeeze.

'He wanted to devote more time to the things in life that

really matter. Look where that got him,' her mother went on. Sighing deeply, she leant her cheek against Anna's shoulder.

They both looked up at the sound of soft footsteps crossing the hallway. Aunty Jane appeared, carrying a tray with three steaming mugs of coffee. 'I'm afraid these are all I could find. Two are chipped and the third has a crack in it.'

She looked around for somewhere to put the tray down. The only surface left was the coffee table; the chairs had been pushed into one corner ready for collection and the antique bureau had already been taken by a specialist removal firm. As Anna quickly removed the necklace and whisked away the scarf, she wondered how all the furniture would fit into her mum's new bungalow. 'Here, let me take the tray,' she said. 'I was just showing Mum something I found of Dad's. Pretty, isn't it?' She held up the necklace for her aunt to admire.

'Oh, that takes me back. When I first saw it, I thought it was odd the way the coin was all bent. That's what I said to your dad.' Aunty Jane took the necklace and spun the coin round and round on the chain before handing it back to Anna. 'But it's nice you still have it.'

'How come you've seen this before? He never showed me,' said Anna's mother, glancing anxiously at Anna.

Aunty Jane must have noticed her sister's hurt expression, but carried on, 'He didn't show me it. Remember when I was helping you both move in here? I was passing him stuff from the boxes to put into drawers and onto shelves. You must have been sorting things somewhere else in the house. I found the necklace at the bottom of one of the boxes. It was under some papers and I nearly missed it. I handed it to Paul and asked if it belonged to you, but he looked surprised and said it was his. When I asked how he came by it he didn't say, just that he'd had it a long time and was pleased it hadn't been mislaid. I remember that scarf too because it's such a lovely colour. He wrapped the necklace up in it and put it in a tin for safekeeping. I'm sorry I didn't tell you, Eileen, but there was so much going on that day – it must have slipped my mind.' Aunty Jane glanced at her sister apologetically.

'Well, there you are. It was just something of insignificance, a trinket that meant nothing much, stuffed away and forgotten about. I must say, it's a relief to hear it was nothing more. Now, let's drink our coffee and Jane can help me pack up the last of these things. The removal men will be here any minute.' Anna's mother gulped down her cooling coffee and put the mug down, so she could get on with taping up the cardboard boxes and marking them up with a thick marker pen.

Anna exchanged a look with her aunt as they went off into the kitchen. 'I'm a bit worried about Mum,' she whispered when they were out of earshot. 'This move, it all seems so sudden – it's barely six weeks since the funeral and she's so determined to put everything behind her. I'm worried about her giving all this up. Don't you think the bungalow will be a bit small after living here for so long? I don't want her to regret it.'

'Give her time. She'll get used to it. It'll do her good to get away and make a fresh start. And remember, she'll be just up the road from us. She'll be just fine.'

But Anna was doubtful as she swept her gaze around the spacious kitchen with its long counters, tall cabinets and scrubbed pine table. She swallowed down the lump forming in her throat, remembering the happy times they used to share here as a family and with friends. If she closed her eyes, she could still summon up her father's deep hearty laugh as he told one of his jokes, holding a bottle of red at the ready to refill everyone's glass. She wished she hadn't been so hasty in giving her approval to her mother moving away from the family home that held so many memories for them both.

'Anna?' said Aunty Jane. 'It's OK to be sad. Think of it as a new beginning for her.'

They were interrupted by a shrill ring on the doorbell and

the arrival of four burly removal men, led by a foreman who cheerfully told them that they should leave everything to them and that their belongings would be in safe hands. There was nothing more for Anna to do except say goodbye to her mother and aunt and promise to visit soon. Reluctantly, she left them to it, still clasping the precious necklace wrapped up in the scarf.

FORTY-TWO

Throughout the hour-long flight to Amsterdam Anna kept her eyes tightly shut, forcing herself to think about anything other than the fact that she was suspended in a metal box 35,000 feet above the Earth. The thought terrified her, no matter how hard she tried to rationalise that the chances of being involved in a plane crash were substantially lower than being in a car accident. Her irrational fear of flying had begun during one particularly bumpy flight to Italy, when she'd become convinced the plane was about to crash into the Alps. Hugo's flippant remarks had done little to reassure her – in fact quite the opposite. Since then, she had chosen to travel by any other means, even if it meant a journey lasting many more hours, or even days. But today she had no choice and she knew she simply had to put up with it.

Closing her eyes, she tried to focus on a time when she'd found flying exciting. She had been on her first big holiday, which had meant taking a flight with her parents to Los Angeles. Visiting Disneyland was the highlight; they were met by a giant waving Mickey Mouse, and went on a ride where she was whirled round and round in an enormous pink teacup. After that, Dad had driven them all up the coast to San Francisco. Her memory of that holiday was patchy, but she remembered a cycle trip along the shoreline, pedalling a bike that was attached to her dad's, and stopping for lunch to eat the most enormous sandwiches filled with layer upon layer of peanut butter and 'jelly', a description that made her giggle, however many times Mum had told her that jelly was just American for jam. Another vivid image came to her of seals – or were they sea lions? – hundreds of them, sleek, mottled grey and sandy-coloured, draped on top of each other as they sunned them-selves languorously on the rocks. That noise they made was like the deep-throated barks of a collection of dogs; but it was the revolting acrid smell she could still remember so vividly. But her strongest memory, and the thing she'd loved most about that holiday, was the flight. She'd been only a little scared and appre-hensive when they'd set foot on the enormous aircraft, holding tightly on to her father's hand. They had been met by a flight attendant, dressed in a scarlet uniform topped off with a big white smile, who'd handed her a canvas backpack in the same glorious colour as the uniform. Inside were snacks and a carton of juice, along with a colouring book, pencils and a miniature toy aeroplane, the exact one they were travelling in. It had been Dad who'd kept her entertained throughout the twelve-hour flight, and she'd snuggled into the crook of his arm to watch cartoons on the small screen set into the back of the seat in front of theirs, while Mum had pretended to sleep.

The tannoy crackled into life with the announcement that they were arriving at Schiphol and the instruction to put their seats into the upright position. Anna's eyes flickered open. She was relieved that her ordeal was at an end. They were taxiing towards the terminal buildings, and Anna allowed herself a glance out of the window. Next to her sat a woman who looked to be about her mother's age, with large eyes magnified behind the thick lenses of her steel-rimmed glasses. She was packing up the remains of the picnic she'd brought with her, and smiled sympathetically at Anna.

'Are you feeling better now? I saw how white you looked back there. Here, have a cheese sandwich. You must be hungry now. I always bring too many.' She spoke fast and with a heavy Dutch accent as she unwrapped a sandwich and tried to press it on Anna, who was reminded of the busybody who had engaged her in conversation the first time she travelled to Rijswjik on the local bus.

Anna gave an involuntary shiver and lifted her hand in refusal. 'No thank you. I'm fine. Really.'

'Ah, I knew you were English! Is it your first time in Amsterdam? It's such a wonderful city. I've lived here all my life and can't think of anywhere I'd rather be. You must go to the Rijksmuseum – there's a new exhibition of the old masters. It's just opened. You like art, don't you?'

Anna nodded, pretending to listen as she let her mind drift back to the events that had led her to be here now.

* * *

Five days ago, she'd been working late in the evening when her mobile rang. She glanced at the screen and her stomach gave a pleasurable jolt. 'Hi, Luuk. I was going to call you,' she began, noticing as she spoke an error in the article she'd been writing.

'Hey, are you OK? You sound stressed.'

Anna turned away from her computer screen. The article would have to wait. 'Sorry, it's work. I'm trying to finish off something and it's not going as well as I'd hoped.'

'Well, I have something to cheer you up. It's all been

decided. Mum spoke to Ilse Meijer on the phone today and has arranged for the three of you to meet.'

'She has?' Anna sat up straight, all thoughts of the article forgotten.

She heard Luuk's easy laugh down the line, but knew he was serious.

'What did your mum say to persuade her?'

'She introduced herself as the daughter of an old friend, and explained that they used to come and visit Ilse and her parents in Rijswijk. The old lady was a bit suspicious at first, saying it was too long ago for her to remember. It took Mum a couple of attempts, mentioning the names of Ilse's parents and describing the street they used to live in, before she accepted her explanation.'

'But we still don't know if this is *the* Ilse Meijer. It seems deceitful turning up when we don't have proof.'

'Anna, now listen to me. I wouldn't be telling you this if I wasn't a hundred per cent sure that I've found her. I've been through as many sources online as I can think of. Admittedly there are quite a few records of women calling themselves Ilse Meijer. But there's only one born in 1921. All the others were either much older or younger. And she's also the only one who was born in Rijswijk. It has to be her, doesn't it?'

'Yes, I suppose so,' Anna said cautiously, her heart beating faster. She so wanted to believe him, but still she stalled. 'There's another thing that's bothering me.'

'Go on, tell me,' he said.

Anna could detect a weariness in his voice but she went on. 'You said that Ilse agreed to meet me. Why would she do that?'

'Well... it wasn't quite like that. My mum said she had a family friend staying and would she mind if she brought her along.'

'That's a lie,' said Anna, though she was smiling.

'Well... perhaps just bending the truth a little. I assumed

you'd want to come and meet her for yourself. I'm sitting at my computer. I can book your flight right away. Please say you'll come.'

Anna hadn't had the heart to tell him that she was frightened of flying.

Now she was on the tarmac at Schiphol airport and all that was left to do was to take the train to Baarn the next morning and meet the woman who might or might not be her grandmother. And if she wasn't, what would she do then?

Anna breathed out in relief when the plane finally came to a halt. Click, click, click, went the unbuckling of seatbelts all around her. Anna rose from her seat at the same time as most of the passengers, murmured a quick goodbye to the woman in the next seat, grabbed her overnight suitcase from the overhead locker and disappeared into the throng exiting the plane.

After a long walk through the terminal, she reached the long, snaking queue for passport control and switched on her mobile, which immediately buzzed with incoming messages. Most were from her phone provider, repeatedly informing her that she was now connected to the Dutch network, one from Caro wishing her luck and signed with four kisses, and another from Luuk saying he'd arrived and was standing to the left of the arrival doors – 'You'll recognise me by the silly grin on my face.' A smile lifted the corners of Anna's mouth, accompanied by an unexpected surge of happiness.

Two months ago, she could never have imagined feeling this way about anyone again. Back then, she'd thought she had her life mapped out, and hadn't questioned whether it was what she really wanted. Hugo was all she'd ever known, the handsome boyfriend who was kind and a steady, dependable presence, but, dare she admit it, rather boring. Perhaps it had been her fault, the way she'd been prepared always to put Hugo first, often to the exclusion of what she wanted – from his career to what they did at weekends, making sure that she was always around for him, regardless of his erratic working habits. But it wasn't just about Hugo, Anna had come to realise as she automatically followed the queue edging closer to the passport control desk. Nor was it her father's death and the unexpected discovery of the precious necklace he'd kept safe all these years that had led her to his birthplace. Nor even Luuk, who had come back into her life so fortuitously with the promise of a tantalising link to her past. It was all these things and more, she concluded, suddenly impatient to get through security and see him again.

Anna arrived at the front of the queue and handed her passport to the uniformed woman sitting in her booth. She wore a disinterested expression on her face as she flicked through the pages, then looked up at Anna, before slapping the passport down on the counter with a curt nod.

Anna slipped her passport into the bag slung over her shoulder and looked for the green 'Nothing to Declare' sign leading to the exit. Her heart beat fast as she was propelled forward by the passengers surrounding her, and found herself through the automatic opening doors, to be confronted by a sea of expectant faces. All around her men held up boards inscribed with the name of hotels, travel companies, or simply somebody's name scrawled in big letters in felt tip pen. Was it always like this, she wondered? Glancing wildly about her, she caught sight of the time and realised it had taken forty-five minutes to get through security. Luuk was nowhere to be seen. Surely he couldn't have given up already? *To the left of the doors*, she repeated his instruction to herself, and set off purposefully, dragging her suitcase behind her.

'Anna! Here, Anna!'

She stopped in her tracks, trying to place where the voice came from, and turned to see Luuk half running towards her with the big grin on his face that he'd promised. He came to a stop, slightly out of breath, at her side. How could she have forgotten the way his wavy fair hair fell across his forehead and the blueness of his eyes? She was mesmerised all over again by his steady gaze. Thrown off guard, she said, 'You weren't where you said you'd be. I mean, there's so many people here...'

'That's airports for you,' Luuk said, still grinning. 'I knew it would take a while for you to clear security, so I thought there'd be time to grab myself a quick coffee. Sorry I wasn't in position.' He lowered his head and glanced sheepishly at her, his mouth pursed, as if trying to suppress a laugh.

Returning his smile, she stepped forward at the same time that he did. His arms surrounded her to hold her tight against him. His strong arms, his warmth, the faint smell of cologne clinging to his shirt... everything felt right.

'It's so good to see you, Anna,' she heard him whisper against her ear. She clasped her hands around his back.

'It's so good to see you too,' she whispered back, reluctant to let go.

FORTY-THREE

Weeks had elapsed since the three of them had last been on Kersten's balcony eating lunch. The glint of the duckpond was no longer visible through the trees, which were now in full leaf. Luuk sat with his long legs outstretched as he gazed into the middle distance. Anna stood beside him, looking out too, while occasionally glancing over to wonder what he was thinking. Then, when she was distracted by the loud chatter of sparrows hidden in a clump of bushes below. 'Look there!' she cried, pointing at the flock as it burst from the foliage with an enormous commotion and flew en masse to another roosting spot several gardens away. A cat came dashing out of the bushes in hot pursuit. Only then did Luuk tear himself away from his view so he could catch Anna's eye. 'It's all go here,' he said with the twitch of a smile, as he reached for her hand.

Moments later, Kersten appeared with a tray, her pale-blue kaftan swirling round her ankles. The glasses of tea chinked against one another as she placed the wooden tray on the mosaic tabletop covered in shimmering shades of blue and green sea glass. She handed round the tea and offered a plate of crumbly *moppen* biscuits, before settling herself in her seat and crossing her long legs. 'Welcome, Anna. I'm so pleased you're back,' she said, beaming.

'Me too. It's so kind of you to let me stay,' said Anna, returning her smile, before regarding the spacious airy apartment through the open glass doors and admiring again the oversized abstract paintings hanging on the white walls. There was something so calming about this place; it was a world away from London, Hugo and the life she'd always known up to now.

Anna concentrated on stirring a spoonful of sugar into her glass of steaming tea. 'It's been a long day, but I'm pleased to be here. I can't quite believe I'm about to meet my grandmother, though I admit I still have a lingering doubt it's actually her. But I am curious to find out,' she added hastily.

Kersten nodded. 'I'm curious too, and I really hope she is the same woman who was friends with my mother all those years ago.'

'You don't sound too sure. What was your impression when you spoke to her?'

'It's hard to say from one phone call. If I'm truthful, she didn't remember me until I mentioned meeting her parents in Rijswijk, and even then she was a bit hazy about the details. After all, she is nearly eighty and may be losing her memory. We should be prepared for this when we meet her.'

Anna hadn't considered this possibility. Her heart sank as she thought she might never get to the truth about who her grandparents were.

'Don't jump to conclusions until you've met her,' Luuk interjected. 'The chances are she was wary of taking a call that came out of the blue. She probably gets cold calls all the time.'

'Let's not worry about that now,' said Kersten with a dismissive sweep of her hand. 'Anna, the important thing is that you came back. I'm sure that by being here you'll find the answers to the mystery of both your grandparents. Luuk's already found out quite a lot, haven't you?'

Both women turned to Luuk, who shrugged. 'Nothing yet on your grandfather, but that's for you to ask Ilse. But I have found a few photos online that intrigued me and made me want to find out more about Ilse's connection to you. Ever since I saw that old photo of her in Leiden, I've been looking for more clues. It's incredible how much stuff you can dig up on the internet.' He got up and disappeared inside for a few moments before reappearing clutching a sheaf of papers. Pushing the tea tray to one side, he laid them out. 'I printed these off so you can see what she was like all those years ago. This was the first one I found, if you remember, and the most promising.'

Anna recalled that moment in her hotel room when Luuk had told her he'd found someone by the name of Ilse Meijer, along with photographic evidence. Despite her misgivings at the time, she remembered clearly the rush of adrenaline she'd felt at having a reason to keep in touch with him. It seemed incredible that she was back here again.

Luuk turned back to the photo. 'It's of a student gathering at Leiden University just after it reopened, and Ilse's name is mentioned in the caption underneath. I'm not entirely sure which one she is.'

Anna leant forward to peer at the black-and-white photo-copy and was struck by how joyful the students all looked as they posed for the camera. They were a typical group of students, larking about, some smoking cigarettes, laughing uproariously at a joke one of them had just made. She was surprised at how smartly dressed they all were compared to modern students in their uniform of jeans and T-shirt; she marvelled at the women's well-cut dresses with cinched waists and pleated skirts. The men were also well-turned-out, with their natty jackets over slacks and shirts with long pointed collars.

Kersten put her reading glasses on and bent forward to look. 'This could be her,' she said, having moved her finger across each person in the group while reading out loud the names printed below. She stopped at a woman who was smaller than the rest, with chin-length wavy hair. She appeared to be smiling up at a woman with her back to the camera. Disappointingly, she stood in profile, so it was difficult to determine her features.

'Hmm. That's a shame as it was the best-quality photo I could find. But I'm sure there was another here somewhere,' said Luuk. He leafed through the copies he'd printed off, which were mainly official ones of the reopening of the university by various dignitaries.

'Ah, here we are,' he said.

The photo was smaller than the rest. It showed a summery scene and featured a group of people standing around beneath trees with sunlight dappling through the leaves. Three men wore dark suits with coat-tails and white shirts, each tied at the neck with a white bow tie. One of the men was in conversation with a woman in a tailored dark coat dress and a small stylish hat that was attached to her hair with a fancy hatpin. 'That's Princess Juliana, who studied international law at Leiden in the thirties. You can see it was some function or other from the way everyone is dressed. But what interests me is that woman there, the one in the background. Don't you think she looks just like the one in the first photo?' Luuk placed the two side by side, but Anna didn't need more than a glance to see that the evidence was flimsy. Apart from her small stature and hairstyle, there was nothing to distinguish her from the other women in her group.

'There are two other women with her and either one could be her,' she said. 'I'm not sure these photos prove anything.'

But Kersten wasn't ready to give up. 'There's something about her that's familiar, and not because she's smaller than the others. I remember now that Else had a similar hairstyle.'

Anna was unconvinced. It wasn't that she didn't want to believe it was Ilse Meijer, but she was suddenly afraid to have confirmation that this photo would somehow prove that Ilse had returned to study at Leiden while five months pregnant, knowing she intended to give up her baby – her own father.

But Kersten wasn't finished. She was examining another photo for any clue they might have missed. 'Wait a minute. Look at this. It was taken a couple of years after the war. It seems to have been taken at an end-of-year celebration. There's Ilse again, and see the tall woman to her left? I can't be sure, because she's turned away from the camera, but she does look like my own mother.'

'Oma?' said Luuk incredulously, as he leant in for another look. 'Why would she be in this picture? You never mentioned she studied at Leiden.'

'No, that's because she was there for less than a year before the Germans closed the university. She went on with her studies for a while at Nijmegen University, but never returned to study in Leiden after it reopened. By the time this photo was taken she had had me.'

'But that doesn't explain why she's in this photo with a load of Leiden students,' Luuk said with a sigh as he began to shuffle the papers together.

'Luuk, wait. Please listen to me,' pleaded Kersten. She touched his arm and he stopped what he was doing. 'My mother may not have gone back to study at Leiden, but it's possible she attended social gatherings as a guest of Ilse's. It all seems to fit. After her stroke, if you remember, she talked to me about the friend I thought she called Else and how close they had been during the war. Seeing Ilse with her in this photo surely proves that Else and Ilse Meijer are one and the same woman.'

FORTY-FOUR

Luuk drove Anna and Kersten to Baarn the following morning. The plan was for him to drop them off at Ilse Meijer's retirement home, find somewhere he could have a coffee and return after an hour.

'We're here,' he said, turning into a broad tree-lined residential street with imposing houses set back behind perfectly manicured emerald-green lawns. 'Give me a call when you're ready and I'll come and fetch you.' He glanced at Anna beside him, but she was looking intently at the large houses on either side.

'Can this be the right street? These places all look like they're owned by very wealthy people,' she said, her eyes nervously flitting from one large mansion to the other. There was certainly nothing to suggest there might be a retirement home among them.

'If you look, you'll see they're not all private houses,' said Luuk, peering ahead for somewhere to park. 'This is where you find a lot of private practices – solicitors, accountants, dentists, that kind of thing. And Ilse Meijer's retirement home.' He slowed the car to a crawl and found a parking space in front of a long three-storey building. Huge picture windows filled with potted plants overlooked an abundance of blue and pink hydrangea bushes. In front was a wide, neatly clipped lawn. Anna expected to see residents sitting in armchairs in the windows, but the foliage did a clever job of concealing the shadowy shapes within.

From the back seat, Kersten read out the name on a board placed discreetly to one side of the main entrance. 'It looks more like a hotel than a retirement home. Ilse Meijer must be well off to afford this place,' she said. Just at that moment, the glass entrance door slid back and a man in a crisp white uniform with an emblem stitched on his chest pocket came out, pushing an elderly man in a wheelchair. They were met at the kerb by another uniformed man wearing a chauffeur's cap, who helped the carer wheel his charge up a ramp into the back of the adapted van. Kersten widened her eyes at Anna. She didn't need to say that this place was definitely a cut above the rest.

Luuk pointed at the clock on the dashboard. 'Come on, you two. You don't want to keep her waiting.' He turned to Anna and gave her an encouraging smile.

Anna took in a deep breath and smiled back. 'Thank you for all you've done,' she whispered.

'You might want to keep your thanks till after you've met your grandmother,' he said, raising an eyebrow.

Together, Anna and Kersten walked up the paved path and waited to be buzzed in. The glass door slid back and they stepped into what resembled a smart hotel lobby. Along one wall was a shiny front desk, where two women sat tapping away at computers. Opposite were several purple plush velvet armchairs beside a glass coffee table stacked with glossy maga-zines. A filter coffee machine made hissing and spluttering sounds in one corner and the smell of coffee filled the air.

Kersten went over to one of the receptionists and spoke in

rapid Dutch, while Anna stood by, trying to work out what they were saying. Ilse Meijer's name kept coming up and she began to worry if Kersten had got the wrong place. Then the receptionist put a map of the layout of the home on the counter and drew a circle on it. She pointed to the lift.

'Let's go,' said Kersten, slotting her arm through Anna's.

'Is there a problem?' Anna asked, tensing her brow.

'No, not at all. I introduced us and asked how long Ilse's been living here and whether she likes it. I was trying to be friendly, but the receptionist didn't want to give away too much about her.'

They went over to the lift and the doors immediately opened, releasing a smell of disinfectant that reminded Anna of hospitals.

'She's on the third floor, which is nice. She'll have a view.' Kersten pressed the top button.

Anna looked at the notices announcing the days and times of various activities under pictures of residents participating in tai chi, flower arranging and music performances. 'Looks like there's a full programme going on here. Somehow from the image I have in my head I can't imagine her doing any of them.'

'You can always ask her,' said Kersten, as the lift stopped at their floor with a loud ping.

Anna followed her out, feeling apprehensive. It all seemed so much bigger and more slick than she'd been expecting. She was beginning to feel sorry for the woman she'd never met, living in an institution with its programme of events that all seemed rather soulless. They walked past an occasional table. It held an elaborate floral display, but the heady scent of freshly cut flowers didn't mask the disinfectant smell and seemed only to make things worse. It can't be easy moving into a place like this and calling it home, Anna thought sadly.

'Here we are.' Kersten stopped by a door halfway down a long corridor. Ilse Meijer's name was typed in bold letters on a piece of card slotted into the brass nameplate. She rang the bell in the centre of the door. It sounded loud and shrill. Moments later, the door was opened wide by a small smiling woman wearing a white coat.

'*Goedemorgen*. Mevrouw Schenk?' She spoke in accented Dutch.

Kersten nodded and introduced Anna as her English friend.

'How nice!' the woman said, switching to English. 'Mevrouw Meijer is waiting for you. I just finish with pills. I give her every morning and evening. Please, come in.'

The entrance lobby was cramped for three people, but led to a spacious sitting room with an enormous picture window overlooking the front lawn. An array of well-tended houseplants covered the windowsill and large pieces of antique furniture, landscape paintings and several upholstered chairs filled the living space. Anna's eyes were drawn to the diminutive elderly woman ensconced in a green velvet-covered chair with a tall back. It looked like she'd made an effort for their visit; her wavy reddish hair, pale at the temples, was neatly styled and she was dressed in a dark-blue tweed skirt and a navy cardigan with a turquoise dragonfly brooch pinned at the shoulder. Anna searched her face, carefully made up with powder and lipstick, hoping to find a resemblance to her father, but could see none. It was disappointing, and she hoped this visit wasn't about to turn out to be a complete waste of time.

This Ilse Meijer seemed friendly enough though, her blue eyes sparkled as she greeted her visitors. Kersten stepped forward and took hold of both bony hands in her own. She said something quickly in Dutch, then looked sideways at Anna, saying, 'Did I mention that my friend is English?'

'*Nee, maar dat is leuk!*' the old lady exclaimed. 'How nice! I now have a chance to practise my English. I don't have much opportunity these days.'

'But your English is very good, like so many Dutch people.

I'm afraid my Dutch isn't, though I do have a few phrases,' said Anna, feeling the need to apologise.

'Ah yes, we had English lessons at school and I always watch the BBC. It is so much better than Dutch television. It is all game shows and talk these days,' the old lady said disdainfully.

'Mevrouw Meijer?' said the carer, who was hovering beside the tall armchair.

'What is it, Carmelita?'

'*De koffie is klaar.* I serve it for your visitors now?'

'*Nee, ik doe het zelf.*' Then switching back to English, she went on, 'You can go now. And I will see you at five o'clock.' She smiled at the carer and waited until she had pulled the door closed behind her. 'She's such a help to me,' she went on. 'I don't know how I would manage without her.' She briefly closed her eyes. '"*De koffie is klaar*". Do you know that phrase?'

'The coffee is ready?' Anna recalled the phrase from her childhood visits to Holland, remembering the warm feeling she used to have when her Dutch grandmother served coffee from the pot brewing on the stove. She felt her cheeks grow hot and exchanged a brief glance with Kersen. It was too early in the conversation to start mentioning her father. She wanted to be sure this woman was her grandmother before she did.

'You know a very important phrase. We Dutch love our coffee,' Ilse Meijer said, and made her way carefully over to the small galley kitchen.

'*Kan ik u helpen?*' asked Kersten, getting up to offer to her a hand.

'*Nee, dank je,*' said Ilse, refusing, but Kersten persisted by following her into the kitchen, where the two of them continued to chatter away in Dutch. Anna frowned as she tried to guess what was being said. She caught one or two words she recognised but nothing that made any sense. It was frustrating, as they appeared to be having quite an intense conversation.

From her seat, she watched Ilse move about her kitchen, carefully pouring coffee from a glass filter jug into three small cups before gesturing to Kersten to take the tray.

Once they were settled with their coffee, Kersten took up the conversation in English. 'Mevrouw Meijer and I were just talking about how I used to visit with my mother when I was a little girl. I remember being excited about the sweets you kept for me in the bag beside your chair. You were always so kind to me.'

There was a pause while Kersten waited for Ilse to finish stirring her coffee. Then, smiling, Ilse raised her head. 'You are so like your mother. So tall, and you have the same-shaped face and fair hair. I used to tell her how you looked like her and that made her glad. I also told her how lucky she was to have you. I suppose I was envious of her, but never showed it. I would have liked a little girl, you see, but it wasn't to be.' Her wistful eyes drifted to Anna.

Anna wondered what she was thinking and cleared her throat nervously. If she was going to say anything, now was the time. 'Mevrouw Meijer,' she began. Suddenly, addressing her formally felt all wrong and she had an inexplicable urge to call her Oma. She swallowed the urge away and instead said, 'You did have a child, didn't you?'

Something like suspicion mixed with confusion crossed Ilse Meijer's face and Anna instantly regretted her words. 'I didn't mean to upset you. But it's true, isn't it?'

'Is that why you came here?' The cup rattled as the old lady tried to steady it with trembling fingers.

'Yes. It is,' said Anna firmly, feeling more brave. 'Mevrouw Meijer, I have something to show you.' Her heart began to pound as she reached into her bag for her purse and brought out the peacock-blue scarf, which she unfolded on her knee. Then she placed the scarf and its contents on the table between them. Ilse put her hand to her mouth and

stared at the little crooked medallion nestled in the folds of
the fabric.

'This,' Anna said, with a sharp intake of breath, 'belonged to
your son. But I think you already know that. You gave it to him
when he was a baby.' It was a guess, but she was certain it was
correct.

Ilse's creased face went very pale as she slowly reached out
to pick up the silver medallion. Her hand trembled as she held
it up close to her face to examine it, twisting and turning it over
and over. 'It's just as I remember it. I never thought I would ever
see this again,' she said quietly, as though talking to herself. 'But
I don't understand why you have it... what are you telling me?'

'That I'm your granddaughter.' Anna's voice was unsteady
and she pursed her lips in an attempt to prevent the rush of
emotion rising high in her chest.

'*Een kleindochter*... a granddaughter.' Ilse Meijer fixed her
blue eyes on Anna's face, as if she couldn't believe what she'd
just heard. 'Come here,' she said. Anna rose to her feet so she
could lean down to embrace her. It felt awkward and unfamiliar
to be hugging this stranger to her, but also oddly comforting.
After a long moment like this, she gently let go.

'Mevrouw Meijer—'

'Please call me Ilse.'

'Ilse,' Anna repeated, trying her name out for real. 'I need to
tell you why I came here and not my father. It should be my
father sitting here having this conversation with you. He
tracked you down, and even bought a ticket to come and see
you. But... he never had a chance to. I'm afraid Dad died before
he was able to.' Her breath caught in her throat – she felt
terrible to be the bearer of such bad news.

'You are saying... he is dead?' Ilse leant forward a little, and,
seeing her clear blue eyes shine with tears, Anna was over-
whelmed with sadness.

'He fell dangerously ill with pneumonia and never recovered. He was abroad at the time... it was all so sudden... I'm sorry,' she said haltingly, as raw memories of the past weeks came flooding back.

Ilse reached over and laid a bony hand on Anna's. 'How terrible for you to lose your father so young. Were you very close?'

Anna didn't know how to reply. Shouldn't she be the one comforting this woman who had just learnt that she'd lost her only child, even though she had given him away at birth? She couldn't allow herself to think that, so turned her attention to telling the story she'd been practising in her head, though it now came out differently to the way she'd intended. Instead of just recounting the events leading to his death, she felt compelled to talk about the father she loved and how much she missed him now he wasn't around. How he'd always been there for her, listening sympathetically whenever she'd a problem, but never criticising or telling her what she should do. The more she talked, the more she wanted to prove to Ilse that her son – Anna's father – had been a special man: kind, loving, patient, funny, hard-working, honest – and that he hadn't deserved to be rejected by his mother. But when it came to it, she was unable to accuse her grandmother for what she might have done. Suddenly, all that mattered was that she'd lost her dad.

All the time she was speaking, Ilse didn't take her eyes away from Anna's face. When Anna had finished, she nodded sadly, then looked down at the medallion. 'It means a lot to me that he kept it all this time. It's a miracle to see it again.' Wistfully, she rubbed the sixpence between her finger and thumb, before holding it out. 'Here, it's yours now. You must keep it.'

Anna was surprised by this gesture and refused to take it. 'Surely you want it back after all you've been through?'

'No. I gave it away when I gave up my baby.' Ilse spoke more firmly now. 'I'm sure he would have wanted you to have it.'

Tears welled up in her eyes as Anna took the necklace and laid it back on the scarf. She knew her grandmother was right.

'What about you, Anna? Tell me something about yourself. Do you have any brothers or sisters?'

Anna's face softened as she shook her head. She didn't know where to begin, so Ilse prompted her by asking about her childhood. And so Anna told Ilse how she had grown up in Oxford, the only child of an academic father and schoolteacher mother, how she had left home at eighteen to go to university to study English, and on to London to work and live. She considered whether to mention Hugo, but somehow it didn't seem relevant.

When Kersten's mobile pinged loudly, all three women glanced towards it. 'Excuse me,' Kersten said apologetically, quickly glancing down at the message. 'It's my son, Luuk. He's downstairs. Anna, why don't you stay a while longer? You can call us when you're ready.'

'May I, Mevrouw— Ilse?' said Anna, feeling she had so much more to learn about her grandmother's past.

'*Natuurlijk*. We still have so much to talk about,' she said, echoing Anna's own thoughts.

FORTY-FIVE

ILSE

Ilse stood by the window, watching the snowflakes falling more thickly than they had all day. It was getting dark and still her mother hadn't returned with the midwife. *What can have taken her so long?* She gasped in a breath as another contraction started up, forcing her to lean heavily against the window frame.

'I'm here!' called a voice from the hallway, followed by the click of the door closing. Then another voice. 'Lies, go and put a pan of water on the stove and bring some towels.'

Marisa, her mother's friend and the local midwife, who lived two doors away, came bustling into the room. 'Ilse, what are you doing down here? You should be in bed where you'll be more comfortable,' she scolded.

Ilse wasn't listening. She had moved to the armchair and was gripping the back of it tightly as another wave of pain broke over her. 'When will it ever stop?' she wailed at Marisa through her tears.

'Just hold on. The worst will soon be over.' Marisa rubbed her back as she looked around the room. 'I see there's a divan bed. Perhaps it's best to make you comfortable in here.'

Ilse groaned, but didn't protest. She waited till Marisa had finished plumping up cushions and smoothing out the eiderdown, before gratefully lowering herself onto the bed. *If only this nightmare would stop*, she thought, as the pain grew in intensity.

'Mama.' Ilse reached out a hand to her mother, who had appeared at the door with a pile of towels. She handed them to Marisa, saying she'd bring the hot water presently, and went over to her daughter, who lay with her hand across her brow.

'Mama, am I making the right decision?' Ilse said, turning her face to her.

'Shh, not now. Just concentrate on what you need to do. We can talk about things later.'

'I'm scared...'

'There's nothing to be scared about. It's all perfectly normal.' Her mother's dear face swam in and out of view as Ilse succumbed to the next contraction.

It was nearing midnight when the room was filled with cries of Ilse's newborn son. Ilse lay back, exhausted from her exertions, relieved the pain was finally at an end.

Marisa appeared at her side, cradling the crying baby, which she'd wrapped snugly in a blanket knitted by Ilse's mother. 'Do you want to hold him?'

'Of course,' said Ilse, surprised Marisa was even asking, and held out her arms to receive her son. As soon as he was in her arms, he ceased his crying. In wonderment, she gently parted the sides of the blanket so she could glimpse the tiny face and the bright unfocused eyes that seemed to search out her own. She studied them, trying to make out their colour, and settled on dark grey. *Weren't newborn babies' eyes meant to be blue*, she wondered, as her eyes assessed the perfectly formed face, the rosebud mouth, and up to the top of his head to gaze at the dark, downy hair. Then, loosening the blanket a little further, she pushed her finger against the baby's tight little fist. Unable to stop herself smiling, she watched as long baby fingers grabbed onto her own with a strength that took her breath away.

The agonising doubt that had tortured her all these months, that the baby she was carrying could be Rudi's... finally, she could put it to rest. Seeing the fingers, and the delicate features, so familiar, confirmed what Ilse had hardly dared hope for. There was no doubt in her mind that Levi was the father of her child. But after months without any definitive news of his whereabouts, Ilse had no choice but to accept Levi was dead. Tears rolled down her face as the realisation hit her that this tiny defenceless human being would never know his father. She lifted him up to kiss the top of his soft head and breathe in his warm newborn scent.

'What a sweet little thing,' said her mother, moving in to take a closer look.

Ilse wiped her tears away and nodded. 'I suppose they all are at this age.'

'Not always,' came Marisa's voice from across the room, where she was cleaning and tidying things up. 'But mothers always love their babies, whatever they look like.'

Ilse tried to smile, but Marisa's words stung. She hadn't been expecting to fall so completely in love with this little human being who so reminded her of the man she had loved and lost. More tears cascaded down her cheeks.

'Here, let me take him. I expect he'll be wanting a feed,' said Marisa briskly.

Reluctantly, Ilse handed over her baby. Marisa laid him in a makeshift crib she'd fashioned from the bottom drawer of the desk, then left the room to go and prepare his first bottle.

The baby began to cry, a soft mewling sound that was unbearable to Ilse's ears.

'Mama, bring him back. He needs me.'

'Are you sure?' said her mother uncertainly.

'He's my baby. Of course I'm sure.'

When Marisa returned with the bottle, she looked taken aback to find Ilse with the baby and tried to take him from her.

'No, Marisa. I will feed him.'

She named him Paul and he remained with her for two days and two nights, while she fed and changed him and tried to commit every little bit about him to memory – his little face that crumpled just before he cried, the snuffling sounds he made when he latched on to his bottle, his sweet baby smell – these were the things she would miss most.

At the end of the second day, and minutes before she handed him over to the woman who had come to take him to his new home, she came to a decision. Unfastening the necklace that she'd worn ever since Levi had lovingly secured it round her neck, she folded it into the peacock-blue scarf Connie had given her the last time she'd seen her. It felt right to do so, having lost first Levi, then Connie, whom she hadn't seen since that fateful night. She tucked the treasured package into the blanket her baby was wrapped in, hoping that eventually he would work out that it had come from his mama. She looked down at the sweet sleeping face of her baby and gently kissed him, her heart breaking in the knowledge this was the last time she would ever see him.

Later, as her mother sat comforting her, she berated herself for not slipping a note in with the precious gift. She hadn't expected to be so tormented with doubt over her decision to give up her baby boy.

'I can't bear the idea that he'll go to a family who won't love him the way I do. Poor little thing, he doesn't deserve this.'

Her mother's voice was firm, but kind. 'Ilse, I know it's hard for you, but it would be a lot harder if you were to keep him.

Apart from the burden of a bringing up a child on your own, you'd have to face people's disapproval. There's not a lot of sympathy for babies born to single mothers, especially those babies fathered by Allied soldiers who left Holland as soon the war was over. Now I know that wasn't true of you and your young man, but still. You know how the Dutch like to judge. Little Paul will be better off growing up in a family with two parents who care for him.'

Ilse listened, wanting to believe her mother but not quite managing to.

Her mother went on, 'You'll be able to finish off your studies, have a social life. Maybe you will even meet someone new—'

'I don't want to meet anyone new,' Ilse said sharply. 'Levi was the love of my life. Had he lived, I know he would have come to find me and been the father I want for my son.'

They talked on, until Ilse was exhausted with it all. Eventually she accepted that she couldn't give her child the life he deserved and that giving him away was the right thing to do. With Levi gone, she had to think about her own future, and that didn't include looking after a child. She needed to let him go.

Three weeks later she was back in the lecture theatre at Leiden University, on her way to obtaining a medical qualification to practise as a doctor. At first, she found it hard to focus on her studies and baby Paul was never far from her thoughts. It was small solace to learn that he was settling in with his adopted family in a small town in Friesland, to the north of Amsterdam. It had been her mother's doing. She'd spoken with Clara, who knew a couple who were unable to have children and longed for a baby. Clara promised to visit from time to time so she could report back on how the boy was faring.

Alone at night in her room that she rented in the centre of town, Ilse would write in her diary, telling him what she was up to and how much she loved him. It was the only way she could think of to keep his memory alive. She kept her diary locked in her desk drawer, hopeful for the day that he came looking for her.

FORTY-SIX

Ilse was in her usual spot in the library, surrounded by textbooks, as she crammed for her anatomy exam. She liked to arrive as soon as the doors opened and, after taking only a short break for lunch, she would be back at her desk, where she would stay for the rest of the day. She was in her third year and her marks had been good so far, but she couldn't afford to slacken her pace now. Anatomy was one of the topics she least enjoyed and if she failed this exam, it would mean a resit, just when she needed to be focusing on the rest of her course.

It was 4 p.m. when Ilse closed the book she'd been reading and rubbed her eyes. She was tired, but decided to take a quick break and go down to the coffee bar on the second floor.

The place was filling up with students who had a similar idea and she bumped into Tina, the girl she shared digs with. Days often went past when they didn't see each other, but they were friendly enough.

'How's it going?' said Tina, edging forward in the queue for the counter.

'So-so. I just need to keep drumming the facts into my head

if I have a chance of passing. I'll be pleased when the exams are over.' Ilse moved forward to stand next to her.

'Me too. Then we can party,' said Tina with a grin. They arrived at the head of the queue and she ordered them both a coffee, Ilse promising she'd pay next time, and they found an empty table. They chatted for a while about their plans for the end of term, until Ilse said she ought to be getting back to her revision. She was taking a last sip of her coffee and had her back turned to the entrance to the coffee bar, so didn't see the tall young woman come up behind her.

'Oh, I forgot to mention – your friend came to the house looking for you just before I left for my tutorial,' said Tina, looking past Ilse. 'She's here now.'

Ilse swivelled round and gasped. A sudden flashback to the night Levi was arrested zigzagged through her mind as she stood up, almost knocking her chair over. The night they'd last seen each other.

'They told me at the library I could probably find you here. I've been looking all over for you,' said Connie with a broad grin on her face.

'Connie, I can't believe it's you.' Ilse couldn't take her eyes off her friend, whom she hadn't seen in more than two years. She looked even taller than she remembered, if that were possible, and wore her hair longer, in a chignon at her neck. They wrapped their arms round each other tightly, as if they never wanted to let go.

'I wanted to come sooner, but I couldn't leave the baby. It was Rik's idea to have my mother look after her while I came and surprised you.'

Tina stood up. 'I'll, er, leave you to it. See you later, Ilse?'

'Yes, sorry, Tina. I'll catch up with you when I get back.' Then she said to Connie, 'I was on my way back to the library. I'm revising for my end-of-year exams, but they're not for another week and I could do with a break. Come with me and I'll fetch my books. We can talk on the way.'

They set off up the stairs.

'It's so good to see you,' Ilse said, touching Connie's arm as if she wanted to make sure she was real.

'And so much to catch up on. Listen, I thought I could stay over. I'm happy to doss down on the floor, like old times,' Connie said with a laugh, then turned to gaze at the oil paintings of past luminaries of the university lining the walls. Sighing, she went on, 'I've missed the old place so much.'

They arrived at the library and Ilse asked Connie to wait while she collected her books.

She couldn't quite believe how long it was since they'd last seen each other. They'd kept in touch, exchanging letters in which Ilse learnt that Connie had gone into hiding for the rest of the war and for some weeks after. Rik had advised her to stay away from Hilversum, in case someone who didn't know her true role as a resistance worker reported her for collaborating with the enemy. He'd wanted to protect her from the very real possibility of being shamed in public by having her head shaved. It was a tense time. Months had passed when the two women weren't in touch, apart from a short note from Ilse sharing the news about the birth of her baby. Connie promised to come and visit, but soon got swept up with her job working at a refugee centre. Then last year, Connie had written to say that she and Rik had got married and she was expecting a baby. Ilse had wanted to be happy after all Connie had been through, but she found it hard, having so recently given up her own baby.

Seeing Connie stirred up the old emotions she thought she'd managed to bury, but she couldn't help but be delighted to see her friend after so long. It didn't take much persuading for her to take the evening off, and they went to their old haunt, a tiny café bar tucked down a side street, where they shared a bottle of wine and a plate of cheese and sausage and talked late into the night about the old days when they'd both been students at Leiden.

'Will you come back to Leiden to study?' asked Ilse.

'Not at the moment, but I don't want to rule it out. It's probably not what you want to hear, but it's hard looking after a toddler.' Connie looked embarrassed, as if she'd said too much. She changed the subject. 'I admit there was another reason for coming to see you. I have some information about Levi and wanted to tell you face to face.'

Ilse thought she knew everything there was to know. Some months after the war, she'd received confirmation that Levi had been taken to Kamp Amersfoort and that there was a strong likelihood that he had perished inside the camp. 'But Levi is dead. What more is there to know?' she asked, bracing herself for more bad news.

'Something Rik has only just found out. It turns out that no records were kept about Jewish prisoners at Kamp Amersfoort. That means we can't be sure that Levi was among those who were executed there.'

A tiny flame of hope ignited inside Ilse. 'Are you saying he survived?'

'Not exactly, but it is the last piece of information anybody has about the fate of those Jewish prisoners. It may be possible that he was one of the lucky ones who escaped.'

It was almost too much for Ilse to bear after all the heartache she'd suffered. She had given away her baby because she'd believed Levi had died. How could she ever forgive herself if he now turned up alive?

'No, I don't believe it,' she said firmly. 'After all this time, wouldn't he have tried to find me?'

'There may have been a good reason why he didn't. It's impossible to say.'

'What do you mean, Connie?'

Connie shook her head. 'I wish I knew more, but there's so

little information. It was wrong of me to get your hopes up, but you seem so sad. Is there nothing I can do to make you happy again?'

Ilse could see that Connie was well intentioned, but what could she do, if all it meant was giving her false hope?

'You're back home. That's the best thing that's happened to me in a long time,' she said, and gave her friend a sorrowful smile.

FORTY-SEVEN

ANNA

The doors of the lift slid open with a ping. Anna stepped out into the lobby to see Luuk sitting by himself on one of the purple armchairs. He looked anxious and immediately stood up to greet her.

'Oh, Luuk, you stayed,' she said, relieved to see him. 'It's true, Ilse Meijer is my grandmother,' she added with a laugh, and let him hug her.

Outside, it was noticeably warmer than when they'd first arrived. Anna noticed the birdsong and scent from a nearby rosebush in full bloom. Inhaling the sweet delicate fragrance, she felt as if a weight had been lifted from her shoulders.

'Where's Kersten?' she said, glancing up at Luuk.

'I took her to the station. She needed to get back home for something or other. But we can stay.'

'Don't you need to get back yourself?'

'No, I took the day off. I suspected this wouldn't be a quick visit.' He squeezed her hand, which sent a shiver of pleasure through her. *Stop this*, she told herself, and quietly extracted her hand from his. It was pointless getting her hopes up when she knew she was returning to her old life in London in less than twenty-four hours.

Luuk put his hands in his pockets and went on, 'While I was waiting, I walked over to the town centre and found a nice-looking restaurant. I don't know about you, but I'm starving. And you can tell me all about your *grandmother*,' he said with a teasing smile.

Yes, it is unbelievable that Ilse Meijer is my grandmother, she mused to herself, as she fell into step beside him. It was turning out to be the most extraordinary day.

The restaurant was situated on the leafy market square, with customers seated outside under a blue-and-white-striped awning. It was a busy lunchtime, but Luuk and Anna managed to grab the last remaining outdoor table. Their waiter came with a jug of water and two menus and took their order for drinks before leaving them to make their choice.

'Steak and salad for me,' said Luuk, after glancing at the menu. 'What do you fancy?'

Anna couldn't make up her mind, so Luuk advised her to try a platter of North Sea fish, a Dutch speciality.

'So, what makes you so sure we have found your grand-mother?' said Luuk, once they had placed their order and the waiter had brought their drinks.

'I showed her the necklace and she immediately recognised it, so I knew it had to be her. I knew I should be angry with her for even contemplating giving up her baby... giving up Dad. But hers was such a sad story, I ended up wanting to comfort her. It's so odd, feeling that way about a woman I'd only just met. And she wasn't at all what I'd been expecting.' Anna paused to think about how welcoming Ilse had been and her surprise at discovering that Anna was English. And it pleased her that Ilse had so obviously made an effort with her appearance – for her sake, Anna wanted to believe.

'What had you been expecting?' said Luuk, leaning forward and touching Anna's arm. She looked up, not realising she'd become lost in thought.

'I'd built her up in my mind as an embittered old woman and in denial about the past. I was also worried she'd be too forgetful to remember much. But I couldn't have been more wrong. After the initial shock of discovering I was her grand-daughter, she opened up to me. It seemed like she genuinely wanted me to understand what she'd gone through and how hard her decision had been.'

Anna took a large sip of her wine for courage, before contin-uing with Ilse's story: the hardship she'd gone through to put food on the table to stay alive, her anguish at leaving her elderly parents behind to cope for themselves and the miracle of meeting and falling in love with Levi, the Jewish boy in hiding from the Germans in her friends' attic, only to be discovered and deported to a concentration camp, where he had died.

Anna broke off as the waiter appeared with their food and placed a large platter of several varieties of fish in front of her.

'I can't eat all this,' she whispered to Luuk in dismay. It didn't seem right to be eating so much food when her mind was full of the deprivations and hardship her grandparents had experienced. 'Can you help me out?'

'Eat what you can. You'll feel better with something inside you,' Luuk said gently, and speared a piece of smoked eel with his fork.

Anna ate little and toyed with her food, appreciating that Luuk didn't make an issue of it. The little she did try was deli-cious and she made a point of saying so, before pushing her plate aside and pouring herself a glass of water. Her head ached with Ilse's story and she was impatient to share more of it with Luuk.

'Remember I was quite upset when you first told me about that article you found about Ilse enjoying herself at university? Well, I know now that her heart must have been breaking because the father of her baby and the love of her life – for that's how she described Levi – was dead.'

Hot tears pricked at Anna's eyes as she found herself grieving for Levi, the grandfather she would never meet. She quickly wiped them away. 'I wish I'd known my grandfather. He sounded such a wonderful, kind and loving man. It's heart-breaking to think that he never saw Ilse again after he was arrested, and never knew he'd fathered a son. I can't imagine how Ilse felt, discovering she was pregnant and all alone. She told me it was her mother who urged her to give up her baby, and that it was commonplace then for single mothers to give their babies for adoption, especially if the father was absent or had died. You've probably heard the term "liberation baby" for the offspring of wartime liaisons.'

'Yes, I have,' said Luuk, nodding.

'Well, it was frowned upon for a woman to bring up a baby outside marriage on her own. But who are we to judge, when we have no idea what it was like to live through a war when ordinary people were starved, persecuted and sent to their deaths for no reason other than they weren't part of Hitler's grand scheme for his so-called Aryan race?'

Anna drank deeply from her glass of water before going on, 'It felt like Ilse was begging me for forgiveness. And I'm ashamed to say I'd been quite quick to judge her. It must have taken considerable courage to part with her baby. She just did what she believed was right.'

Luuk was listening intently, and looked thoughtful. 'Women like Ilse were dealt a bad hand because of the war. It was a tragedy, and there were so many in her position. Strong and brave in the face of adversity, and not afraid to put themselves at risk. There were also many women resistance fighters who used their sex to their advantage. I've been reading about Hannie Schaft – she was known as "the girl with the red hair" who became a symbol of female resistance after the war. She was involved in the resistance with her friends, Freddie and Truus Oversteegen. They were just teenagers, but they bravely plotted to kill Nazi officers and collaborators. They weren't the only ones. Many Dutch women were involved in small resistance acts – working as couriers delivering vital information, or leading young Jewish children to safety before the Nazis could get their hands on them. It's an aspect of my research that fascinates me. But I digress...'

'No, not at all. It's fascinating,' said Anna, intrigued by what he had told her. 'Ilse talked about her best friend and her resistance work to save Jews from the Nazis. Her name was Connie. Was that your grandmother's name?'

'Yes, it was,' said Luuk. 'I'd already guessed it had to be her, even though it's a common enough name – and everything we now know confirms she must have been the woman who put her life at risk for Ilse. What else did Ilse say?'

'That it was Connie who brought Levi to her parents' house in Hilversum next door to a sanatorium, which was considered to be safe from the Germans. They never went near the place for fear of catching tuberculosis. And it was Connie who tried, but sadly failed, to help Levi escape when two Nazis came searching for him. She was a member of a local resistance group and married the man who helped her go into hiding herself. Did you really not know any of this?'

'I knew my grandfather had had dealings with the resistance,' Luuk said, 'but he never talked about it. And I had no idea about my grandmother's involvement either. Neither of them ever spoke of the war, so the subject never came up. When I was a teenager, I remember doing a project on the Second World War and I thought it would be brilliant to get a first-hand account from her, but she refused to talk about how it was for her. She said her memories were still too painful. She could be quite blunt, and when she was like that I knew I shouldn't probe. I never asked her again after that. I wish I had. Ironic, isn't it, that I ended up taking such an interest in Dutch women in the resistance but never knew that about my own grandmother?'

Anna smiled. 'It's sad that so many people have never wanted to talk about their war experiences. I'm so grateful for all you've done, Luuk. If it hadn't been for your efforts to uncover my family history, I wouldn't be here now.'

Luuk reached for her hand, interlinking his fingers with hers. 'And I'm grateful you came back, or I might never have discovered the truth about my own family.'

FORTY-EIGHT

It was early evening when they arrived back at Kersten's apartment to find her kneeling on the floor, surrounded by piles of papers and cuttings from old newspapers and magazines. By her side were two empty cardboard boxes and another from which she was lifting items onto the floor.

'What's she doing?' Anna asked Luuk, inhaling the musty scent associated with old things that have been locked away for a long time.

'Looks like she's finally decided to go through Oma's things,' said Luuk. He strode over to look and began speaking rapidly in Dutch as he pointed at first one item, then another. Kersten replied in even faster Dutch. Anna heard nothing much more than the word 'Oma', which cropped up several times, but it was enough for her to have a pretty good idea what they were discussing.

When they had finished, Kersten sat back on her haunches and pushed her reading glasses onto the top of her head. Her face glowed as she beamed at Anna. 'Isn't it incredible that Connie and Ilse were friends? I've suspected as much all along, and after I left Ilse's, I couldn't wait to get straight back home and look through the boxes. I've been meaning to fetch them up from the basement for ages, but never got round to it. The task was simply too daunting. These are only some of them. I never imagined I'd find such a treasure trove, and I've only just begun. Here, take a look at these.' She picked up two yellowing, tattered cards. 'These are original identity cards from the war. And this is my mother, Connie,' she said, with a look of pride, as she pointed to the photograph on top.

Anna looked at the black-and-white picture of a young fair-haired woman with her face turned slightly away from the camera, and with two thumbprints in the right-hand corner. The family likeness with both Kersten and Luuk was striking.

'But I don't know about the other one,' Kersten went on. 'Do you have any idea who it might be, Luuk?'

Luuk took a closer look, frowning as he peered at the photograph. 'I can't be certain, but I think this one is a forgery.' The card bore a picture of a woman with wavy black hair with a scarf tied at the neck. 'I wouldn't be surprised if this was a man disguised as a woman. The search for people working for the resistance was so intense that disguise was used as a way to evade detection by the Nazis. I only wish I'd been able to ask her about it when she was still alive.'

'I'm not sure she'd have told you anything,' said Kersten with a sigh. 'But it is odd that she still had it in her possession. Why do you think that is?'

A thought occurred to Anna. 'Perhaps she was intending to give it to Levi on the night she was meant to bring him to safety. If that's the case, it's rather touching that she held on to it all that time.' She kept gazing at the card with an aching sadness as she thought of what might have been. Next to her, she felt Luuk slide an arm round her waist, and was comforted that he understood how much this discovery meant to her.

Gradually, the three of them managed to sort the papers into some kind of order. Much of it was of little importance; an accumulation of items that only had meaning to their owner. Connie had either been reluctant to part with them, or simply hadn't got round to getting rid of the clutter.

Anna had just finished leafing through a pile of old Dutch magazines dating back to the 1950s, when she spotted a slim photo album lying at the bottom of one of the boxes. It was in poor condition, worn at the corners and held together with a faded pink ribbon, frayed at the ends. She carefully lifted the album out and opened it at the first page. Several black-and-white photos fluttered into her lap. She studied the solemn faces staring out at her and tried to place when the photos might have been taken from the stiff formal clothes and head-coverings, reminiscent of the Dutch national costume her father had once shown her in a magazine.

Putting them back at the pages where they had fallen out, she started at the front and turned each stiff black page, all separated by thin yellowing transparent paper. The first few pictures looked as if they had been taken by a professional photographer and showed women in long evening dresses, some wearing fur stoles round their shoulders, while the men were dressed in dark suits and white tie. *Leiden 1950. Ilse (in het midden)* she read, under one photo that took up the whole page. The photograph had been taken from above, looking down onto an auditorium of young people dressed in academic gown attire with attentive expressions on their faces as they watched or listened to whatever or who was out of shot. Anna scanned the photograph and recognised her grandmother, sitting right in the middle with a radiant smile on her face.

'What's that you've found?' said Luuk, crouching down beside her. 'Mum, come and look.' He took the album from Anna and laid it on the floor so the three of them could all see.

'I think it's my grandmother's graduation ceremony, when she qualified as a doctor. Why do you think Connie had it?'

'I imagine Ilse wanted to show Connie how much she'd achieved after everything she'd been through,' said Luuk.

'That's me and that's my kitten I was given for my third birthday,' said Kersten with a laugh, leaning across Anna. The little girl in the photo had curly white-blonde hair and was struggling to hold on to the tiny striped kitten that looked intent on escaping her clutches. There were three or four of Kersten as a young girl, a little taller in each one. Then, over the page, there were several pictures, neatly stuck in, of a man and woman and two children on the deck of a boat, a view of fields and a church spire in the distance.

'So Mama did have photos of our holidays in Friesland. I can't say I remember ever seeing these,' Kersten said. 'Anna, look here. This little boy is your father.'

'I was looking at pictures just like these with my mother recently,' said Anna. 'There was one of a family group with my dad at the centre. Now I know for sure who the adults are, and that you were the little girl.'

She looked intently at the boy in the picture, who had a children's fishing net in one hand and proudly held up a jam jar with his catch in the other. He had a shock of black hair and a cheeky grin. Beside him stood the same curly-haired girl as in Anna's picture, who had her head turned towards him. The next showed the boy, wearing a sailor's cap, at the wheel of the boat, concentrating on the direction they appeared to be going.

'He was too young to be in control of the boat but he loved to pretend, until his father started allowing him to steer. He must have been five in that photo. Those were wonderful holidays.' Kersten sighed.

'He looks happy,' Anna said simply, trying to keep her emotions in check. Seeing so many photos of her dad as a little boy, she was struck by how sweet and innocent he appeared. She fervently hoped he had been as happy as he looked.

'Oh, he was. There was no doubt about that. His parents

loved him dearly,' said Kersten, as she pointed out more photos from the holidays she'd shared with the family.

Anna took the album from her, eager to commit these early photographs to memory. There weren't many, a reflection of how few photos people used to take in those days, but the more she looked the more she pondered on their significance. 'It's strange how your mother became friendly with my father's family. I can't work out why that was,' she said out loud, more to herself than to Kersten.

'I'm afraid I can't answer that. All I know was that we were friends of the family from when I was a little girl.'

Anna nodded, but she wasn't satisfied with Kersten's explanation. It seemed too much of a coincidence. Did Connie have a reason to keep in touch with her friend's child after he'd been adopted? Dismissing the thought, she asked if she might take one or two photos of her father as a keepsake.

'Of course! Let me find you an envelope to put them in. Take as many as you like,' said Kersten.

Anna had reached the last page of the album. She saw a picture of a young man and woman standing side by side, dressed in their finery. She was carrying a small bouquet of flowers; he had a matching corsage pinned to his jacket. Anna caught her breath. There was no mistaking that the woman was Ilse. Below the photo was a date: *September 1950*.

'This looks like a wedding photo. My grandmother never mentioned to me that she was married. I wonder if it was someone she met at university. Kersten, do you know who the man in this photo is?'

'No, I'm afraid I don't. My mother never mentioned anything to me – but then why would she? I was only four at the time. It seems you still have a lot to discover about your grandmother.'

FORTY-NINE

The flight back to London was delayed due to bad weather, adding to Anna's already mounting anxiety about flying. Staring up at the departures board, which showed the new departure time as two hours later than scheduled, she realised that she wouldn't be home before midnight. It was like a bad omen, she thought, before telling herself to stop catastrophising. There was nothing she could do except calm down and wait.

The departures lounge was teeming with people, but eventually she settled in a plastic seat with a cup of tea, facing the window, with a view over the tarmac and stationary planes in the pouring rain. Closing her eyes, she wished she hadn't been in such a hurry to rush through security after Luuk had offered to wait with her when it looked as if her flight would be late.

They had in fact already said their goodbyes the night before, standing at the door of Kersten's apartment when he was about to go home. Kersten had gone to bed, saying she needed to be up early for a business meeting, though Anna suspected she wanted to give them some space to be together. After all Kersten had done for her, Anna felt a pang of guilt that she was going to disappoint her.

There was an awkward pause, when neither said anything but just looked intently into each other's eyes. It would have been so easy to fall into Luuk's arms and forget about Hugo and work and London. Instead, she gently took his hands while she gave the little speech she'd prepared in her head but had still been dreading.

'Truly, this has been the most incredible few days and none of it would have happened if it hadn't been for you. And to discover that our grandmothers were actually firm friends... it's been really special. I hope we'll keep in touch.' Anna's heart pounded, knowing her words sounded hollow.

Luuk dropped his hands, but kept his eyes locked on hers. 'It was special for me too, but this was never just about finding your grandmother. Sure, that was the connection, but I thought there was so much more between us. I got the impression you felt the same way, but perhaps I'm mistaken.' He sounded hurt, and turned away as if to go.

'Luuk, wait. If you think this is about Hugo, it's not. He and I... things haven't been great between us for a while. The minute I met you again I felt a rush of something I can't explain. I felt you understood me... perhaps I always did.'

'So what's stopping you?' Luuk raised an eyebrow, a familiar gesture that now filled her with sadness.

Anna couldn't bear to see the look of hope in his eyes. She had no choice but to let him down. 'I really like you, really I do, but my life is back in London. I can't just give it all up to be with you. It wouldn't... it couldn't work. Please understand.'

He shrugged. 'Of course it's impractical. But I never was a practical kind of guy. If you ever change your mind, please let me know.' He gave her a sweet lopsided smile, and then reached out to hug her. She slid her arms round his waist and thought, briefly, how warm and safe he made her feel.

'Tomorrow, I will collect you at eight,' Luuk said, after

breaking apart. 'I'll take you to the airport and we will say goodbye as friends.'

Anna nodded and pressed her lips together as she looked into his eyes. 'Thank you for being so understanding. And we will stay in touch. We have to, don't we? I seem to have more questions about my grandparents than when I arrived.' She laughed and he laughed with her, and briefly the tension between them melted away.

* * *

It was almost midnight when Anna arrived, exhausted, back at her flat. She'd tried to ring Hugo as soon as she'd landed, but his phone had gone to straight to voicemail. Assuming he must have gone to the pub, she'd thought nothing of it, but when she found the flat cold and in darkness she wondered where he'd got to. Flicking the heating switch to on, she grumbled to herself about how thoughtless he was and went to fill the kettle for tea. As she waited for it to boil, she was sure she heard more than one voice, and laughter, coming from outside the front door, and then the unmistakeable sound of a key grating in the lock. It could only be Hugo. Instantly she knew he was not alone.

'Shit, she must be back. You'd better not come in.' Hugo's whispered voice floated to her from the hallway.

Anna remained perfectly still, listening to the sounds of scuffles and the front door closing, and waited for Hugo to appear. When he did, she saw one side of his shirt was untucked. He hurriedly adjusted it.

'Who was that?' Anna asked nonchalantly, focusing her attention on pouring boiling water into her cup.

Hugo thrust a hand through his hair. 'Hon, I can explain. It's not—'

'—what I think it is? What is it then?' Anna leant back

against the kitchen counter, cup in hand, and gave him a long hard stare. 'Who is she?'

Hugo nervously shot a look behind him as if he expected the woman to appear. 'Nobody. I mean, she's a friend of Olly's.'

'Olly? With the deep-sea diving website?' It was Hugo's latest obsession; he was forever poring over pictures of pristine white beaches against impossibly blue skies, underwater shots of exotic marine life and people on boats smiling and waving at the camera. And she knew he hankered after joining his university dropout friend Olly, who ran a diving school in the Philippines.

Hugo's face lit up. 'Yeah... you remember! Look, I'm sorry, hon. We only went out for a few drinks and she's flying back to the Philippines tomorrow. Hon, don't look at me like that. It's nothing.'

'Let's sit down. I think we've got a lot to talk about.'

In the end it was a relief to have it out.

They talked deep into the night like they hadn't done in years. Anna realised she'd been as much to blame for the failure of their relationship as he had. The signs had been there for a long time but neither had been prepared to admit it to the other. Hugo had been suffering from the pressure of his Boston job for months, thinking he had to keep at it because the money was good and that Anna expected it of him. Being fired had been painful, but the longer he had been out of corporate life, the less he wanted to be a part of it again. Anna simply hadn't realised it when she'd been badgering him to get another job – she'd always assumed he was driven by the need to succeed, but nothing could have been further from the truth. He was serious about taking the gap year he'd never had and intended to spend time travelling around Southeast Asia, maybe even getting that diving qualification she'd always been so scornful about.

Anna was pleased for him, and even forgave him for his lack of interest in the things that were important to her. She skated over the details of her latest trip, omitting to mention how Luuk had made it happen, because it was best that way. It was pointless expecting Hugo to show an interest in her search for her father's family – it was too late for that now. She'd already made up her mind to move on.

FIFTY

As soon as Anna told Caro she had split from Hugo, Caro insisted they spend a long weekend together and booked the next available Eurostar train from Paris.

'I know it was more about you than him, but it'll hit you harder if you're alone,' she said. 'Anyway, I haven't been back to London in ages for anything other than for work. We can do stuff, go to an exhibition, take a walk along the river. Please say yes.'

'Yes,' said Anna, happiness surging up inside her. It was impossible to feel anything else when she was in the company of her best friend.

Anna went to meet Caro from the train, and caught sight of her waving frantically as she came hurrying over the concourse pulling her small silver suitcase behind her.

'Anna!' she cried, letting go of her case so they could embrace. 'How long has it been? A month... two?'

'Too long. That's for sure,' said Anna with a laugh. 'You're looking great. Paris suits you.' She looked Caro up and down, taking in her blonde highlights and the crimson lipstick that matched her high-heeled shoes. 'Very Parisian,' she added.

Caro laughed. 'But, Anna, you don't look so bad for someone who's just ditched their boyfriend. Is there something you aren't telling me?'

'Nooo,' said Anna, feigning surprise at being asked. She didn't mind, but suspected it wouldn't be long before Caro started questioning her about Luuk.

They linked arms and walked away from the station, falling into easy conversation as if they'd never been apart.

It was five o'clock and Caro decreed it was time for a drink, and steered Anna towards a wine bar a stone's throw from the station. 'It's convenient for meetings when I come over on a flying visit,' she said over her shoulder as she pushed open the door.

They settled down at a quiet table with a bottle of Pinot Grigio. 'I want to know everything about your trip. Don't leave out a thing. Promise?' urged Caro, pouring them each a glass and handing one to Anna.

'Promise,' said Anna with a smile, and lifted her glass to Caro's. She needed no coaxing. She was relieved to have Caro to talk to; she knew she could tell her anything. They may not have seen much of one another recently, but she knew Caro was with her every step of the way.

Anna told Caro all about how her grandmother had had no choice but to give up her baby for adoption. 'And you say she never saw her baby again? That's so sad,' said Caro.

'What's even sadder is that she discovered from Connie that there were no records of Levi having died. By then it was too late – Ilse had already given up her baby and gone back to her studies. Just imagine the heartache if he'd unexpectedly turned up on her doorstep to find she'd given away their son. You know, it haunts me to think that he might have survived that awful concentration camp and that something else prevented him from reaching her.'

'Then you must find out,' said Caro directly. 'You said he

came from a family of well-known jewellers in Amsterdam. What did you say the family name was?'

'Abel. His name was Levi Abel.'

'Well, there you go. That's a start. Why don't we go back to yours and pick up a takeaway on the way? I think we might have a long evening ahead of us.'

Caro had passwords to several genealogy websites Anna hadn't even known existed. She had to try a few before she tracked down what she was looking for.

'Look here,' Caro said, and read from the screen. '"Abel Jewellery were a fine jewellery company, founded in 1885, based in the heart of Amsterdam. They were a successful Jewish business that traded up to the 1930s."' She broke off and looked at Anna, before saying, 'There's nothing to say what happened after that.' The rest of the text was written in Dutch, so Caro applied an online translator and read out the list of Abel Jewellery's prestigious clients, including the Dutch royal family. Abel necklaces and brooches had apparently been prized examples of rare gemstones set in gold and silver.

'What do you think of that then?' said Caro, grinning at Anna.

Anna couldn't resist a smile. 'If it's true that they are my family, it makes me incredibly proud to have Jewish roots. But let's not jump to conclusions.' She scanned the rest of the document till she found what she was looking for. It was a short entry stating that the company had ceased trading in 1938, after it had been vandalised and forcibly shut down by the Nazis.

'It's what I suspected. But is there nothing to suggest they started up again after the war?' asked Anna, desperate for confirmation.

Caro concentrated as she tapped away, looking for any evidence of Abel Jewellery after that date, but there was none.

'Don't be disappointed. I'm sure there must be more,' she said, with a quick glance at Anna. A few minutes later she directed her mouse at a website describing Birmingham's Jewellery Quarter.

'What's that to do with the Abels?' said Anna, suddenly weary of the lack of progress they were making.

'Shush. I've got a hunch about something,' said Caro, who was now staring intently at the screen. 'Now listen. "The Jewellery Quarter was a target of bombing raids by the German Luftwaffe during the Birmingham Blitz. There was a great deal of devastation, but many companies changed their operations to support the war effort, producing buckles and belts for soldiers' uniforms, and military insignia." And here's a list of jewellers involved. Look, right at the top – Joseph Abel.'

'But how do we know if that's anything to do with the Abels in Amsterdam?' said Anna, not wanting to get her hopes up.

'We don't, but many Jews fled their homeland and Birmingham was famous for its high-class jewellery. It's possible the family made it out of Amsterdam and restarted their business in Birmingham.' Caro kept scrolling for more evidence.

Anna was doubtful. 'I'm trying to see how Levi fits in to all this. Ilse met him towards the end of the war when he was in hiding. Why didn't he just go straight to Birmingham if his family were safely there?'

Caro stopped her search and pondered this thought a moment. 'I can't say, and I'm afraid I don't think there's much more I can do with the information here. But I do have a friend who works as an archivist in Birmingham. I'm sure she'll be able to help.'

Caro wanted to ring her friend right away; Anna had to remind her that it was past midnight. 'I don't think she'd appreciate a call this late, as much as I'd like to find out more. We both need a break. Let's call it a night and start again in the morning.'

. . .

But Anna was unable to drop off to sleep; she kept mulling over the possibility that her grandfather could still be alive and living in England. And if that were the case, did she have a whole new family she knew nothing about? The thought was both intriguing and exciting.

It was past nine the next morning when after spending a restless night she came to, and noticed Caro's voice coming from the spare room. She tiptoed over and found Caro sitting up in bed, talking into her phone. She smiled, and spoke to Anna in an excited whisper: 'It's Kelly, my friend the archivist. She's looking up some stuff for us.'

'I'll put the coffee on,' Anna mouthed back, unable to bear the suspense of waiting for Caro to tell her what might be bad news. But she'd hardly switched on the coffee machine before Caro came through, her phone clamped to her ear. 'Hang on a minute, while I tell Anna.' Then, turning to Anna, she went on, 'It's good news. Kelly tells me that Abel Jewellers in Birmingham specialised in gold and silver pieces. And this is the best bit – under the list of directors is one Levi Abel.'

'No! Is she sure?' said Anna, her heart starting to race. 'Is there any more information on him?'

Caro repeated her question into the phone and kept looking at Anna while she waited for the answer. 'She's looking it up on another database. It'll take a few minutes,' she whispered.

The coffee had finished brewing and Anna busied herself filling two mugs and topping them up with milk from the fridge.

Caro was still hanging on. It seemed to be taking an awfully long time, Anna thought, as she nervously handed Caro a mug.

'Ah... Right, I see... I'll tell her. Thanks a million, Kelly, you've been so helpful.' Caro switched off her phone and took a deep breath. 'What she says seems to fit, but it's not all good news.'

'What did she say?' said Anna with a feeling of growing unease.

'Levi Abel had a wife, Theresa, and one daughter, who was born in 1951. Her name's Joanna. He also had a sister, Rebecca, who was a non-executive director of the company.

But sadly, it seems that Levi, his wife and sister are no longer alive. Levi died in 1993. I'm so sorry. It's not what you wanted to hear.' She sat beside Anna and placed an arm round her.

'It's almost too much to take in. But how can we be sure this was my grandfather?' Having come this far, Anna couldn't bear to think it was all a waste of time.

'Well, the company is still trading, so they're bound to have records of past directors. There's an address and a telephone number on the website, so you can contact them,' said Caro, upbeat as ever.

Anna took a sip of the coffee, which made her feel a bit better. 'I wonder if his daughter, Joanna, works for the company. Maybe she's even a jeweller herself.'

'Exactly! I've a good feeling about her. I think she could be the one to settle your family roots once and for all.' Caro helped herself to more coffee and went to look out of the window. 'It's going to be a lovely day. Let's forget about all this for now and enjoy the rest of our time together.' She smiled at Anna. 'Oh, and you haven't yet told me if anything is going on between you and that Dutch guy. Remind me of his name... Luuk, was it?'

FIFTY-ONE

August 2001

'Mevrouw Meijer is waiting for you on the terrace. Go through the lounge, then the conservatory and the glass doors are in front of you.'

'Thank you,' said Anna to the woman on the desk, whom she recognised from her previous visit. Now she was here, alone this time, she felt apprehensive about meeting her grandmother in person again. It was a special day – Ilse's eightieth birthday – and the last thing Anna wanted to do was upset her, yet she feared that was what she was about to do.

Through the double doors, she could see her grandmother sitting by herself in the warm sunshine that caught the reddish glints of her neatly coiffed hair. She was wearing a blue dress and cream jacket that made her look younger than her eighty years. As before, Anna was struck by the effort she'd made with her appearance.

When Ilse caught sight of Anna coming through the glass doors, she began to get out of her chair, her face breaking into a smile.

'Stay sitting, Oma.' Anna surprised herself at how naturally she used the Dutch word. But her grandmother was already standing and holding out her arms.

'Happy birthday, Oma. You have a lovely day for it,' said Anna, accepting her embrace.

'And I insist we kiss three times. For luck,' said her oma, as she offered each cheek in turn. 'Come and sit down. The coffee will be here in a minute.'

'*De koffie is klaar,*' Anna said, sitting down beside her. 'I've been brushing up on my Dutch, but that's still my favourite phrase.'

They both laughed.

'Now, let me take a good look at you. There's something different about you. Is it your hair?'

'I had it cut before I came. It's shorter than I normally have it.' Self-consciously, Anna ran her fingers over her smooth bob, which wasn't to her liking. She was still annoyed that the hairdresser hadn't listened to her instruction to trim only a little off the ends.

'Well, it suits you and shows off your lovely face. Believe me, that's a good thing at your age.'

Anna was just wondering if now would be a good time to raise the subject that had filled her mind all morning, when a fresh-faced young woman in white uniform arrived with the coffee tray. She took her time pouring the coffee, adding milk and offering sugar, while Anna grew increasingly tense about the news she was about to impart. She waited till the attendant had gone back inside.

'Oma, I want to speak to you about something you said the last time I was here,' Anna began as she stirred her coffee.

'Oh, must we talk about the past on my birthday?' said Ilse, offering her a cinnamon biscuit. 'I'm so happy to be in the company of my delightful granddaughter. That's more than enough for an old woman.'

Anna swallowed nervously. She needed to have this conversation before they met the others for lunch. That, hopefully, would be the time for celebration. So she persisted. 'I wouldn't mention it, but there's something important I've found out that I think you should know.'

'I can see you're determined to tell me,' said her grandmother with a sigh, and lifted her coffee cup to her lips. 'What is it?'

'It's about Levi... my grandfather.' The words sounded strange said together, but saying them gave her a little frisson of pleasure.

'Levi? What more is there to say?' A look of worry crossed Ilse's face.

'You told me you thought that he must have died inside Kamp Amersfoort, even though there was no record of it. Well, I made a discovery that he did make it out, and emigrated to England after the war.'

'But that's impossible.' Ilse shakily replaced her cup and saucer on the table.

'No, it's absolutely true. A friend of mine showed me where to find the information on the internet. She worked out the connection between Levi's family and a jewellery company in Birmingham, and Levi's name was listed as one of the directors. I now know that his uncle arranged for his safe passage to England after the war. Because he had no other family left.'

Ilse shook her head sadly as she processed this information. 'Birmingham. Of course. I remember now. Levi's uncle left Amsterdam with his family when the Nazis made life impossible for them to stay. It was a mistake that his brother didn't join him. And for all these years I thought that Levi had perished, along with the rest of his family. Do you know anything more?'

Anna nodded. 'He had a sister, Rebecca, who joined him in Birmingham around the same time. Levi got married in 1949, and had a daughter, Joanna, in 1951. All his life he worked in his uncle's business, crafting high-value pieces from gold and silver.'

At this, a smile spread across Ilse's face. 'It gladdens me to hear that. He once showed me his drawings and they were very good, very original.' She gazed into the middle distance as if she could see them now. 'He will have been so pleased that Rebecca made it out of Amsterdam alive. She went into hiding, like Levi, and I always wondered what happened to her. But where did you find this out?'

'I spoke to his daughter, Joanna. She's a director of the company, which is still trading. I was nervous making the call, in case she wouldn't want to speak to me. But she was really friendly, after the shock of discovering I was her father's grand-daughter. She had no idea her father had a son. I asked her more questions and she told me that her father had been successful in the jewellery business, with a reputation for high-class jewellery. But she regretted never really knowing him as a person. He was a difficult man, quite distant towards his wife and daughter, and was always shutting himself away in his workshop. She knew little about his life during the war, only that he had suffered terrible traumas when he'd been inside the concentration camp. He never talked about what had happened to him, or anything else from that time.' Anna bit her lip as she waited for Ilse's reaction.

'You talk as if he is no longer alive. Is that the case?' Ilse's face was still.

'I'm afraid so. He died a few years ago. I didn't want to upset you...'

'No, my dear Anna. You haven't upset me. It's too late for that. Nothing good would have come of Levi coming to look for me. By then, my darling baby was settled with his new family, and I was studying to be a doctor. I had my own life.' She looked away with an expression of deep sadness. 'And Rebecca?'

'She's no longer alive either, nor his wife.'

Her grandmother slowly nodded, lost in her own thoughts.

'Oma,' Anna said, and gently touched her hand. 'Can I ask you something else?'

Ilse blinked several times and inhaled a deep sigh. 'You're a determined young woman, aren't you? I like that about you. Carry on.'

'Kersten had an old photo album of Connie's, and she showed me photos of my father as a young boy. I don't understand why she had them.'

'It was Connie's idea. She brought me photos of Paul when she came to visit me in Leiden because she wanted me to see that he was fine. Paul's adopted parents were friends of her family, and she regularly used to visit them to make sure he was getting on all right. I think she felt she owed it to me as she hadn't managed to save Levi the night he was arrested. It was such a generous, kind thing to do. I admit receiving regular photos of my dear boy did help me come to terms with my grief.' At this memory, tears came to Ilse's eyes, which she dabbed with the corner of a handkerchief.

'At the back of the album was another photo, of you and a man,' Anna went on. 'It looked like a wedding photo. Who was he?'

They were interrupted by the arrival of the assistant who had served their coffee. She exchanged a few words with Ilse and left.

'The car has arrived. I asked her to tell the driver to wait a few minutes. Now, you were asking me about my husband. Is this your last question?' she said, with a weary smile.

'Yes. I promise. No more after this one.'

'His name was Willem. I think you say in English that I was his childhood sweetheart, but I never loved him the way I loved Levi – Levi was always the love of my life. Willem knew about my past, but never judged me for having a baby outside marriage with another man. Nor for giving him up for adoption. We never had children of our own. But he was always my kind loyal companion, until he died ten years ago. And that really is all there is to say. Now, Anna, will you please take my arm and walk me to the car?'

FIFTY-TWO

The water slopped gently against the dock as Anna watched a motorboat slide away from its moorings, its engine sputtering quietly as it headed out towards a small island in the middle of the lake. Beyond the island, a handful of white sailing boats were moving imperceptibly across the tranquil blue water. She walked a little way along the boardwalk to a wooden seat, where she could look back at the restaurant terrace and the table where Ilse, Kersten and Luuk were still chatting and laughing together. Keeping her eyes on Luuk, she noted his easy manner, his laugh, the sparkling blue eyes against his tanned face, the way he pushed his thick hair from his eyes, and realised how much she'd missed him. The last time they'd met she'd made it abundantly clear that things couldn't work out between them, but when she'd met him today at the restaurant, straight away she'd forgotten her resolve. All it took was for him to clasp her gently to him as they embraced hello, and compliment her quietly on her new hairstyle, for her to realise how wrong she had been.

Anna reflected on what had been a perfect summer's day for Ilse's birthday celebration. She hadn't wanted it to end. It was a small gathering, just the four of them, and was the first time Ilse had met Luuk.

'You are so like your grandmother. Incredible,' she had said, reaching up to touch his cheek, as if she didn't quite believe it. 'The whole family was so tall and blond. You should have seen them – Connie and her parents,' she said, turning to Anna with a fond smile. 'Now, Luuk, you must tell me all about yourself. Am I right in thinking that you are a historian at Leiden?'

'That's right, Mevrouw Meijer,' he said, bending his head to speak to her, all politeness and charm.

'Call me Ilse, please,' she said with a coquettish laugh.

Luuk took her arm and, with a quick wink at Anna, led Ilse to her place at the table overlooking the lake, which shimmered in the afternoon sunshine.

Ilse clearly enjoyed being the centre of attention on her special day, with Luuk on one side, Anna on the other and Kersten sitting opposite, as she regaled them with stories about Connie as a young girl, who was often getting into trouble but always able to argue her way out of every situation. Every so often, Anna glanced up at Luuk, to see him looking back at her, and each time he smiled.

Kersten had arranged for a cake topped with fresh fruit and whipped cream to be brought out at the end of the meal. After the coffee, Anna quietly placed a small square box wrapped in gold paper and tied with a blue ribbon in front of her grandmother.

'What is this?' she said, clearly delighted, as she picked it up and made it rattle. 'You'll have to open it for me. It's too much for my old fingers.'

Anna made a show of undoing the ribbon, opening the box and showing her the contents, before laying the twisted gold-and-silver brooch encrusted with tiny rubies in the palm of her hand.

'It's beautiful. But this is too much,' her grandmother protested.

Anna caught Luuk's eye again and he gave her a tiny smile of approval. She wasn't able to stop herself from smiling too, as she announced that the brooch had been designed and crafted by Levi's own hands. She wasn't expecting her oma to break down in tears, and felt guilty that she'd been the cause of it, till she realised her oma was shedding tears of happiness.

'I can almost imagine he was thinking of me when he made this,' she said, running her fingers over the brooch's smooth curves. 'How did you come by it?'

Anna helped pin the brooch to Ilse's cream jacket as she explained how she'd asked Joanna if there were any examples of his work in existence. 'She had none herself but she found this one on a website for vintage jewellery. I just knew it would be perfect on you.'

Shortly after, Anna excused herself and slipped away to have a few moments on her own. Sitting at the water's edge, she savoured this moment of quiet and felt herself relax in the knowledge that her father would have been proud of her efforts to track down his biological parents. She thought back over the past few weeks, remembering the moments of profound sadness she'd experienced, especially when she'd learnt that Levi had died, never knowing that Ilse had given birth to a son. What horrors had Levi experienced that had so damaged him that he was incapable of returning to Ilse, the love of his life? Anna would never know; nor had she any wish to, for she would have felt obliged to tell Ilse. And after everything she'd been through, Anna didn't think she deserved that.

Anna only realised she'd been watching Luuk for some time when he turned his head, caught sight of her and waved. She waved back, feeling the heat rise in her cheeks. He stood up, said a few words to the others and left the table to walk down the boardwalk towards her. This was the first time they had been on their own that day and she was acutely aware they had both been avoiding this moment.

'Is everything all right?' he said, as he approached her.

'Yes, everything is fine. Come and sit down,' she said, looking up at him. She patted the empty seat beside her. 'It's such a beautiful spot. I thought I'd wander down here and watch the boats and have a few minutes to myself. It's been quite an intense day, hasn't it?'

'You could say that.' Luuk sat down with a sigh. He leant forward, elbows on knees, and turned to look at her. 'I don't know how your grandmother does it. She's been chatting non-stop since the moment we arrived and still isn't showing any signs of flagging. It's like she's catching up on all those lost years, the way she and Mum talk. Mum has been asking all about what Connie did during the war and some of the stories are incredible. Apparently, Connie risked her life on so many occasions to help Jews to safety that she was exceptionally lucky not to be caught herself. You know I've been doing research of my own into Dutch women in the resistance? Well, you should have seen the look of surprise on Ilse's face when I told her that Connie wasn't just working for a local resistance network – she was actually running a group that covered the whole of Hilversum and beyond. She built a complete network of contacts, each with responsibility for persuading people to take in Jews on the run from the Nazis. It's believed she saved over a hundred lives.'

Anna listened, spellbound. 'What incredible courage that must have taken. And Ilse never knew?'

Luuk shook his head. 'Connie hinted that she did more than she let on, but she never told Ilse the full truth. I suspect she did it to protect her and Levi. You know, I feel proud knowing she was my grandmother.'

'So you should. It's incredible how much our grandmothers went through together. You must use this information for your research paper. How is it coming along?'

Luuk sat back in his seat so he could face her. 'The paper's finished. I only found this out about Connie after I'd submitted it. You see, something came up that meant I had to finish it off more quickly than I'd intended.'

'Oh. What was that?' Anna said, wondering why he was suddenly so serious and hoping he wasn't about to reveal that something terrible had happened.

Luuk didn't answer immediately. 'After you left, I did a lot of thinking about what I want to do with my life. Here I am, at twenty-nine; I've always lived in Rijswijk and am doing the job I always knew I'd end up doing. I could see myself in twenty years doing exactly the same and that scared me. I needed a change. Then, by chance, a colleague of mine heard about a research post at Oxford University for this coming academic year. He encouraged me to apply for it. I meant to tell you sooner, but when you said you were coming over, I thought I'd wait and tell you face to face. Like now.' He scrutinised her face expectantly.

'Oxford University... this year? You mean in the next few weeks?' Anna said the words out loud as she tried to process what he was saying to her. She found herself holding her breath as he went on to describe what the work would involve. It meant little to her and she guessed he was stringing it out to gauge her reaction. He still hadn't said whether he had accepted the job. Eventually, she became so impatient that she grasped him by the arm and said, 'Well, are you going to take the job or not?'

Luuk gazed into her eyes for a long moment, and said, 'I am. I'm starting in October. Everything's arranged and I'll be living in college. Apparently, my rooms overlook the quad. I think that's meant to be good, isn't it?' He covered her hand with his and held it there.

'It's very good. I mean, Luuk, this is wonderful news.'

'It's a one-year post.' He kept looking at her.

'Ah. One year. That's good too.'

'That's what I thought. I mean, I wouldn't want to come between you and your boyfriend...' The corner of his mouth twitched.

'Hugo?' Anna shook her head vigorously. 'It's over. It has been for some time. He's moved out... he's gone to the Philippines.'

'So... you are saying you like the idea of me coming to Oxford?' He spoke softly and moved his hand so he could touch the silver medallion that nestled in the hollow of her throat.

'Very much so,' she said, happiness brimming up inside her.

'Oxford isn't too far from London, is it?' he murmured.

'No, not far at all.'

'And as it's just for one year, I was thinking... shall we see how things go?'

Anna had heard enough of his questions, and silenced him with a kiss.

A LETTER FROM IMOGEN

I do hope you enjoyed reading *The Boy in the Attic*, and if you did, I would be grateful if you could write a review. I'd love to hear what you think, and it makes such a difference helping new readers to discover one of my books for the first time. If you did enjoy it and want to keep up to date with all my latest releases, just sign up at the following link. Your email address will never be shared, and you can unsubscribe at any time.

www.bookouture.com/imogen-matthews

Few of us can really appreciate the extreme hardship the Dutch experienced when their country was occupied by the Germans during the Second World War. Following the bombardment and utter devastation of the centre of Rotterdam on 14 May 1940, the Germans made life increasingly difficult for the Dutch, culminating in the terrible hunger winter of 1944/45 when tens of thousands of Dutch people lost their lives to starvation.

My mother was one of the survivors. Thanks to her grit, determination and courage, she kept her parents and herself alive by trudging out into the frozen countryside in search of anything that could pass for food. When the farmers' fields were all entirely stripped of their crops, my mother discovered a new food source: tulip bulbs. Tasteless, but nutritious, in the end tulip bulbs were all they had to eat. And had she not kept on venturing out on her dilapidated bicycle through snow, ice and bitterly cold winds, my mother's family would have died of starvation and I would not be here today to tell the tale.

The Boy in the Attic is the closest I've come in my wartime Holland novels to reliving the extraordinary stories she used to tell me and my sisters. Through my character Ilse, I've remained faithful to my mother's own description of enduring hardship under German occupation. Like my mother, Ilse had her whole life before her when she was forced to give up on her studies after the Germans forcibly closed Leiden University. But this is where my mother's and Ilse's stories diverge and the reality becomes fiction.

Though as much as *The Boy in the Attic* reflects my mother's own experiences, it is also about the very real threat posed to Jews by the Nazis, who systematically sought out Jews in order to deport them to concentration camps with the intention of killing them. While researching my book I discovered this shocking and chilling statistic: three-quarters of Dutch Jews lost their lives in concentration camps during the Second World War, more than any other European country. Those who did survive did so because they were lucky enough to get out before being discovered, or through the selfless acts of people prepared to give Jews a safe haven and protection from a ruthless and brutal enemy.

We are constantly reminded of the need to learn the lessons of the past, though sadly the persecution of innocent people because of their race, beliefs or simply for who they are continues to this day.

I hope that in some small way my book serves to show that there is goodness in people, and that many will go to extraordinary lengths to protect those they love.

It gives me great pleasure to hear from my readers – you can get in touch through my website, my Facebook page, through Twitter or Goodreads.

Many thanks,

Imogen

www.imogenmatthewsbooks.com

twitter.com/ImogenMatthews3

instagram.com/oxfordnovelist

ACKNOWLEDGEMENTS

With thanks to Matthew, who knows me best and has always provided helpful and insightful comments when I can't see a way forward with my writing. Our many long walks during lockdown resulted in several eureka moments for me. Long may they continue.

Thanks to my editor, Susannah Hamilton, at Bookouture, who has always made herself available at a moment's notice to help me navigate the trickier parts of the plot. Her clear-sighted comments never fail to hit the mark and have contributed to making my writing the best it can be.

Thanks also to all the hardworking team at Bookouture who never fail to impress me with their professional approach and commitment to every aspect of the publication of books and support for their authors.

Made in United States
Orlando, FL
22 March 2023

31319371R00178